The *Trip*

James McWhorter

and

Jon McWhorter

ISBN 978-1-64492-193-7 (paperback)
ISBN 978-1-64492-194-4 (digital)

Christian Faith Publishing, Inc.
832 Park Avenue
Meadville, PA 16335
www.christianfaithpublishing.com

Printed in the United States of America

Chapter 1

Dr. Martin

Dr. Joseph Martin had been trying to ignore the discomfort in his chest for the past few days, and he knew better. Sixty-nine years old and still a very active general surgeon, early to the hospital most days, usually late leaving. The Nexium and TUMS were not working on his chest pain, but like most doctors, he continued to treat himself.

Joseph Ewell Martin, MD, respected surgeon, devoted husband, father of three, deacon in the church, and active in foreign missions. He had practiced in Monroe, Louisiana, for thirty-six years after finishing his specialty training at Big Charity Hospital in New Orleans, the LSU division. He was regarded by many to be the best general surgeon in North Louisiana. It is two o'clock in the afternoon on Tuesday, and he is in OR 3 finishing up a laparoscopic gallbladder.

"Susie, how many times do I have to tell you to hold the scope still and point where I'm looking?"

"I've told you for years that I can't tell where you are looking."

"Well, at least you could hold the scope still."

"It ain't moving. Your head must be moving."

Dr. Martin let out several phrases in Spanish and ended that with, "Get me somebody in here who knows what they're doing."

"You got the best there is, and you know it."

"That's scary."

He had always enjoyed operating-room humor and appreciated the people he worked with. The feeling was mutual among the OR crew. They were all like family.

He finished up and was pulling off his gloves when his cell phone rang.

"Hey, Maggie."

"Do you think you'll be home early tonight? You know Anna is excited about fixing dinner."

"I don't know. I have a full clinic that I am late for and an appendectomy after that."

"You know how much Anna is looking forward to feeding us."

"I can't help it, baby. It is what it is."

"Did you check with Phillip Carter like you promised you would?"

"Not yet."

"Don't come home till you do. I've seen you eating all those TUMS. You of all people know better than to take chest pain lightly."

"I know, but it's not like I've had all the time in the world."

"No excuses."

*****

Clinic was busier than usual. There were the people who had an appointment that day and then the ones who had been rescheduled from the day before. His nurse, Becky, was so used to juggling things around that it had become second nature to her.

"Surgery go well?"

"It did, thank you."

"You look a little tired today. Do you feel okay?"

"Between you and Maggie, I'm not sure."

"She called."

"I'm not surprised, and if I know you, you have already called Dr. Carter's nurse."

"I have. They're going to wait for you and see you after clinic."

"What about the appendix?"

"It'll take them a little while to set up for it anyway. I called surgery and told them you might run a little late."

"What would I do without y'all?"

"I shudder to think."

*****

Dr. Carter, one of the clinic cardiologists and good friend, stood looking at Joseph's EKG. He studied it for a long time like cardiologists do and then said, "Joseph, there are some changes that I don't like. We need to do more testing especially since you are symptomatic."

Joseph replied, "Are you talking about a heart cath?"

"I am."

"When?"

"I wouldn't put it off. I'd go ahead this afternoon."

"I've got a lot to do this evening. Can we plan for tomorrow?"

"I don't really feel good about waiting."

"I'll be okay. I know what signs to look for. What time you want me at the hospital in the morning? I'm going to have to move some surgeries around."

"If you're gonna be stubborn about it, come in early, and we'll work you in. I hope you have enough sense to call me if you get in a bind." He muttered to himself, "Doctors do make the worst patients, and general surgeons have got to be the worst of the lot."

"I heard that."

"Well, if you're honest with yourself, you'd have to agree with it."

Dr. Martin got real pious and said, "It's only because we work so hard and don't have time to take care of ourselves."

Dr. Carter managed a smile and replied, "Never have really thought of your specialty as martyr types. Anyway, your non-compliance will give me time to make sure Mark Hughes is close by."

"Heart surgeon on standby. Getting a little dramatic?"

"Not at all. Just cautious."

*****

On the drive home, Dr. Martin did feel tired. He tried to attribute it to a long day, but he could not ignore the pressure that he kept feeling in his chest. He was not a man that was prone to worry, but he knew enough to know the potential seriousness of the problem. His hope was that if he had any coronary blockage that it could be fixed with stents, and he wouldn't be down long. The one thing that he absolutely hated was idle time.

His thoughts turned to dinner. He was wondering what Anna may have conjured up this time. Lord knows she tries, but she is not a good cook. He couldn't help but smile when he thought about his youngest child. If there ever was a daddy's girl, it was her. The circumstances surrounding her birth were not good memories, but she had been nothing but a joy since then. He was hoping that she would get her life together before long, but he was enjoying her living back at home.

His thoughts shifted to tomorrow and how that would go. He couldn't help but have some anxiety. Doctors don't ever like to be on the other end of the knife. Well, at least Maggie would not be on his case since he had followed orders and seen the cardiologist.

*****

The next morning, Dr. Martin was in the outpatient department as he said he would be. Maggie was with him. They had convinced Anna to come a little later. He wondered to himself whether he would have come in if the pain had stopped, but it hadn't anyway. It was actually worse.

Dr. Carter came in and spoke to Maggie, shook hands with Dr. Martin, and said, "I see you made it through the night."

"I'd have called you if I had passed on."

"I'm sure you would have. I know that you are familiar with what I'm going to do, but do you have any questions?"

"Just promise me that if you find any blockage, you'll try real hard to fix it with stents. I don't have time for a cabbage."

"Maggie, just so you'll know, he is referring to a coronary artery bypass graft."

She replied, "I think I've heard that one before."

*****

In the cath lab, Dr. Martin was sedated but could hear what was going on from time to time. He very clearly heard when Dr. Carter said, "This is bad, and I can't get a stent in. We need to get him to the OR now!"

Chapter 2

The Airport

Matt Martin sat waiting in the Atlanta Airport for the flight that would take him to his hometown of Monroe, Louisiana. He had been here many times before, but it was different today. He was going home for his father's funeral. If that wasn't bad enough, he would have to interact with his younger brother all weekend, and he never looked forward to that.

Matthew Aldridge Martin, age forty-three, great wife and two kids: a son, nine; and a daughter, seven. Kids were younger because he married later. He never liked his middle name. His parents claimed they just liked it, and it had no connection with family or anything else. His first name came from two sources: the Gospel of Matthew and one of his father's best friends, so Matt was always okay with that. He was a good-looking, clean-shaven man who had an air of confidence about him. His clothes were upscale, not because he was flashy, but he felt that a successful businessman should look the part.

By any standards, Matt would certainly seem to have it all. He was co-owner of a very successful medical equipment company that he and a longtime friend had started together after college. It had exceeded their expectations and seemed destined to do well for a long time to come. He had no financial worries, and he took pride in that. Other than help from his dad for his education, he had never taken anything from anybody. His self-sufficiency was a source of pride to him, and he could on occasion be caught boasting about it, especially to his two younger siblings.

His wife and kids were another source of pride for him. He always joked that he often had to pinch himself to make sure he was really married to the woman that shared his house and last name. She was from Virginia and was the essence of a Southern lady in every good sense of the designation. She had a degree in psychology, but Matt's business success had allowed her to be a full-time mom. Matt swore that she used her degree to analyze him from time to time.

They had met while attending college at Ole Miss, both of them sharing that trait of attending a school outside of their native states. They were friends in college but never really had a serious relationship till some time after graduation when they reconnected at a five-year reunion. Matt always said that he almost didn't go and that would have been the worst mistake he ever made in his life. He loved his wife with all his heart, and if he had ever worried about finding one as good as his father's, he had at least come close.

His kids were both apples of their father's eye. His attitude over the years had been that he didn't like kids and never intended to go to the trouble of raising any. His wife had other ideas, and now he could not imagine life without them.

School had just started back as it was early fall, so Matt had made the decision to leave his family in Atlanta. His mother had shown great disapproval, but Matt would deal with that later. He felt that it was the best decision, all things considered.

*****

"Young man, is there anything I can do for you?" Matt looked up to see a middle-aged lady standing in front of him holding a tissue.

"No, ma'am," Matt replied. "My father passed away, and I guess I'm just a little emotional."

He thanked her, and she squeezed his shoulder as she walked away.

Matt could have crawled under the chair that he was sitting in. He had no idea that it was that obvious. He had gone to the rest room several times to dry his eyes in an attempt to hide it. He never understood why some tears could be suppressed and others could not. Everybody knows that feeling you get that appears suddenly, somewhere deep within, and then wells up in you as it is heading for your eyes.

He had never been sentimental or emotional. Real men don't cry, and if one of them did by accident, it wouldn't be Matt Martin.

Why now? Flight delayed and too much time to sit, think, and reflect. No way to be ready for the death of your father. Matt had thought of him as a good friend more and more as time went by. He had not appreciated his wisdom and experience till he had a family of his own. He was going to miss that.

*****

Joseph Ewell Martin, MD. General surgeon, dead at sixty-nine. Just didn't sound right. "Aren't we supposed to get into our eighties at least?" Matt said to himself. His father's middle name seemed a little odd to Matt, and his dad never liked it either. He said that his parents must not have liked him because he felt like he was named after the Southern general that was responsible for losing the Civil War. When asked to elaborate, he would say that it was very simple: "The war was ultimately lost at Gettysburg, and if General Ewell had taken the high ground as he should have, the South would have won that battle and forced the North into negotiations." He loved his Civil War history, and nobody ever really argued with him. He and Matt's younger brother would debate the politics of the war at times, and their dad would simply say, "I'm not a politician. I just love to study the history." Matt told him that at least his middle name was connected to something.

He continued thinking about his father, a good man who in many ways was the personification of the American Dream. He grew up in modest circumstances. His father was a functioning alcoholic who worked in a post office and never accomplished much of anything else. He had a loving mother who was an encourager and always told him that he would do well in life. He credited her a lot for his motivation and desire to seek higher education.

Matt never knew his paternal grandfather as he died when Matt was young. He also had a heart disease, and it was said to run on that side of the family.

He was able, however, to spend time with his grandmother before she suffered a stroke and had to be admitted to a nursing home. He remembered her as a fantastic cook who always fixed what he wanted. She would make all three of her grandchildren feel that they were the most special people in the world. Matt never forgot that she was the one who taught him how to ride a bike.

Matt's father also had a brother, but he died when Matt's father was in high school. It was said that it was an accident of some kind, but Matt thought there may be more to it. His dad would never talk about it, or much about any other aspect of his past for that matter. Matt wondered if he might have been a little embarrassed about it.

Dr. Martin's education was all LSU. He went to college at LSU in Baton Rouge, Louisiana, and medical school and specialty training at Charity Hospital in New Orleans, the LSU division. Charity was also home to Tulane University's medical school in those days. Tulane is a private school, and Dr. Martin always said it was for the prima donnas that couldn't get into LSU.

Matt felt that his failure to follow in his dad's footsteps by not attending LSU was a slight problem between them. This, he thought, was compounded by the fact that he did not choose medicine as a career either. And to make matters even worse, he chose to attend Ole Miss, an arch rival of LSU in everything, especially football. His dad's only remark when he told him of his plans to attend Ole Miss was, "Boy, I don't know if I am genetically capable of writing a check to that institution."

Even though his dad would tell him that he was proud of him and seemed genuinely pleased when he completed his studies for his MBA from Ole Miss, Matt felt that he just didn't quite measure up to what his dad would have wanted. He had a feeling that he would had to have been a doctor to really speak his dad's language. He thought, *Doesn't really matter now, does it?* Still, it bothered him.

Matt couldn't keep from a brief smile when he thought about his dad trying to wear an LSU cap to his graduation and his mom reprimanding him and making him put it back in the car.

*****

His mind wandered as one does at times like this. One thing about his father that kept coming back to him was his integrity. He had never in his life heard or heard of his father being dishonest. Whenever he said anything, Matt would never question as to whether that was his true and honest opinion. He vividly remembered one of his dad's friends saying, "Joseph Martin's handshake carries more weight than any contract you'll ever get from a team of lawyers." That meant a lot to Matt.

His father's work ethic was legendary. He went to work early and came home late. He was, in the opinion of many, the best general surgeon in Monroe, and possibly, all of North Louisiana. Matt would hear comments through the years such as: "If you need surgery, Dr. Martin is the one you need," or "Dr. Martin is the only one I'd ever let cut on me," and on and on. His dad could never go anywhere that patients wouldn't come up and speak to him, and tell him how much they appreciated him. Matt remembered one story of a man coming in to the ER having a heart attack, and when asked who his doctor was, he said Dr. Martin. When he was told that Dr. Martin didn't treat heart attacks, he simply stated that he wasn't having anybody else. All of this was brought home to Matt when he thought about the fact that his father had a full day of surgery the day before he died.

Matt also reflected on his father's attitude about money. He became aware over time that it wasn't his focus. He did enjoy a good income and the lifestyle that went along with it, but money never seemed to be what motivated him. Matt's mom was the one that tended to the banking and the bills, and Matt never heard his father say much about it. He had asked him once about investments, and his dad said that he never fooled with them. However, his mom let it slip that he had invested in the cell phone business in its infancy, at the insistence of a friend, and had made a great return on it over the years. She told Matt that he had told her that he had special plans for the money after his death, if the timing was right, but she knew nothing else about it. She was aware that he had consulted an attorney, but she never pressed him for any more information.

Matt was sure of the fact that he would hear a lot said about his father and think a lot more about him over the next few days, but now he remembered something his father once said, "It's hard to be a good doctor, a good husband, and a good father all at the same time." Matt thought he had done a pretty good job of it. He got up and went to the restroom again.

As Matt sat back down, hoping for an announcement about his flight to come soon, his cell phone rang.

"Hello, Mom," Matt said, trying to sound as upbeat as possible.

His mother said, "Thought you would have been here by now. It is a short flight from Atlanta."

"I texted you earlier that my flight was delayed," Matt said with obvious irritation in his voice.

His mom replied, "I don't appreciate your tone, and remember, I am still unhappy with you for not bringing my grandchildren."

"I am sorry, Mom, on both counts, but we covered all of that on the phone last night." Matt's tone was more respectful.

"I know we did, but I still don't understand why they couldn't have missed a couple of days of school"

"We'll talk about it when I get there. Is the golden boy there yet?" Matt immediately knew that he said the wrong thing. His mother did not like him calling his younger brother by that designation, especially when he used a sarcastic tone of voice.

She replied short and to the point, "Call me when you know something about your flight." She hung up the phone.

Matt sighed and mumbled to no one, "This day really is not going that well so far."

*****

Matt thought about his brother and felt that acidy feeling in his stomach that he always seemed to get when he came to mind. He never had been able to accept Samuel's free-spirited ways and his constant lack of any kind of stability and maturity. Their differences went back a long way, but Matt could not remember any specific event that started it, with the exception that Samuel was angry with him for not attending the state high school championship football game in Samuel's junior year. He broke about every quarterback-related record the school had. Matt used the excuse of having to study for an exam, but nobody really bought it. Matt's parents felt strongly that jealousy was the main reason Matt was not there.

Samuel Jackson Martin was three years Matt's junior. His middle name was always felt to be after General Stonewall Jackson, but his parents denied it. Matt thought his dad would someday own up to it, but he never did.

The golden boy. Both Matt and his younger sister claimed having come up with the nickname, but if the truth was known, neither one knew for sure.

He was called that for two reasons: he had thick blonde hair that everyone was envious of. It looked great long or short, but most of the time, he kept it at what his dad called the surfer's length. The second reason was that both of his siblings were absolutely convinced that he was their parents' favorite. If not so much with their mother, for sure with their father. If it ever came up, it was always strongly denied.

Matt, in a somewhat self-righteous way, was constantly upset with his brother for squandering his father's money on one so-called business venture after another. He had tried everything from a scuba shop in Puerto Rico to a bike shop in San Diego. There were others, all funded by Dr. Martin, of course. Samuel would be coming in from Winter Park, Colorado, where he had been staying for a month, exploring the possibility of starting a ski rental business, as if they needed another one. None of Samuel's dealings were Matt's business, but he constantly expressed his displeasure to their father.

Samuel excelled in almost everything he did, especially in sports. He was one of the best quarterbacks Neville High School ever had, and his dad had visions of a scholarship at LSU. Samuel, however, never really had any interest in organized sports past high school and fizzled somewhat in his senior year. Matt had started to recognize a pattern where his brother would take something to the edge but never quite finish it.

Samuel's prowess in the area of sports was not the only thing that caused Matt to have jealous feelings. He was always the center of attention. It didn't seem to take any effort on his part. Whether at a family get together or anywhere there were people, everyone would naturally congregate around Samuel. Matt was sure that he would see that again this weekend. A funeral would be no different, just a different crowd.

There was one thing, however, that Matt did admire in his brother even though it also brought on jealous feelings—that Patrick Swayze type of persona. It is a level of cool that is rare. Matt could not think of many more that displayed it, maybe Joe Namath or Clint Eastwood. Steve McQueen would be another. One had to be born with that; it is not something that you can acquire with effort. With Samuel, it was as much a part of him as his blonde hair. Along with his good looks, it had a lot to do with numerous broken hearts over the years. Matt had to smile when he thought of all the girls that came and went during their teenage years.

Finally, the announcement came. "Delta Flight 2315, non-stop service to Monroe Regional Airport, is now ready for boarding."

Matt texted his mother and boarded the plane.

Chapter 3

Home

Matt looked out the window of the plane and recognized all of the familiar landmarks as they made their final descent into Monroe. He was glad it was a short flight. He was tired of sitting, something that he did not do well.

As he approached the baggage claims area, he saw Billy Slocum standing there. He had not known who was going to meet him at the airport but would have bet anything that it would be Mr. Slocum, who simply wouldn't have let anybody else do it.

He had been their next-door neighbor for as long as Matt could remember. He was seventy-nine-years old and still as active and sharp as ever. He was a retired attorney and one of Dr. Martin's best friends. He was always working on something, about as often at the Martin's house as his own. Over time, it got to where he did all their yard work and any landscaping that needed taking care of. Said that Dr. Martin didn't have time to do it, and wouldn't pay anybody to do it, so that left him to do it.

He took Matt's hand and gave him a warm handshake.

"How was your flight?"

"It was fine, sir. Thank you."

Mr. Slocum turned to look as the bags began to come out and said, "I made sure that everything was in order with the house and the yard. This time of year, the yard didn't need mowing, but there was some trimming and such to do."

Matt replied, "I figured you would do that, and we sure do appreciate it."

Matt's suitcase came around, and of course, he was not allowed to carry it.

During the drive home, they exchanged some small talk for a while and then there was silence for what seemed like a long time. Matt noticed a single tear run down Mr. Slocum's face and then he said quietly, as if talking to no one, "I'm not ever going to get used to Dr. Martin being gone, not ever."

Matt just shook his head and said, "Me neither," so quietly that he did not know if Mr. Billy heard him.

As they turned down the street that their houses were on, Matt was shocked. He had never seen so many vehicles in his neighborhood in his entire life. It was getting close to four in the afternoon, and Mr. Billy said it had been like that all day.

They pulled into Mr. Slocum's drive as there was no room at Matt's house. As they made their way through the front yard, the first person to shake Matt's hand and offer condolences was Stan Roberts, the administrator of the clinic where Dr. Martin had practiced for thirty-six years. There were two of his father's colleagues there also who did likewise.

Matt walked in the front door and saw a large crowd of people, most of whom he knew. He immediately saw Ruth Shelby walking toward him with some degree of purpose to her steps. She hugged him and announced to the crowd that they were to leave him alone for now because she had to have him for a few minutes. Everybody knew Ruth, and nobody argued.

Ruth was their neighbor who lived across the street. She was about the same age as Matt's parents and was a widow. Her husband had died of colon cancer about ten years ago as near as Matt could remember. Their families were always close, but Matt's parent's help to Ruth as she was going through her husband's illness and death seemed to take their friendship to the highest level.

Ruth was the type of person that was a doer and an organizer. Whenever there was sickness or death in her circle of friends, she was the first one there and the last one to leave. When Matt talked to his mother shortly after his father's death, it was no surprise to hear her say that Ruth was already at their house working.

"Your mother is in her bedroom. I sent her in there to get away from the crowd for a while. She wanted to talk to you as soon as you came in," Ruth said.

She added, "I have all the meals arranged over the next several days, as well as people coming in to take care of cleaning and doing the dishes. I have you all meeting with Rick Parker at the funeral home tonight at seven, and visitation will be from five to seven tomorrow night. The funeral is set for two o'clock on Sunday afternoon. All of this has your mother's approval and, of course, needs you to give the final approval since you are the oldest."

Matt replied, "It all sounds good, Ms. Ruth and I hope you know how much we all appreciate your taking care of all that."

"Y'all are family," she said. "Now go on and talk with your mother."

"How is she?" Matt asked.

Ruth replied, "She is doing pretty well, all things considered. I think the crowd got to her and she needed to get away for a minute."

Matt related his earlier conversation that he had with his mother and said that he felt bad for being impatient and disrespectful, especially at a time like this.

Ruth smiled and said, "Matthew Martin, you know as well as I do that your mother has always been a sucker for your charm. I doubt you'll be in trouble long."

Matt said, "I sure hope you are right."

Matt's mother was sitting in a chair by the bedroom window, and she looked up when he came in. She appeared to be a little weary, but her face brightened some when she saw it was Matt. He walked over and hugged her, and immediately apologized for his earlier behavior. He also told her how bad he felt that she was so disappointed that his wife and children had not come.

"Don't worry anymore about it, son," she said. "I know that the kids are too young to be in the middle of all this. I guess I just wanted to show them off, but I know it is not the time."

Matt said, "Looks like Ruth has got everything under control."

His mother replied, "That is for sure. I haven't had to make a single phone call to anyone about anything. I hope that you are okay with the arrangements she has made so far. She just took off with it."

Matt answered, "It all seems good to me. How is Anna?"

She answered, "Not doing well. She is upstairs in her room now, resting some, I hope. She's taking her father's death hard. You and I can talk more later. I would like for you to go up and see her now. You know, she worships the ground that you walk on, and she needs to see you. She's been asking for you all day."

Matt kissed his mom on the cheek and headed for the stairs. When he walked into Anna's room, he found her asleep on her bed. He was going to try to get out without waking her up but she opened her eyes and saw him.

She immediately sat up on the side of the bed, held out her arms to him, and started crying. Matt took her in his arms and held her for the longest time. She was crying so hard that he was afraid she wasn't going to be able to catch her breath. He felt helpless and just kept patting her on the back and telling her that it was going to be all right.

Anna Miller Martin. Matt always thought that she had two last names and no middle name. He thought that there was a reason for that, but he couldn't recall what it was. She was eight years younger than Matt and five years younger than Samuel. Matt always felt that she was the cutest female ever born, and he told her that all the time. That may have been the main reason that Matt was her favorite, or so he liked to think.

Anna had been back at home for the last two months after a breakup with a man that she had followed to North Carolina. They had planned to get married. Her parents were not happy with that at all, and now it was obvious why. His abusive personality finally had gotten to Anna, and she understood what people had been trying to tell her. Also, she had dropped out of nursing school with only one more semester to go, making matters worse.

Anna had been in and out of school over the years and had never quite settled on anything. Romantic relationships had never panned out. It seemed like she had bad luck with men.

She finally gained some control and said, "How could this happen, Matt? How could this happen?"

Matt replied, "Nobody knows, baby sister. It just does."

They talked back and forth a while about the crowd, their mother, plans over the next couple of days, and then Matt asked, "Have you heard from Samuel?"

Anna said that she had, and he told her that he would be driving in tomorrow.

"Why is he driving, and what time did he say he would be here?" Matt asked with irritation in his voice.

"He said that driving would give him time to clear his head, and he didn't know what time he would be here."

"Clear his head of what?" This time, there was disgust in Matt's tone.

He added, "Wonder if he'll make it in time for visitation?"

Anna teared up a little and then said, "Matt, you know I love you to death, but you have to realize how awful it makes everybody feel to see how bad your and Samuel's relationship is. I don't understand it."

Matt said, "I don't think it's that bad."

Anna became animated and said, "Not that bad! What about last spring when y'all almost came to blows over some stupid political point?"

Matt replied, "I can't help it if he has become a liberal idiot."

Anna said, "That is not the point! Y'all are brothers for God's sake!"

Matt lowered his voice and said, "I really don't want to talk about it right now. I will do my best to focus on what is going on this weekend and not cause any trouble." He smiled at her and said, "Wash that face of yours, baby sister, and let's go down and work the crowd."

She punched him on the shoulder and replied, "I love you, you old troll."

*****

The people had not thinned out much. Matt figured that Ruth had not yet gone into the crowd-control mode. He knew she would at some point.

As he and Anna made their way toward the kitchen, they got numerous handshakes and hugs. That was coupled with all of the usual: "So sorry about… Your dad was… We're gonna miss… I can't tell you how sorry…" Matt was glad when he finally made it to the kitchen. Anna had beat him there and was already spooning something out of one of the numerous casserole dishes. He was glad to see that she had an appetite.

His mother was sitting at the breakfast table talking to their pastor, Dr. Ted Johnson, and their minister of missions, John Lyons. Matt paused a minute and just looked at his mother. He was struck by the fact that she was still a great-looking lady. It was the first time he could remember thinking that Anna favored her a lot, and he found that odd.

Margaret (Maggie) Barrett Martin, age sixty-eight. Dad always said that he had married a younger woman. She was the fun mom when they were growing up. Theirs was the house where all the kids congregated. Everybody had a comfort level there and knew that Ms. Maggie was pretty easy to get along with. She had some rules, but they were never rules just to have rules. She was never legalistic.

Maggie's philosophy was that kids had to learn, and they had to grow up, but they also had to be kids and have fun. Matt remembered with a smile a weekend when she spontaneously gathered up her kids and any of their friends that wanted to go and set out for Dallas. Dr. Martin was on call, so he couldn't go. The kids thought it was hilarious that when their mother called their dad to see if it would be okay for them to go, they were already halfway there. There were countless other stories like this one.

Maggie was one that treated everybody the same, regardless of who they were or where they came from. She was as impartial as a supreme court justice is supposed to be. Matt remembered many times when she would rule in favor of one of his friends over him. It irritated him then, but he admired her for it now.

She was heard to say on numerous occasions, "I call 'em like I see 'em." She and Matt would butt heads now and then, and Maggie said it was mostly a birth-order issue. Both she and he were first-born children. Maggie had two younger sisters.

Matt walked over to the table, and both ministers stood up and shook his hand.

Dr. Johnson spoke first and said that he was glad to see him but sure did wish that it had been under different circumstances. He was a good preacher who really did seem to care about his people. Matt's dad said that he had a sixth sense and could tell where you stood with your spirituality, your church attendance, and your tithing. Matt was hopeful that his dad was joking.

John Lyons spoke next. "Matt, I am sorry for your loss, and I have to say I have suffered one myself. I have lost my best man in our Nicaragua missions. You know how involved your dad was there."

Matt did know. His dad had been going to that country for over thirty years. He started by going on a medical mission trip, which he still did every year, and then began going on what he called his freelance trips. He would go by himself and spend one to two weeks. He learned Spanish and became fluent in the language after a few years. Some would say that he could speak it better than most Spanish-speaking people. It was also said that he had more contacts and friends in Nicaragua than he did in the U.S. He was respected by several physicians there, and many times, he would operate during his visits. One of his patients was a family member of the president, and the fact that he did well was a feather in Dr. Martin's Nicaragua cap. The president would offer him first-class accommodations from time to time, but he always declined and stayed at a compound in Diriamba.

The compound had a one-story, five-bedroom house owned by the Nicaragua Mission Outreach Board, a group of men mostly from the Baton Rouge area. Its primary purpose was to house mission teams from churches all over the southern and southeastern part of the U.S. It had a sprawling veranda, and Matt's dad said it was his favorite place on earth. He said more than once, "If I departed from this world while sitting on that porch, sipping Nicaraguan coffee, and visiting with an old friend, I'd go a happy corpse."

After they had talked for several minutes, Pastor Lyons excused himself and left. Matt shifted his attention to the conversation between Dr. Johnson and his mother.

She was saying, "I don't know how I'm going to pick six people out of all the possible candidates for pallbearers. I don't want to hurt anybody's feelings."

Dr. Johnson said, "Well, Maggie, you're going to make all the doctors in the clinic honorary pallbearers. That will help avoid some hurt feelings. And I know that Billy Slocum will be one of the six. You also mentioned that John Lyons said that Dr. Romero is going to make it in from Nicaragua. I would feel sure that you would honor him by making him one. That only leaves four."

Maggie sighed and said, "Who can think at a time like this? Matt, maybe you can help me."

Matt said, "Thought for sure that you would ask Pat Sanders. He is not only a fellow surgeon but he and Dad were real close friends."

Maggie said, "I have about decided that I'm going to ask him to do the eulogy. You know how great a speaker he is, and no one knew your dad better than him."

Dr. Johnson interjected, "He can do double duty, Maggie. There is nothing wrong with that."

Matt leaned forward and said, "See how easy this is. We are now down to three. What about that African American male nurse that Dad thought so highly of? That choice, coupled with the Latino we already have, will bring diversity to the group." He couldn't suppress a laugh.

His mom was laughing and said, "Leave it to you, Matt, to make me laugh at a time like this. But I do want to point out to you that we are choosing pallbearers, not a presidential cabinet or delegation to the United Nations."

Matt composed himself and replied, "Nevertheless, I have gotten us down to two, and surely, we can think of them soon. What about music, a soloist, programs, and all of that?"

Maggie replied, "Of course, Ruth is helping with that. She says all she needs is the names of the pallbearers by tomorrow morning and a rough idea of what we want the program to look like. She will take care of the details. Of course, she will require us to give the usual final approval."

Matt thought that if anyone ever displayed genuine, down home Christian service, it was Ruth Shelby.

Dr. Johnson asked Matt, "How is your family?"

"Doing really well, sir," Matt replied

Dr. Johnson got into the pastor mode and asked, "You have been in Atlanta for several years now. Do you have a good church home?"

Matt felt a little uneasy and replied, "To be honest with you, we haven't been attending regular lately. I hate to make excuses, but I've been so busy with my business that I just feel like I need to rest some on the weekends."

The pastor didn't want to preach at Matt and simply said, "Maybe you can slow down some before too long."

Matt was a Christian, saved and baptized at the age of eleven. He was taken to church regularly as he was growing up and had never drifted too far until the last several years. It was not a conscious, intentional thing with him as much as it was a slow process of just not making the effort. When he thought about it, and at times analyzed it, as he was prone to do, he felt like his success and subsequent self-sufficiency had a lot to do with it. He had a hard time giving God the credit for all of his own hard work that had led to that success. He was, however, bothered a little by that verse that talked about the rich man, the camel, and the eye of a needle.

Matt's maternal grandparents came into the kitchen. They had just gotten there, and Matt got up to greet them. His grandfather was wheelchair bound and had some dementia, but he still knew who Matt was and shook his hand. His grandmother was still in good health and was still attractive at the ripe old age of ninety. Matt could see his mother in his grandmother's face.

Matt's grandfather had been a banker and was president of The First National Bank for twenty years. His grandmother had some old family money that came from the timber business. She was high on the social ladder, and she liked to flaunt her status whenever she could. She was initially thrilled that her oldest daughter married a doctor, but became disappointed over the years because her son-in-law never really had any interest in high society. Said that he didn't have the background or the time for such things.

Elizabeth and Jason Barrett. Even the names sounded distinguished.

Matt hugged his grandmother and said, "How are you, Gran?"

She replied, "Well for my age. How was your flight? Flew first class, I'm sure."

"Yes, ma'am," Matt lied.

She then said, "I was hoping someone would do something with that hideous car that Dr. Martin insisted on driving. I noticed it in the driveway when we drove up. I don't think it makes a good impression at all."

Maggie said, "Mother, it's a good old Land Cruiser, and Joseph always said that it had a lot of good miles left in it. Besides, everybody in town knows he drove it anyway."

She replied, "Well, that doesn't mean that we have to have it on display now. And, Maggie, I am going to insist that you get a new dress for the funeral, and I want you to promise me that you will wear your grandmother's brooch. It will certainly be a good reflection on the family."

Maggie replied, "I am not that interested in some kind of display that reflects on the family. I am going to be there to bury my husband! Who cares what I look like?"

Elizabeth was now getting angry, "I for one care, and I would think you would too. There is no reason that you have dressed like a pauper over the years except to irritate me, and after all I have done."

Maggie lost it. "I am sitting here, planning my husband's funeral, and you walk in and make it all about you and your status in the community! Is that what you think is important? I'm going to go to my closet and find the plain-Janest-looking dress in there and wear it as I am driving that old car to the church. And I'm going to make sure everybody sees me and knows who I am!"

Tears were now streaming down his mother's face, and Matt didn't know what to do. He had seen some exchanges between them over the years but never quite like this one. His grandmother had always taken pride in her self-control and never would have had a public outburst like that. Matt wondered if maybe she was suffering from dementia like her husband. She had turned and was making her way back toward the living room. Matt got his mother a glass of water, and Ruth Shelby said it was time for crowd control.

Matt noticed how pained and weary his mother looked. She also seemed a little embarrassed that she had lost her temper to that degree.

She said, "I am sorry, but I am not going to let mother create a scene with all of her 'reflection on the family' nonsense. You would think she would know by now that nobody cares about all of that."

Matt said, "She just has to create the drama and get the attention. It's always been that way."

Maggie replied, "Well, I don't need it right now, and I hope she got the message."

Matt said, "I bet she did!"

*****

When they got to the funeral home, Rick Parker met them with that warm greeting that only a funeral director can accomplish. It is a special gift how they can do so well with people at such a terrible time in their lives.

He said, "Any problems with your flight, Matt?"

Matt replied, "Just the inevitable delays, nothing major."

Rick said, "I take it that Samuel hasn't made it in yet."

Anna didn't give Matt a chance to reply and quickly said, "Driving in tomorrow."

Rick hugged Maggie and patted Anna on the back, and ushered them all into his office. He offered them something to drink and they declined.

Then he looked at them all, kind of going from one to the other, and said, 'I wish for all the world that we didn't have to be here tonight. I would like to say how sorry I am for your loss. I knew Dr. Martin well, and it is going to be hard for this community to get along without him. You know, he was always so good to visit the family members of patients that had passed away. All doctors don't do that."

Maggie said, "Thank you, Rick."

Rick went on, "Maggie, you and Dr. Martin have a good burial policy, so there is really nothing to be concerned about from a financial standpoint. What we have to do tonight is let y'all choose a casket and discuss a few details. It shouldn't take long."

They all nodded their heads in agreement.

It was not difficult for them to pick out a casket. Everyone knew that a fancy one was not what Dr. Martin would have wanted. Rick related how he once told him that he would rather be buried in a pine box but was sure one wouldn't be available because there wasn't any money in them. Maggie said she had also heard him say that before. They all agreed that the copper colored one without any frills would be fine.

They spent some time going over some of their preferences for visitation and the funeral, and the whole meeting was over in less that an hour and a half.

*****

Back home, everybody was gone except for Ruth. She made sure they didn't need anything else to eat and finished cleaning the kitchen. She assured them that she would be back early in the morning and left.

Maggie, Matt, and Anna sat around the kitchen table and talked for a while, glad to just be the three of them. Matt couldn't help but remember that the last time he was home and sitting at this table, he was talking to his dad. He got that sick feeling that one gets when all of a sudden, it comes to their mind that they have suffered a great loss and can't undo it. It's almost like your mind had forgotten for a while and then in an instant remembers. The cruelty of the grief process.

Anna seemed exhausted and said, "I think I would cry some more but my tear tank must be empty."

Maggie gave her a hug and said, "I bet you got some left, but I do think you reached your quota for today."

Matt said, "I would have to agree with that observation."

Anna managed a smile and said, "Well, if y'all are going to gang up on me, I think I'll go to bed."

******

Saturday began with Ruth and two other members of Maggie's Sunday school class cooking breakfast. They got an early start, and judging by the volume of food, they must have been expecting a crowd. Mr. Slocum was in and out doing various maintenance work that he felt was necessary. He also had the leaf blower out and in good running order. He did not intend for one leaf to be on the sidewalk at any time during the day.

Anna and Matt went to the airport midmorning to meet Dr. Romero. They were relieved to get out of the house for a while. They recognized him easily because he was the only Hispanic passenger among the arrivals. Matt was impressed that even though they had never met him, he called them by name and acted as if he had known them all their lives.

Dr. Romero was in private practice in Nicaragua but also taught part time at a medical school. He was the primary one that set up surgical cases for Dr. Martin to do while he was there. He spoke English very well and seemed to Matt and Anna to be very personable. When they got home, Maggie was in her usual spot in the kitchen. He bowed slightly, took her hand, and kissed it.

He said, "Mrs. Maggie, I am very pleased to see you again after all these years. The biggest honor of my life has been to work with your husband and to call him my friend. I do not have adequate words to express my sympathy and deep sorrow that I feel for you and your children."

Maggie's eyes were moist, and her lip quivered a little. She said, "Dr. Romero, it is an honor for us to have you here. I wish the circumstances were different. Joseph always said that he had lost one brother but found another one. He talked about you all the time, and I know you were a big part of what he was trying to accomplish in your country."

Dr. Romero replied, "He accomplished a lot. There are so many stories but not enough time to tell them."

Ruth appeared and said, "Let's tell them later. It is time for lunch so y'all fix your plates."

Maggie introduced Dr. Romero to Ruth and related to him as to how she was in charge. They all fixed a plate and sat down.

Matt and Anna had a lot of questions about Nicaragua and Dr. Romero's practice. He tried to relate as best he could some of the contrasts between their two countries. They were fascinated with the information, which was somewhat new to them since they had not talked about it that much with their father. Anna was about to ask Dr. Romero when he had met their mother, but she didn't get a chance to. There was a commotion in the living room, and they heard someone say the name Samuel. The golden boy had made it.

Matt stood up, began walking toward the living room, and met Samuel coming into the kitchen. He shook his hand and said, "Good to see you, brother. Glad you're here."

Matt was mildly irritated that he was just now getting in, but he did not show it. He had promised Anna that he wouldn't make a scene.

Samuel could barely return the greeting before having to brace himself as Anna came running full force and gave him a huge hug. She was smiling ear to ear, and Matt was glad to see her feeling better. She had been through some tough days and had some more ahead. Anna made no bones about being crazy about her brothers. She had always enjoyed the dual position of being the only girl and the baby of the family. If anybody ever told her she was spoiled, she simply thanked them and said that she deserved it and was proud of it.

Matt looked at Samuel and was impressed as usual. He was wearing shorts, a polo shirt, and deck shoes with no socks. His hair was slightly long and just a little windblown. Sunglasses perched at the top of his forehead. Matt thought, *Yeah, Patrick Swayze.*

Maggie made a big fuss over him and said, "Go and kill the fatted calf, Ruth. Look who's home."

Matt leaned over to Anna and said under his breath, "That sure is appropriate. The prodigal son returns. If dad were here, I bet he'd give him a robe and a ring. Then we could be biblically correct."

Anna punched him and said, "Matt, you promised!"

Matt replied, "I know, I know. I'm just kidding."

Anna added, "And besides, the jealous brother in the story is not a good 'reflection on the family.'"

Matt punched her back.

Ruth gave him a big hug and told him that she was going to do something with that mop of hair of his if he didn't take care of it. That was a running thing between them. Samuel smiled and said, "Yes ma'am." Samuel was definitely Ruth's favorite. That went all the way back to his childhood, and she never tried to deny it.

The kitchen table had become kind of a headquarters, and they all sat around it through the better part of the afternoon. There weren't as many people in and out as there were yesterday. They talked through most of the afternoon, and Samuel filled everybody in on his latest venture. He felt that opening a ski rental and supply shop in Winter Park was not going to be a good idea. Matt, of course, had already come to that conclusion.

Anna was sorry that she had dropped out of nursing school and was afraid she would have to start all over if she went back, so she was not sure of her plans. Nobody said anything about her failed romance.

Matt was the only one who seemed to have it together with his job and family, but he didn't say much about it. He just joined in the small talk.

About three o'clock, they decided to try to get some rest and then get ready for visitation at five.

******

Rick Parker met them at the side door of the funeral home as they had planned. He had told them the night before that a lot of people would be there early, and if they came in the front door, they would never get to where they needed to be.

They were setup in the chapel, with the casket down front. The family did not have to be in a formal receiving line, and some of them could come and go, taking breaks as needed. Rick thought that would be better since he expected so many people. The chapel was full of flowers, and they found out that some had been sent on to the church since there was not enough room for them all.

The casket was open and that took some getting used to, especially for Anna. Matt had to take her in another room for a while before she was able to come back into the chapel. She did pretty well after that.

Samuel, in his usual fashion, drew crowds. The faces would change from time to time, but he was never without a group around him.

There were more people than anyone could imagine. Visitation was supposed to be over at seven but went on till almost eight. Matt had never shaken so many hands in his life. His mother had settled into a routine of standing for a while and then sitting for a while. He thought he saw her shoes off at one time. They were all glad when they could say their goodbyes to Rick Parker and go home.

Chapter 4

The Funeral

Sunday morning was quiet around the house. It was the first time since Dr. Martin's death that there were no people there other than family. Ruth Shelby had left instructions for breakfast, and even labeled everything and left warm-up instructions so there would be no confusion. She asked for the morning off so that she could attend church. Maggie said that she didn't think Ruth had missed a day of Sunday school, or church, in years.

Maggie decided to go to Sunday school but said she wasn't going to stay for church. She opined that she would be attending a fairly large service there later in the day. She knew she could have gotten an 'excused absence' from her class but said that she got a lot of comfort from her church friends.

Maggie left, and Matt and Anna took their usual perches around the breakfast table. Samuel had not come down yet. He was a night owl and stayed up much later than the rest. He had indicated that he might want to go to church but was realistic and knew he probably wouldn't get up on time. Matt did think it a little odd that Samuel was thinking about church but did remember that he always was a little bit more "spiritual" than Anna and him. Their dad had even kidded that with his gift of gab, his looks, and his religion, he could probably make it as a TV evangelist.

Samuel made it to the kitchen around 9:45 a.m. and took the breakfast casserole out of the refrigerator. He declared that of all the different casseroles brought when somebody passes away, he would bet that the breakfast casserole was the most popular. He heated a piece in the microwave and sat down.

Matt asked, "What time did you turn in last night?"

Samuel answered, "About 12:30. I'm reading the book, *Not a Fan*. It's about how Jesus has a lot of fans but not that many followers."

Matt said, "I didn't realize you were going so religious on us."

Samuel said, "Oh, I don't know about that. I'm trying to work on a few things. You know, find peace and happiness and all that."

Matt's reply was sarcastic, "A job might help with that."

Anna jumped in before Samuel could reply and said, "Let's don't get into all of that today, guys."

Samuel looked at Matt with a combination of hurt and anger in his eyes, but he let it drop.

Anna quickly changed the subject and asked, "Are we going to have to go to a lawyer's office and have some type of reading of the will, or will Mom take care of all of that?"

Matt answered, "Mom said that we were all supposed to go to Bill Haynes office on Monday morning, but I think it is just a formality. I don't think it will be dramatic like in the movies when someone really rich dies."

Samuel said, "There is one thing though. I was talking to Cynthia Reynolds at visitation last night. She is Bill Hayne's paralegal and said that Mr. Haynes was handling all our legal affairs. I told her that I guessed it would all be pretty straightforward, and she said she thought so. But she went on to say that there was a manila envelope in the file that Mr. Haynes had handled without her help, and he never commented on what it was. Said when she asked about it, he was evasive. When I pressed her about it, she said that she had already told me more than she was supposed to."

Matt remembered what their mother had said about his father's special plans for the money from his one investment. He wondered if that was related to the mysterious envelop. He decided not to say anything about it. Besides, he didn't know much about it anyway.

Maggie came in from Sunday school, and her eyes were all puffy and red. Her children asked her what had happened?

She related as to how Jim Norred spent almost all of the open assembly time talking about their father, and there wasn't a dry eye in the place. She said that she felt like she must already be at the funeral.

Matt said, "I guess it turned out to be a bad idea to go."

Maggie replied. "No, it was all right. I love all those folks and they love me. It's just part of the process. Besides, like Anna says, maybe my tear tank won't be quite as full this afternoon."

Maggie added, "Ruth will be over at eleven o'clock to make sure we are fed and presentable for church. Billy Slocum will drive us up there at about one o'clock."

Nobody was very hungry at lunch, but Ruth insisted on them eating some.

She said, "It's gonna be a long afternoon, and y'all have to have something on your stomach. I'll declare you act like you want to get sick right in the middle of the service. One more bite of that green bean casserole Samuel and you can be through."

Before they left, Ruth lined them up in chronological order and began her inspection. One would have thought she was a commanding general inspecting the troops. Everybody got some comment when it was their turn. It was under her breath, as if she were saying it to herself: "Didn't think you were serious…threatened your mother with a plane dress…makes your hips look too big. Big businessman…can't tie a tie straight. Samuel Martin, you're going to… another combing of that mop. Shoes don't even begin to go with that dress, young lady. Thought y'all could do better."

When revisions were made and they were all finally pronounced to be good enough, they loaded up and went to the church.

*****

The Second Baptist Church was a sprawling complex with a large sanctuary that had been remodeled two years ago. People were already arriving when they pulled into the parking lot at 1:20 p.m. They were met by Rick Parker who told them that they would be riding to the graveside service in one of the cars provided by the funeral home, so they didn't have to park in line.

As they walked toward one of the side entrances of the church, they were met by the minister of education, Mike Smith. He ushered them into the church and on to Dr. Johnson's study. When they entered the study, they found Dr. Johnson sitting in a chair with his elbows on his knees and his head in his hands. He quickly stood up and tried to compose himself. He seemed embarrassed. Matt thought about how he had felt in the airport in Atlanta two days ago.

Maggie said, "Are you all right, Ted?"

He replied, "To tell you the truth, Maggie, I am not. I am supposed to be the strong shepherd, but I guess I am also human. Some days are tougher than others, and this is one of them. But thankfully, the Lord will see us all through it."

They all sat down around the table in the study, and Dr. Johnson asked if anyone had any last-minute concerns or details.

Maggie said, "I wanted to be sure that we had agreed that the casket would be closed."

The pastor replied, "I talked to Rick a few minutes ago, and he is aware of that."

He continued, "Mike will escort you all to the foyer just prior to the start of the service, and Maggie and Anna will be ushered to their seats by Dr. Sanders and Dr. Romero, respectively. Matt will walk along behind his mother and Samuel with Anna. The service will start when you all are seated. Everything will simply follow the program after that. Of course, Rick and his assistant will be sure everything runs smoothly, as will I."

Time passed quickly, and Mike took the family to the huge foyer in the back of the sanctuary. Everyone stood as they were escorted to their places on the first pew.

When they were seated, Matt saw his grandparents seated a short distance from them. His grandmother looked fantastic. That was not by accident, of course. He wondered if she was over the quarrel that she and his mother had.

One of Maggie's sisters and her husband had made it and were seated next to the grandparents. The only other person seated with the family was Ruth Shelby. Maggie had insisted. Billy Slocum would have been next to them also but he was seated with the pallbearers.

The church was full with some having to stand. The crowd noise quickly died down when Dr. Johnson stood up and walked to the pulpit. He welcomed everyone and then voiced a prayer.

Some music followed, the first piece was a contemporary song called "Follow You There." Dr. Martin had heard it on a mission trip, and it had become one of his favorites. Two of his favorite hymns followed: "The Old Rugged Cross" and "Just as I Am." Matt remembered his father saying on many occasions that he always showed up just as he was and figured he would show up in heaven someday the same way.

Dr. Johnson spoke again and talked about how full a life Dr. Martin's had been and his dedication to his family, his church, and his profession. He told of the many times that he was present with family members when Dr. Martin would come in and talk with them. He spoke of how he had a bedside manner that created an air of comfort and confidence for patients and families in times of difficulty and uncertainty. He concluded his remarks by speaking about Nicaragua and the passion that Dr. Martin had for the people of that country. He introduced Dr. Pat Sanders, saying that he would now come and say a few words about his friend and colleague.

Dr. Sanders was slightly over six feet tall and still had all of his hair. It was gray and made him look all the more distinguished. He was three years younger than Dr. Martin, and they had met when they were in training at Big Charity Hospital. Matt always thought that he was the essence of a Southern gentleman. To top it off, he had a slow, clear Southern drawl that he now employed to its fullest.

He began, "Maggie, Matt, Samuel, and Anna; Mr. and Mrs. Barrett; other family members; and guests. I would first like to thank you, Maggie, for the honor you have given me in allowing me to speak about your husband, Dr. Joseph Martin. I hope I am up to the task.

"Joseph Martin was my friend and colleague for over thirty years. When I say 'friend,' I do not use that designation lightly. Time does not allow me to tell of all the times he proved his friendship, but I will tell of one time in particular that affected me in a big way. Twelve years ago, when my father was suffering from the terminal stages of

Lou Gehrig's disease, it was very hard on me and Joseph knew it. He did some things that I will never forget, and without which, I may not have made it through that time. He would take my night call from time to time without me asking him to. For the non-medical people in the room, that is a tremendous thing for someone to do. Remember, he would still have his own call to do. He would also make it a habit to come by my office most days at the end of clinic. He would spend a lot of time talking with me instead of making his rounds and going on home to his family. The third, and perhaps the most significant thing he did, was to pray for my father, my family, and me at the end of those visits. To do those things for a short time would be exemplary, but Dr. Martin kept it up for three months.

"That he was a good doctor is a matter of record, and many of us here today are testimonies to his skill. It has been said that it takes three things to be a good surgeon: compassion, competence, and confidence. And I can attest to you that Joseph Martin exemplified all three. He was an intuitive surgeon who knew when to operate, but just as importantly, he knew when not to operate. His confidence was born of humility in that he never took credit for the skills he possessed. He believed that they were God-given gifts, and he had no right to be prideful about them.

"I want to tell a story now that illustrates his sense of humor, and believe me, he had one. I overheard him talking to some family members one day shortly after a patient had expired. The family spokesman said to Joseph, 'Well, you know, Dr. Martin, it was the Lord's will.'

"He replied, 'That is true, no doubt.'

"When I saw Joseph later, I said, 'You sure did let the Lord take that hit.'

"He said back to me, 'You have to understand that when things don't go too well, it is okay to let the Lord carry most of the blame. But when things go well, you need to take most of the credit for yourself.'"

The congregation erupted in laughter.

When the noise died down, he continued, "Another thing I always enjoyed involved his fluency in Spanish. Whenever he got irritated or impatient in surgery, he would break into rapid-fire Spanish. Nobody could understand a word he was saying. It reminded everybody of Ricky Ricardo from the old *I Love Lucy* show. Joseph said he would do it to relieve tension but also to show off a little. He said he thought it sounded like he was worldly and sophisticated when anybody would point out that he was bilingual."

Dr. Sanders paused briefly and then continued, "I think it is hard to know what to say at a time like this to truly express one's feelings. When someone passes away, they just leave a big old hole where they used to be. Joseph Martin leaves several of them: in his family, the clinic and hospital where he practiced, this church, this community, and Nicaragua. We cannot ever fill those holes in. Maybe I can sum it up for me with a quote from Robert E. Lee that Joseph was fond of. Upon hearing that Stonewall Jackson had to have his left arm amputated, Lee said, 'General Jackson has lost his left arm. I have lost my right.' Ladies and gentlemen, I have lost my right arm, and my best friend."

He paused and wiped his eyes. It was several seconds before he was able to speak again.

He continued, "I wish I had time to tell you a lot more, but I don't, and most of you already know it anyway. Let me conclude by simply saying that Dr. Joseph Martin was a good man. He got up every day of his life and simply did his best. There are a whole lot of people who are better off today because of him, and I am one of them. Thank you, Maggie, for allowing me to say these few words."

As Dr. Sanders was making his way back to his seat, the choir and orchestra began "Amazing Grace."

Matt began to reflect on the service, and something kept bothering him. He didn't seem capable of crying. He had shed a few tears at the airport, but he felt like that didn't really count. That was more like the moist eyes we can get occasionally. He had observed his mother sobbing from time to time during the service, and Anna and Samuel seemed to take turns breaking down and having to console one another. He wondered if there was something wrong with Matthew Martin. He loved his father and felt terrible, but he just didn't seem to be able to express it. Had he become a cold-hearted businessman that had lost his compassion for people, even his own family? Would he feel better if he had a "good cry" as he had heard people say? The hymn ended and Dr. Johnson rose to speak.

He thanked Dr. Sanders for his eulogy and thanked the people, on behalf of the Martin family, for attending and supporting them during this difficult time. He admonished everyone to keep them in their prayers. He said the closing prayer, and the casket was then rolled out of the church by the pallbearers under the direction of Rick Parker. The family followed close behind with "What a Friend We Have in Jesus" playing in the background.

The graveside service was made more special by the beautiful fall weather. Dr. Martin would have liked that because he was known to talk about his thermostat not being wired for hot or cold, just the moderate temperatures.

The family took their seats, and Anna was seated between her brothers. She had now reached the point where she was virtually crying continuously. Matt and Samuel took turns trying to console her. Matt felt that the finality of the gravesite was simply too much for her. She kept repeating, "No, Daddy. No, Daddy," and Samuel was having a hard time with that. Matt was moved but held it together as usual. He tried his best to comfort them both. He was thankful that his mother had Ruth.

Dr. Johnson's remarks were brief, and he concluded by quoting the twenty-third Psalm. The pallbearers placed their boutonnières on the casket and then filed by to pay their respects to the family. Pat Sanders got no further than Maggie. He put his hand on her shoulder, and as he was about to say something, he simply broke down and wept. His wife came over in a few minutes and led him away. Dr. Romero was the last one in line. He was fine till he got to Anna. He hugged her and then his tears came. He kept repeating something in Spanish.

*****

Baptists don't do anything without food being provided, and the fellowship hall of the church had plenty of it. Dr. Martin and

Maggie's Sunday school class was in charge of getting it all organized. Fortunately, the crowd had thinned out some from the large numbers at the funeral.

Matt noticed Dr. Romero sitting by himself and decided to go over and talk with him. He felt like he had not been able to visit with him much due to the last two days being so hectic.

Matt did know some things about Dr. Romero because his father had talked some about him over the years. He was from a large family of eight siblings, but he was the only doctor. Two of his brothers lived in the United States, somewhere on the West Coast, as best as Matt could remember. His family was not wealthy but had some old connections to the president's family, and Matt's dad always said that was invaluable help to their work there.

Dr. Romero and Joseph Martin had hit it off on the first medical mission trip that Dr. Martin took over thirty years ago and had become great friends. They shared a common concern for the people of Nicaragua and felt like they made a lot more progress together than they could each on his own.

Dr. Romero stood up as Matt approached him and commented on how nice the service had been.

Matt nodded his head in agreement and said, "I wanted to tell you again how much it means to my family to have you here. We know how hard it is for you to get away from your practice."

Dr. Romero replied, "Thank you, Matt. It would not be possible for me not to be here."

He went on. "As Dr. Sanders pointed out, there is a big hole left by your father in my country, and also in my heart."

After a few minutes of small talk, Dr. Romero said, "Matt, I will be looking forward to you coming to my country before too long."

Matt replied, "Maybe someday, but I don't really have plans anytime soon."

Dr. Romero's expression became more serious, and he said, "Plans are not always made by us. As you see, neither of us had plans one week ago to be here today."

Matt was puzzled and asked, "Dr. Romero, are there some plans that my father talked to you about?"

He replied, "There is something, but I do not feel like your father would want me to talk to you about it now. In this country, isn't it customary to meet with a lawyer after someone has passed away?"

Matt said, "Yes, we are doing that in the morning."

Dr. Romero said, "Perhaps that is when you will get the answers to these questions."

Matt immediately thought about the mysterious manila envelope that Bill Hayne's paralegal had spoken about.

Chapter 5

The Lawyer's Office

Monday morning was a sharp contrast to the previous several days. Even Ruth wasn't there. She said she would leave them alone till around lunchtime, but they could call if they needed her input on anything.

Everybody had made it to the kitchen by about nine thirty and were sitting in their usual places. They were all dressed and ready to go to Bill Hayne's office.

Maggie said, "It sure is a relief to be through with all of that process, but I thought the service was very nice. I especially thought that Pat Sanders did a great job, and I know that was hard on him."

Samuel said, "It really does touch your heart when you realize how many friends your family has and what they mean to you. I am always impressed with that church too, and how sincere everyone seems to be. I'm not sure I really appreciated it before."

Maggie said, "You know your father felt the same way. He said that church was a doing kind of church and not just one that preached about it."

Matt thought about his own church in Atlanta, and how he and his family had gotten away from it. He had seen a great deal of support over this weekend and wondered what that would be like if something happened to him. He definitely did not feel a closeness to his church like what his mother and Samuel were talking about. His discomfort went even beyond his thoughts about his church. He had never seen much answered prayer in his life, at least not the way he wanted it answered, and he did not feel this strong need for God as he felt like he was doing fine on his own. He was still unable to be at peace with that line of thinking. He wondered if his father's death had made him start thinking about his own mortality. His thoughts were interrupted by his mother's announcement that it was time to go.

Bill Hayne's office was not that far of a drive from their house, and they were met in the waiting room by Cynthia Reynolds. She commented on how nice the services had been the day before and hoped they were all doing well. She ushered them into Mr. Hayne's office and asked if they would like any refreshments. They declined, and she said he would be in shortly. One of the first things that Matt noticed were several items of memorabilia from the University of Alabama in various places in the office. Mr. Haynes came into the room, and after the appropriate introductions and greetings, Matt commented on his connection to LSU's archrival.

He chuckled and said, "I'm not sure that I would have been Dr. Martin's lawyer if he had known about that before he got to know me. I did a lot of work for the clinic several years ago and got to know your father because he was on the board. When he came to me for some personal legal work and noticed the Alabama connection, he said it would be okay. We could just agree to be enemies on game day."

Everybody laughed, and he went on to say, "I do want to express my sympathies to you all and express my deep regret at the passing of Dr. Martin. He was a friend as well as a client. What we have to do today is, for the most part, fairly straightforward and should not take that long. There is one item that is somewhat unconventional and may take a little longer. We can handle it last."

Matt knew he was talking about the envelope, and he was getting more curious as time went by to see what that was all about.

Bill opened the file and continued, "Dr. Martin's will is straightforward and of course, leaves his assets to his surviving widow as is customary. Those assets are primarily a retirement fund, and real property that is jointly owned. There is some equity in the clinic and a savings account that will also be included. Life insurance policies will be dealt with in the upcoming weeks. He did make some lists of personal items that would go to each of you, and I have made copies for you."

He paused briefly and then said, "I would like to say something at this point if I could, and I'm not sure exactly how to express it. There was something special about this man, and I know you are aware of that and have heard it from many others. He was cut from a different cloth. I have never in my life worked with someone who not only didn't know his net worth but who didn't seem to care. Said he had plenty and a little extra on top of it, so why worry. I digress, but I just felt like I needed to share that with you."

Matt wondered how many mini-eulogies he had heard through the weekend. He appreciated them all, and he was particularly glad that Anna had done okay with this one. She seemed to have her emotions in pretty good check this morning.

Bill continued, "Unless any of you have questions, I will proceed with the final matter that we have to deal with that is somewhat unusual."

He opened the manila envelope that was in the file folder and took out several documents.

He said, "These documents have to do with an investment that Dr. Martin made several years ago that has done quite well and his plans for that money. This matter, Maggie, is directed only to the children. There is a cover letter that your father wrote, and I am to read it before we discuss any more details."

Dear Matt, Samuel, and Anna,

I am writing to you to at least partially explain my intentions in handling this money this way. I am simply requiring you three to take a trip to Nicaragua together. Do not feel that I am trying to force my love of that country and its people onto my children. That has little or nothing to do with it. Suffice it to say that you are going there because my connections there enabled me to plan such a trip. What I hope is accomplished in each of your lives through this trip may never happen, but I trust you will understand that my motivation is pure.

Dad

Mr. Haynes continued, "Although unusual, the matter is fairly simple. The amount we are talking about is roughly three quarters of a million dollars, which you will share equally. The only requirement for anybody to receive a share is for all three to go. The trip is planned, and for the most part, paid for. And the people who are handling the details in Nicaragua will simply need to know the date you plan to arrive. The length of the trip is specified as three weeks."

He paused at that point to let the information sink in.

Matt was the first to speak, "My first thought is that I don't have three weeks that I can simply take off and leave everything to my partner. And of course, I am the only one of the three of us with a spouse and children. What if I was willing to forfeit my share to Anna and Samuel?"

Their attorney answered, "You cannot do that. It is very specific in that if one does not go, then no one gets anything."

Matt asked, "What happens to it then?"

Mr. Haynes answered, "It is specified in the will to go to a fund in Nicaragua."

Matt was getting agitated and said, "Well, let's just give it to them then. They need it more than we do."

Samuel said, "I certainly don't think that is your decision alone, Matt. Some of us might need that money."

Matt was quick to reply, "We don't need to get into a discussion about the many reasons why some of us might need the money, do we?"

Samuel gripped the armrests of his chair and acted like he was going to get up but then stopped. He was glaring at Matt as if he had something to say but thought better of it.

Anna was getting upset and said, "Do you two have to act like this?"

Maggie spoke up, "Bill, I apologize for this. I guess we are all a little out of sorts. It certainly looks like we are going to need some time to discuss this. Is there anything else you need for us to do right now?"

Bill replied, "No, not at all. I'll have Cynthia bring some papers by for you to sign. They are just routine signatures that are required. Take your time in discussing this matter and get back to me at your convenience, and always feel free to call if you have any questions. There is a three-month time limit for a decision to be made. Dr. Martin felt that there may be some differences of opinion and did not want this to linger as a bone of contention."

Matt said with sarcasm, "This is likely to be a bone of contention for a long time to come."

Chapter 6

The Discussion

Back home, they were all milling around in the kitchen, fixing something to eat from the generous supply of leftovers. Ruth stuck her head in the back door and made sure her services were not needed. She and Maggie talked for a few minutes, and she left.

After lunch, they were all sitting in their usual spots around the kitchen table. They all knew that there needed to be a discussion about the proposed trip to Nicaragua, but Matt's initial reaction had made everyone reluctant to speak.

Maggie broke the ice. "Judging from the brief discussion in the lawyer's office, I think there is definitely going to have to be some more conversation and, ultimately, a decision made. Each of you is in a different circumstance, some between opportunities, and then there is Matt settled in his business. He is also the only one right now with a family to think of."

Samuel said, "I am not sure what the big deal is. People take vacations all the time. And besides, a quarter million dollars for three weeks is a pretty nice pay off."

Matt remained calm but couldn't resist a little sarcasm. "It is easy to talk about time off when you are 'between opportunities,' as Mom so nicely put it. I can't simply tell my partner that I'm going to check out for three weeks."

Anna said, "But, Matt, you have talked about how great a guy your partner is. It seems like he might understand in this situation."

Matt replied, "It's not just him. I have to live with myself and my decisions, and how they affect everybody. And you mention understanding. How can anybody understand something like this? I have always thought that Dad was different, in a good way, I might add, and I admired his sense of humor. But this is hard for even me to understand."

Maggie interjected, "I know this whole thing is unconventional to say the least, but I know that your father had a good reason for doing this. He was never one to engage in some kind of cruel humor or bad prank. He certainly would not do that with his own children and that much money."

Matt replied, "I know that he said in his note that he wasn't trying to 'force' Nicaragua on us, but I have to say that it seems that way. He would always say that he thought everybody would benefit from seeing the world from that perspective."

Maggie said, "I know that your father would not do that. He may feel that you would gain some benefit as a side effect, so to speak, but he would not force his own views on anybody."

Anna said, "I go back to what Samuel said. Three quarters of a million dollars is a lot of money. I don't see how we have any choice in this. I know your business is doing well, Matt, but surely you realize what we're talking about here."

"I can't look at it the same way, Anna," Matt said. "My company is providing me a better living than I ever thought possible, and a good part of the reason for that is that I have been there running it. Y'all are asking me to go for the short-term gain without any consideration for possible long-term consequences."

Samuel asked, "What could possibly happen in three weeks that would have such a dramatic effect on your business?"

"I don't expect anybody at this table to have a clue what I'm talking about," Matt replied. "But you don't just pick up and leave at the drop of a hat and hope for the best.

"And besides, my partner and I were talking about vacations just last week, and he was saying that he was overdue for one. Can I just tell him, 'Too bad. Maybe next year.' And we haven't even mentioned my own family." Matt became real sarcastic and said, "Sorry, kids. No trip to Wally World this year. Dad had to go on a wild goose chase to God knows where!"

Samuel was getting madder and said. "I am not sure what all of your problems are with this, but I have about grown weary with your attitude. You have such a high opinion of yourself because of your great success in business, but I can assure you that there is a whole lot more to life than that. Your relationship with your siblings ought to mean something to you, and I don't know about Anna, but I'm not feeling the love here lately."

Matt started to speak but Samuel cut him off. "And don't hide behind that righteous shield of using your children as an excuse. I am absolutely sure that they will not be deprived of all future joy because you happened to go on this trip. I am going to say one more thing before I'm done. I have taken a lot of your sarcasm and derogatory remarks over the last few days, and I am done with that. I hope you understand what I mean."

Anna was getting upset and said, "I don't understand why it has to be like this. Matt, you and I talked about it before. I don't understand what is wrong!"

Matt had calmed down and did feel some remorse over the way he had been treating Samuel, and he was genuinely upset about the way his behavior affected his mother and Anna. He said in a softer voice, "I am sorry for anything I have said that may have been offensive to anyone. I can't give an answer on this before my flight leaves tomorrow. I have to discuss it with Carol and Tom. Let's try to get along better. I'll try to do my part."

Maggie thought that his form of an apology was probably the best he could do. She was not quite through with the discussion and said, "Matt, I would like to speak with you in private in my room if I could."

*****

When they were seated in Maggie's room, she in her chair by the window and Matt on the side of the bed, she said, "Matt, you have always said of me over the years that I was pretty perceptive, and it was hard to pull the wool over my eyes, so to speak."

"Yes, ma'am. That is for sure. I was always guilty till proven innocent."

Maggie smiled, "I think you got due process most of the time." She went on. "I think you would agree that I haven't interfered in your life a whole lot or meddled where I wasn't wanted. But I feel I need to say some things to you now, and hopefully, you will take them the right way. If any of what I say offends you, I will apologize in advance.

"First of all, for some reason your father wanted his children to go on a trip together. And interestingly, he will have some control over it even after his death. I have some ideas about what he was thinking, but I don't intend to speculate on that. I will say that your father was a very smart man and did not do things without good reason. Remember that Samuel and Anna did not come up with this idea but your father did.

"Second, I feel that the reasons you are stating for not wanting to take the time to go are only part of the story. I have known for quite some time that your relationship with your brother has not been good. It bothers me, and it literally breaks Anna's heart.

"It would be worse if we were together more often, but it is still a problem. I am of the opinion that what I'm talking about is at least part of your problem. I do not intend to take sides in the matter, but I am going to say that I feel that you haven't always judged Samuel fairly over the years. I don't think you have taken the time to try to understand what he has been through at times. He is not perfect but deserves some of the same 'due process' that you expect."

"I'm not sure I ever got the same due process as you call it from Dad. Samuel gets all of the accolades for rock climbing in Arizona, and I get nothing for studying and working hard to make something of myself."

Maggie said, "I think that your perception is wrong, but I guess it has become your reality. It is not my purpose to argue that with you today. I feel like you are going to give a lot of thought to your decision, and I am confident you will do what is right. Remember that you will have to live with it for a long time to come."

Matt walked back into the kitchen. Anna and Samuel were no longer there, and he stood for a while looking out the back window. It was quiet, the way it was after the funeral was over and all of the people were gone. The reality hit hard at this point as the permanence of his loss sunk in.

Matt would fly back to Atlanta tomorrow and discuss this trip with his wife and partner. But he already knew what he was going to do.

Chapter 7

The Tax Attorney

Joel Stein was back in his old law offices in downtown New Orleans for the first time since Hurricane Katrina had run him off. He had relocated to Birmingham, Alabama, where his son lived, and he intended to have a limited practice for the few years before he would retire for good. An old-school tax attorney, he was more than a little bitter over being forced out of the office where he had practiced for forty years. He also resented the computer age that had all but made him obsolete as he refused to give up pencils and paper.

His office building was a victim of the floodwaters and never reopened after Katrina. It was too old to be remodeled, which would have been cost prohibitive. The building was to be demolished in a couple of months, so he was back to go through the old files to see if anything had to be kept. He had put off the task for as long as he could. His offices were on the second floor, which was above the level reached by the floodwater. Some cleanup work had been done, but the building still had that musty, moldy smell. He climbed the stairs to the second floor and walked down the hall to his office. He wondered how many times he had made that trip before.

He loved the old-fashioned appearance of his office door that was wood with a frosted glass window. It had his name and title written in old print. His key still worked the lock, and he was glad of that. He didn't know how the humidity might have affected it.

Once inside, he was reminded of his glory days when he was one of the most respected and sought-after tax attorneys in the New Orleans area. Although dim and dusty, he could still visualize the way his offices had once looked, the old oak paneling and leather chairs, a reminder of the way it used to be. He had simply been too old and set in his ways to change with the times, and maybe it was a good thing that Katrina had all but finished him off.

After sitting at his desk and reminiscing for a while, he got up and walked into the file room to begin the task of going through the old records. The job that he had dreaded for so long turned out having a pleasant side to it. A lot of great old memories came back as he reviewed the files. The Sykes Shipping Line file was one that reminded him of big business and everything that goes with it. Back in the day, that was his biggest client. He had fond memories of the perks that came his way as he would save the shipping giant millions in taxes, and they would show their appreciation without restraint. The bonuses and the parties were memorable.

After going through several files, he came to the Monroe Medical and Surgical Clinic file. He had fond memories of that account, and it was one that he really never should have had. There was an old judge in New Orleans that was a relative of one of the founding doctors of the clinic, and he had recommended Joel to the group. He had provided almost all of their legal and tax work for over thirty years. The trips to Monroe were fond memories for him.

As he looked through the pages of the file, as one would look through an old scrapbook, he saw so many familiar names. He had to smile when he thought about some of the clinic board meetings he had attended and the discussions that would go on for hours. The doctors would argue about the finer points of tax law as if they knew what they were talking about. He remembered coming to an impasse with one of them over a tax question, and he laughed to himself since it was a relatively small sum of money, considering the millions that flowed through the clinic.

Five hundred dollars a month was being sent to Nicaragua from the clinic through the Nicaraguan Mission Outreach board. It was taken out of the doctor's check, and the argument came about when

Joel said that it should be tax deductible since it was going to a charitable organization. The doctor would not hear of it because he said that it was going to a specific person, and the NMO board simply was the vehicle to get it to Nicaragua. Joel had continued the argument and said that if it was going to a person there through a tax-exempt organization, it would have to be a good cause and still should be written off. Dr. Martin said something to the effect that he wasn't so sure that the cause could be classified as charitable. It was more of an obligation. Joel let it drop since it did not have anything to do with clinic taxes, but was a matter of the doctor's personal taxes. He never knew what that money was for or who it went to.

Chapter 8

The Missionary

Daniel Stevens walked down the middle of the walkway in the Sunshine Market. This was a sprawling complex located in the middle of Managua, Nicaragua. It was not the place where you would find the *touristas* looking for souvenirs to take back home. He had been here many times and had some degree of comfort but still had a healthy fear. His wife Sharon was with him, which caused him another level of anxiety, but his protests had fallen on deaf ears.

"I am as much of a missionary here as you are, and I will not let fear keep me from doing what I feel called to do any more than I would expect that of you," she had said when he told her he would feel better if she stayed home.

Daniel did take some comfort in the fact that they were with a Nicaraguan lady named Olivia. She knew her way around the market and would not let them get themselves into trouble. Olivia ran an outreach program that basically tried to find prostitutes some alternative to their chosen profession. This was difficult because there were so many of them and so few jobs available. They plied their trade in the brothels located in the market, and most of them brought their children with them. The kids were left to themselves most of the day in an environment that was unwholesome and dangerous.

Daniel had met Olivia through a fellow missionary that was moving back to the States. He immediately became interested in her ministry and was very concerned with helping the children. He and Sharon wanted to try to set up some type of day care for them, among other things. Lack of funds and a mountain of government red tape were making the project difficult to get off the ground.

Daniel had been a missionary in Nicaragua for the last four years. He worked for the Nicaragua Mission Outreach board, the one that owned the compound in Diriamba. He, his wife Sharon, and two children—Bo, thirteen; and Sadie, ten—lived in a gated neighborhood in Managua. His background was in construction; and it was said that he could build anything, and he could fix anything.

Daniel was introduced to Nicaragua by coming on mission trips starting when he was in his early twenties. This was through his church in his hometown of Mobile, Alabama. He had felt over the years a call to become a full-time missionary and was eventually hired by the NMO board. His primary responsibility was to coordinate and work with all the mission teams that came throughout the year. He was free to work on other projects that came to his attention as was evident by his work with Olivia.

Olivia and Sharon were visiting with two of the ladies whose trust they had gained, and Daniel decided to walk on a little farther into the market. He was trying to establish somewhat of a presence there and get to know more of the people, yet he was still cautious and knew he had to be smart about it. Not far ahead of where he was walking, he spotted Ramon. Ramon was somewhat of a godfather type in the market and controlled a lot of what went on, especially the prostitutes. Daniel had learned what he knew about him through Olivia, who said that he could be dangerous and absolutely could not be trusted. Daniel was one of those who believed in the core goodness of all people and figured that he would talk to Ramon at some point. But not today.

*****

On the drive home, Daniel said, "I saw Ramon today while you and Olivia were talking to those ladies. I may be a little skittish, but I didn't care for the look he gave me."

"You need to be skittish as you put it," Sharon said. "Olivia told me that he was overheard saying that he might have some fun with some gringos that like to mettle in his business." She continued, "She thinks that he doesn't bother us now because we are not having much of an effect on anything."

"Do you really think he would be that big of a problem?"

"That is what I love about you, Daniel. You are gonna look for the good in every single person there is, no matter what. I'm giving you a couple of months, and you'll have Ramon passing the plate at church."

"Well, let me put the question to you as your kids would: what would Jesus do?"

Sharon laughed and said, "You got me on that one."

*****

Back home in his office, Daniel was going over some paper-work, and he picked up the folder he had prepared for the next group coming in to stay at the compound. It was different in that it was not the usual twenty- to thirty-member group from a church that he was accustomed to. This group consisted of only three people. There was a paper in the folder that had been prepared about two years ago that outlined some activities that they were supposed to do. Daniel looked over some of them: cliff diving/jumping, attend some of the feedings of children in the villages, participate in building one or two houses, visit a volcano, and a few others. Daniel had spent a lot of time with the originator of that list and felt that he had a pretty good idea what he was trying to accomplish. He was also very familiar with the names on the folder: Matt, Samuel, and Anna Martin.

Chapter 9

Nicaragua

It had been three months since their father's funeral, and Matt, Samuel, and Anna were on a plane to Nicaragua. Matt had the aisle seat; Anna was in middle, of course; and Samuel was by the window. They had all expressed their pleasure that the flight would only take about three hours. Samuel was already napping due to the fact that he always stays up later than the other two, and they had to get up early this morning to catch the short flight from Monroe to Houston to connect with their flight on to Managua. Matt noticed that Samuel had been reading in the Bible that their father had left to him. It was a Spanish/English translation that Maggie had given Dr. Martin years ago when he began learning Spanish. It had already made this flight many times before. Their father said that he loved it because he always got a Spanish lesson whenever he read the scripture.

Anna and Matt talked for a while about Anna's plans for the future, Matt's business and family, their mother, and various other things. After a time, they just relaxed in their seats and turned to their own thoughts. Anna dozed off, and Matt began thinking about Nicaragua. Being the curious one and the analyst, he had done some reading about the country and now reflected on what he had learned.

Nicaragua is a Central American country that is not very far north of Panama. It is about half way between the top of Canada and the bottom of South America. It had been considered in the early twentieth century for the site of the canal that ended up in Panama. There is still interest in constructing such a canal today.

The first European to visit Nicaragua was Christopher Columbus on his fourth voyage in 1502. Matt didn't remember that he had made four voyages. Of course, not too long after that, Nicaragua was conquered by Spain and did not gain independence from them until 1821. Civil war and revolution became the norm for the country after that. A revolutionary of note was Augusto Cesar Sandino. He led a revolution against the conservatives from 1927 to 1933. He was assassinated in 1934, but as a historic figure, he was the inspiration for the formation of the Sandinista National Liberation Front that was established in 1961.

The Sandinistas came to power in 1979, after a long dictatorial rule by the Somoza family. This led to the formation of a rebel group known as the Contras. Matt remembered that the Iran-Contra affair was a problem for Ronald Reagan during this period as he used funds raised through arms sales to Iran to support the Contras.

A Sandinistan, Manuel Lorenzo was elected president in 1984, defeated in 1990, then reelected several times. He is the current president of the country. Matt was glad that there was no revolution going on at the present time.

Matt reflected on the fact that the three of them would be supporting one of the main parts of the Nicaraguan economy, which is tourism. He did not anticipate, however, that they would be staying in any luxury accommodations. He had heard his dad talk about the compound before, and it did not sound too good to him. The fact that there was no air conditioning seemed to him to be a little too much to bear, especially in a tropical climate. His father had always said that you get used to the heat, but Matt wasn't looking forward to that.

He figured that they would also be supporting the other primary sector of the economy which was agriculture. He had tasted the coffee that his father had brought home, and it was excellent. The fruit was reported to be always fresh and excellent. He also heard that high-grade cigars were made in Nicaragua, and even though he wasn't a regular smoker, he was not opposed to a good cigar occasionally. He figured to get as much out of this trip as he could.

When the plane touched down in Managua, the pilot sure seemed awfully anxious to get it stopped. He rapidly deployed everything he had available to slow down, and Matt was wondering if they had a short runway.

The airport was relatively nice. It was crowded because another flight had landed just before theirs. They were all in line to get through customs, and Matt noticed the diversity of the crowd. He was impressed by how many Americans there were, and he couldn't help but notice how many people had on matching shirts denoting a mission group. It brought to mind that his father once said that the Nicaraguan people were the most "missionarried" people in the world.

There was a fee of ten dollars to get through the agent and enter the country and that seemed funny to Matt. He had never been to a country that had an admission fee.

After they collected their bags, they had to put them on a conveyor belt that sent them through some type of scanner. There was a lady sitting beside it, checking them on the screen as they went through. Occasionally, she would require the owner of a bag to take it over to a counter where there were several official-looking people who would then open the bag and go through the contents. The owner stood by and answered any questions they may have. Matt had a sick feeling in his stomach when the lady indicated to him to take his bag over to be looked at. He was already feeling the heat of the country and felt a little hotter as he picked up his bag to take it over for inspection.

He had not gone but two or three steps when he was approached by an official-looking gentleman with a badge above his left shirt pocket. Matt figured he was some type of government official. He motioned to the lady at the scanner, and she nodded her head in agreement with him.

He smiled and said to Matt, "I am sure that el Presidente would not want to hear that a son of Dr. Joseph Martin was inconvenienced upon arrival in his country. An inspection of your luggage will not be necessary. I am sorry I was not here earlier so that I could have gotten you through the lines faster."

Matt was somewhat dumfounded and said, "That is all right, and I do appreciate your help."

Matt held out his hand and said, "I am Matt Martin. I am pleased to meet you."

"I know who you are, and I know that Samuel and Anna are also here. I am Jose Ramirez, special agent to Presidente Lorenzo. I will be at your disposal if you need anything during your stay in my country. You will be able to get in touch with me through Dr. Romero if I am needed. I am not allowed to give my cell number out to anyone from another country."

Anna and Samuel had made it over, and after brief introductions, they made their way to the double glass doors that led to the hallway out of the building. The area was crowded with people, all of whom seemed to be waiting for arrivals. They immediately saw Dr. Romero and an American that they did not know. He was introduced to them, and they recognized the name, Daniel Stevens. They had been told that he would be their host during their stay. Their father had spoken highly of him before.

As they made their way through the crowd and out of the airport, Samuel asked Matt, "Who was that gentleman that you were talking to back there in the airport?"

Matt answered, "You're not going to believe it. I'll tell you later."

"This is your limo." Daniel pointed to an old white van that had seen some better years. "It belonged to one of the founders of the NMO Board, and he sort of gave it to me when I moved here four years ago. You'll be happy to know that I got the air conditioner fixed last week, and it almost works."

"Sounds and smells diesel," Samuel said.

"Virtually everything here is diesel," Daniel said.

They loaded the bags into the back of the van and climbed in. Dr. Romero insisted that Matt ride up front with Daniel. Said it was the privilege of the oldest. He and Daniel immediately struck up a conversation, and the first thing Matt talked about was his encounter with the government official back at the airport.

Daniel said, "I am not surprised to hear that. One thing you need to know is how popular and well known your father was here. A lot of the people you meet while you are here will either have been operated on by your dad or have a family member who was. Dr.

Romero always bragged about keeping him busy so he would not be bored during his visits."

"I can understand that, but I never quite got the whole connection to the president. I never thought much about it but that meeting in the airport makes it kinda real."

"Oh, it's real alright. The story has become a legend, but it is true. It all took place several years ago. The president's brother was hospitalized and was seriously ill. He had some kind of government job that required very little work which afforded him plenty of time to drink heavily. He started having some internal bleeding that you would have to get Dr. Romero to explain, but it is what can happen to heavy drinkers."

Daniel continued, "Dr. Romero knew that his only chance to survive was with surgery, but it was going to be complicated and risky due to the nature of the problem and how sick he was. Of course, he recommended your father to the president who immediately had him flown to Nicaragua by private jet."

Matt said, "You know, I remember my dad saying something about going one time on somebody's jet and how he could get used to that."

"Well, he sure did. And to make a long story short, he saved the president's brother who went on to drink proficiently for many more years, and your dad went on to become a living legend."

"That is an incredible story."

Daniel replied, "I understand what you are saying, but remember the guy at the airport. Would you say that his presence brings credibility to it?"

Matt replied, "It does that. I guess I just have never thought of myself as being the son of some kind of saint or legend as you say. I loved and respected my father a great deal, but I always thought of him as being mostly human."

Daniel laughed, "Of course, he was human. But down here, people tend to put folks on a pedestal, and I know your father's is pretty tall. And of course, we all know that pedestals tend to grow some after someone passes away.

"I myself am a big admirer. I had occasion to visit with your dad when I was down on a mission trip and cut my arm pretty bad while doing some construction. He was down here on one of his freelance trips and sewed me up. We talked and I shared with him my thoughts about being called to full-time missions. He said he would come back later that evening and visit with me about it. He did, and we talked for about two hours. I really liked his simple theology and that talk was helpful to me as I was trying to make my decision."

Daniel went on, "You have to understand that the work your father did here was very valuable to all of us. You can't view it the same way you do back home. There he was doing work that in a way he had to do, but here, he had a choice. People appreciate that and endear themselves to somebody like that. He didn't have to come here and spend his time helping people. And the fact that he treated everybody with dignity and respect went a long way with people. They don't forget that."

Matt replied, "I guess I never really looked at it that way. Maybe in an odd way, I'm a little jealous."

Daniel said, "The old 'I never measured up syndrome' from the son, I guess"

Matt said, "You may have hit the nail on the head."

"Well, I don't know about all that, but I do know that your father was crazy about his kids. He used to say that one of his faults was talking too much about y'all, but he couldn't help it. I can testify to the truth of that statement."

"I guess you heard a lot about the golden boy."

Daniel laughed out loud. "Sounds like we're adding some sibling rivalry to the situation."

Matt was a little embarrassed, "Maybe I'm bearing my soul a little more than I should considering the short time that I've known you."

Daniel chuckled and said, "Nicaragua seems to bring that out in people, but don't worry, what is said in Nicaragua stays in Nicaragua.

"You know your dad got a little bit of a kick out of the golden boy nickname, but I think he worried some that you and Anna may have really believed that Samuel was a favorite. He said one time that since he never really had to worry about you, that you may have felt that you got less attention."

Matt said, "I guess I've never looked at it like that. It just seemed like Samuel was always in the spotlight."

"Oh, your dad always referred to him as the coolest guy in the world, but would go on to say: 'That don't pay the rent.' Overall, I would have to say that the three of you pretty much got equal air time."

Matt replied, "I have to say that what you are telling me surprises me. I guess I had convinced myself otherwise."

"Happens to the best of us. I have two brothers, by the way."

Matt was glad that the highway noise and hum of the diesel engine would keep Samuel from hearing much of his conversation with Daniel. He was bothered by the fact that he still was unable to shake those old resentful feelings and the jealousy that defined his relationship with his brother. Even though he tried, it was hard for him to be optimistic that this trip would do much to change it.

Samuel had made some changes himself. Matt felt like his remarks and insults to his brother at the time of their father's funeral may have gone too far. Samuel was no longer quite as laid back and easy going as he had been, and was making some comments and remarks himself. Matt said to himself, "May be a long three weeks."

Matt didn't really have any preconceived notion about what Nicaragua or Managua would look like, so he was not really surprised. Managua was not unlike any large city with a lot of buildings and busy streets. One thing that seemed different to him from cities in the United States was that at times, there seemed to be no clear distinction between the poor areas and the more affluent parts. A good street might all of a sudden become not so good, adversely affecting the flow of traffic, which was somewhat crazy at best. People did not always pay much attention to stop signs or traffic signals.

He also noticed the difference in the types of vehicles. It definitely seemed that the most popular type of transportation was the mid-sized diesel pickup truck. There were also a large number of motorcycles but no high end SUVs like those so prevalent in the U.S. Large yellow buses that resembled school buses, and were decorated and overcrowded, were popular and seemed to fit a tropical country. They looked like something you would see in the movies.

During the pause in Matt and Daniel's conversation, Matt noticed that Samuel was conversing with Dr. Romero mostly in Spanish.

Matt leaned over the seat and asked Samuel, "When did you learn Spanish?"

"In Puerto Rico. Remember I lived there for three years."

Matt said with some degree of sarcasm, "Oh, I almost forgot about your dive shop phase."

Samuel just looked at him, shook his head, and resumed his conversation with Dr. Romero.

Anna turned and stared out of the window, her eyes moist. She always had the same question: "Why does it have to be like this between them?"

As they drove on farther and appeared to be getting out of the city, Matt sensed that they were going uphill and asked Daniel about it.

Daniel replied, "Diriamba is what we call 'up the mountain' from Managua, so we are climbing, so to speak. There is roughly a thousand feet difference in elevation. The significance of that is it is slightly cooler where you are going, and most of the time, there is a breeze. That is a good thing. Take my word for it."

"I can stand cooler," Matt said.

"Don't get too excited. It is still hot." Daniel beat on the dash and said, "Speaking of hot, I guess I'm gonna have to get 'em to look at this AC again."

Samuel heard that and said, "Hey, Matt, why don't you just cut him a check for a new van. I'm sure you can afford it. Wife probably wouldn't even have to sell her Range Rover."

Matt felt an intense anger welling up inside, but he made no comment. He figured he had that one coming considering his earlier remark. He knew that he would not handle Samuel's remarks well if he brought his wife into it.

As they rode on, the scenery was getting more rural. Matt was surprised to see some people filling up water jugs from a truck on the side of the highway. He asked Daniel about it.

He replied, "A lot of people don't have running water, especially in the more rural areas. Our ministry will occasionally have water projects, and people really appreciate it more than you and I can imagine."

"Are you serious? No running water?"

"You're going to see a lot of things in this trip that may shock you. For instance, that horse-drawn cart you see over there carrying sticks of wood is hauling firewood. Most people cook on a wood fire."

"Seems like they would catch the house on fire."

Daniel said, "Wait till you see some of the houses. You'll see why several of the mission teams that come down here are construction teams with the purpose of building houses. As a matter of fact, building a house is on the to-do list that your father prepared for the three of you."

"Can't say I know a whole lot about building houses."

"Don't worry about that. I have built a few myself, and there are a couple of Nicaraguans that help us. They have done so many that they can build them in their sleep."

Matt laughed and said, "Well, I can assure you that if I am going to build something, I better be wide awake."

Daniel laughed and reflected on how many houses he had built over the years, many on mission trips when he was younger and many more with mission teams that had come since he moved to Nicaragua. Although he had many duties, building was his first love.

After a short period of silence, Matt said, "I have pretty much aired the family linen. Why don't you tell me a little about yourself?"

"Not real exciting. I am the youngest of three boys. My brothers have always picked on me and said that I got everything I wanted because of my position as the baby of the family. I certainly disputed their claims and was quick to point out that whatever I got, I richly deserved anyway. It is always in good fun, and we are pretty close as it goes with brothers. We had some conflicts over the years but nothing serious.

"My father was and still is the minister of education at the First Baptist Church in Mobile, and my mother is a high school teacher. We always have been a close family."

Daniel continued, "I was saved and baptized at the age of twelve. After high school, I started working in construction, and I still have a fondness for that. Had I not moved to Nicaragua, I probably would have pursued a degree related to that field and maybe even have tried to build my own business. Somewhere along the way, I got married and had a couple of kids. I am real pleased that they have adjusted well to living here.

"My mission journey started when I began coming here on construction trips through my church. I can't really explain it, but I began to feel a call to full-time missions. A lot of discussion and prayer, and here I am."

Matt asked, "Did you feel like you got a real, clear answer to your prayers, and if so, how?"

"I did not hear an audible voice from above if that is what you're asking. I think that it is different for everybody and each particular circumstance. I just felt a peace about it over time and that became my answer."

"That was it? Nothing else to lead you to such a major move?"

"Well, discussions with other Christians like the one I had with your father are also very helpful. Also, if you search the scriptures as you are working on a decision, God will reveal his plans through that process as well."

"You really felt like he talked to you in that way?"

Daniel replied, "Absolutely, without a doubt."

Matt said, "I may need to discuss that more with you over the next three weeks. I don't think I have ever experienced that before."

"I'll look forward to it."

Matt liked Daniel and had a comfort level with him that he never seemed to get with people in the ministry. He did not like to admit it but he had a cynicism toward those who made a living in organized religion, especially the ones who did well financially. Daniel already had credibility with Matt because he had obviously given up possibilities for future financial success to serve in another country, and of course, there was a lot of uncertainty that also went with that. Matt remembered the passage in James that talked about showing one's faith by his works.

Matt, on the other hand, was a paradox of sorts. He had achieved exactly what he had set out to do with his life, and by just about any standard would be considered wealthy. Even so, he did not ever really feel at peace and was now riding down a highway in Nicaragua next to a man that virtually had nothing that the world feels is important, but seemed to be not only at peace, but happy. His own father had always seemed to be content where he was, and never worried about money and the sense of security that it was supposed to bring. He wondered if his feelings about his brother were at least partially brought about by a jealousy that Matt felt toward him because he was happier with less. Did all of this relate in some way to his spiritual apathy that had developed over the years? He would think about these things some over the next couple of weeks.

They had been riding for about an hour when Daniel announced that they were coming into Diriamba. It seemed like a fair-sized town, and they began to notice vehicles that they had not seen before. They looked like a small coach with a motorcycle stuck on the front. Daniel said that they were called motos and were taxis. He was sure that they would ride in them some during their stay.

There were numerous shops in the downtown area, and the streets were crowded with various types of vehicles as well as motorcycles, bicycles, and carts drawn by horses and even oxen. Matt did not see how they all missed each other as the streets were not that wide. There were also larger vans and some larger work trucks.

After they had gone through town and seemed to be heading out again, Daniel turned off the main highway and drove for another two or three miles. He then turned into what seemed to be a long driveway that ran along a fenced-in yard. He pulled up to a gate and announced, "We're home."

Chapter 10

The Compound

The gate was closed, but they were let through by an armed guard. This process would be repeated numerous times over the next three weeks. Daniel assured them that they would be safe and not to worry even if they heard an occasional gunshot in the night. He said that it would only be the guard firing a warning shot, more than likely.

The main house was to their right after they drove through the gate, and there was a drive that bordered the veranda. Matt assumed that this was the legendary porch that his father had carried on about. He hoped it would meet his expectations. The house was painted half-green and half-peach color, and had a green metal roof. It was built on a low hill, the low side being where the porch was, making it somewhat elevated. That added to its atmosphere.

As they unloaded their bags and walked up the steps onto the porch, Samuel said, "I already feel the breeze that we were told is here most of the time."

Anna replied, "I really like this already. I can see why dad talked about it so much. What do you think, Matt?"

Matt said, "Yeah, I think I am going to like this. Looks like a man could do some serious relaxing here."

Daniel added, "There have been more theological discussions right here than in most seminaries, not to mention the philosophizing and storytelling that goes on with it.

"Y'all bring your bags in, and I'll show you where you'll be living for the next three weeks."

They went in the door that opened onto the porch, and they were in the kitchen. There was a long table along the wall on the right and an island to the left. The sink and the stove were on the left wall and corner. The kitchen opened into a large meeting room with couches and chairs scattered around. There were several doors opening into the bedrooms, two on one side and three on the other. Daniel said that they could each choose the bedroom they wanted; there wasn't much difference between them.

After they each had chosen a room and deposited their luggage, they headed back to the kitchen. Dr. Romero was there talking with an older lady and introduced her as Isabella. Daniel said that she would be doing the cooking. Isabella spoke fairly good English and said she was glad to meet them. With tears in her eyes, she said that their father was one of the finest men that she had ever known and what an honor it would be to get to know his children. She gave Anna a long hug and tears began running down her cheeks. She said that Daniel could have the boys, but this one was hers. Her reaction seemed a little overboard to Anna, but she liked the attention.

As they walked back out on the porch, they noticed people coming up the road that ran by the yard. Many of them walked but some were in motos. Daniel said, "I am sure that you had visitation as is customary in the US, but I am also sure that you are getting ready to have a Nicaraguan visitation."

Samuel asked, "How did they know we were here?"

Daniel was a little bit amused by the question and replied, "In this country, if one person knows something, everybody knows. I thought there would be a lot of people wanting to pay their respects, and it looks like I was right."

The guard seemed to know everybody and just let them through when they got to the gate. People would then just walk up the stairs to the porch and talk with one of the three children of Dr. Joseph Martin. Samuel knew enough Spanish to get by, and Daniel translated for Matt and Dr. Romero for Anna. It was just like it was back home with everyone speaking so highly of their father. So many of them would say that they would not be alive today if God had not sent their father and guided his hands to work on them. Mothers would occasionally lift up the shirt of a child and point out a surgical scar that was placed by their father. There seemed to be an endless stream of people, and Daniel just shrugged and said, "I told you how popular your father was here. But to tell you the truth, these numbers have surprised me some."

As the afternoon wore on and the crowd began to thin some, an old lady appeared on the porch and started talking to Daniel. He walked with her over to where Samuel was, and Daniel told him that the she had requested to pray for him. Samuel was a little confused, but Daniel reassured him and told him that she prayed for people all the time. Samuel said it would be okay, and she indicated that she wanted him to sit in a chair. He complied, and she stood behind him with her hands on his shoulders. She began her prayer as Samuel bowed his head. It was in Spanish, so Matt could not understand any of it but he could tell that it was a passionate prayer.

Daniel walked back over to where Matt was and could sense his curiosity. He said, "The lady you see there is well known in this area, and I guess you might call her a prophetess. She will pray for people and seems to know something the rest of us don't."

Matt asked, "But why Samuel?"

"I can't answer that. All I can say is that many times, when she prays for someone, it may have something to do with their health, or their spiritual life, or even something big that may be coming in their future. Only she seems to know what it is about. And many times, we won't know the significance of her prayer till much later."

After a long time had gone by, the prayer ended and the lady left. Samuel appeared to be moved by the experience, and Matt went over and asked him about it.

"You know Spanish, Samuel. Could you tell what she was saying?"

"Her Spanish was a lot different from mine and a whole lot faster. I could only catch bits and pieces. But she said the word *hermano* a lot and, of course, that means brother. And she seemed to be talking some about fever, but I could not make it out. A phrase I heard over and over was, '*No vas a salir de Nicaragua.*' I'm sure that means something about not leaving."

He and Matt walked over and asked Dr. Romero about the phrase, and he said that it meant Samuel would not be leaving Nicaragua.

Matt asked Samuel with some degree of concern, "Did she put some time frame on that?"

Samuel laughed and said, "I have no clue. I only caught that phrase because she repeated it so many times. And to tell you the truth, I don't know how accurate my understanding of it is."

"Why do you think she would single you out?"

Samuel shook his head. "I have no idea."

When all the people had left, Matt began to feel a little weary from the day of travel and shaking hands. He sat down on the bench seat that was built into the railing around the porch and began to reflect on the day. One thing that surprised him was that he liked Nicaragua so far, and he had not thought that he would. There was a comfort that he felt with the compound even though he had only been there a short time. And of course, he could already tell that the porch that his father loved so much was going to be one of his favorite places.

Dr. Romero came over, sat down, and said, "Well, Matt, welcome to my country."

"Thank you. I am not sure that I can explain why exactly, but I like it here so far."

Dr. Romero smiled and said, "Maybe it is genetic. You are your father's son after all."

"Dr. Romero, let me ask you about the man I met at the airport, Jose Ramirez. He said I could get in touch with him through you. Do you know him well?"

"I do. He is my cousin. My family is large but we are very close. One thing you will notice in this country is that families for the most part are pretty clannish as you would say in your country."

He continued, "There is an old connection between my family and the president's family that goes back some generations, but things are not usually forgotten. That is the main reason that some of the members of my family work with the government. Jose works closely with the president and is a good one to call if help is needed. I do try not to call on him that often and overplay that privilege, if you know what I mean."

Matt said, "I know what you mean by that. You don't want to wear out your welcome."

"I will say this though, Matt. He is yet another one in this country that thought very highly of your father and considered him a good friend. I think it will be hard for you to wear out your welcome."

Matt smiled and said, "I guess you can never have too many friends in high places."

Dr. Romero laughed, stood up, and said that he had to leave. He told Matt that he would for sure be seeing them off and on during their stay. He also made sure that Matt had his cell number. He said his goodbyes to Samuel and Anna before leaving. His clinic was right down the road from the compound, so he did not have far to go. He had left his car there and ridden to the airport with Daniel.

Anna walked over, sat down by Matt, and put her head on his shoulder.

Matt said, "What's the matter, baby sister? Are you worn out?"

"I think I am. It has been a long day. I don't think I was ready for another visitation."

Matt said, "I don't think I had really thought about that happening, but I guess it makes sense."

"Matt, I'm feeling a little on the low side."

"What in the world are you talking about?"

"Well, all I've heard lately is how great our father was, and it has started to make me take a look at myself and I'm not sure I've got much of a résumé. I am thirty-five years old. No husband. No job. No degree of any kind because of a stupid decision. Also, from a standpoint of having babies, I'm already considered at an advanced age. With no husband in sight, that is even gonna get more advanced."

Matt replied, "I understand what you are saying in a way. I know we are not supposed to compare ourselves with other people, but I even told Daniel today that I felt some jealousy toward our father."

"That doesn't really make sense, Matt. Look at all you have accomplished already."

"But does any of that come close to the legend our father seems to have become? And don't forget, a lot of his accomplishments were for other people. I don't see that in my business at all."

"Well, sure, it is different, Matt. You're not a doctor."

"Don't remind me. I'm still not sure that he wasn't disappointed in me for not following in his footsteps."

"I think that you might have some feelings that come from being the oldest son. I am not sure what you do with that. Maybe even the makings of a midlife crisis. You know, you are kind of approaching that age."

Matt replied, "Maybe while I'm here in this tropical paradise surrounded by missionaries and prophetesses, I can figure it out."

"Getting to be quite the cynic, huh, Matt? If you do get it figured out, I want to be the first one you pass it on to."

"Well, I do know one thing we ought to do and that is to bury the dead. I mean no disrespect, but I know for sure that Dr. Joseph Martin did not require his children to come to Nicaragua so we could have a wake for three weeks. I was obviously reluctant to come, but I am here now, so I am going to try to enjoy it."

Anna said, "That sounds like a good plan to me. After all, this is really an all-expense-paid vacation."

*****

Daniel and Samuel were talking on the other end of the porch, Samuel leaning back in one of the several chairs that were scattered around.

"You know, Daniel, I felt something when that lady was praying for me. I have never had anybody lay hands on me and pray before. I can't explain it, but I felt like there was something really significant in what she was saying."

Daniel said, "I can tell you stories that I have heard, but there is one story I actually know to be true. There was a man in his forties that had cancer and came on a mission trip with his church. It was a medical team. She came by one evening and singled him out as she did you and prayed for him. She did not know him, and no one who knew he had cancer had told anyone in Nicaragua. I heard some months later that he was cancer free at his next check up with his doctor. I verified that myself the next year when he came back on another mission trip. He said that his doctor was amazed because he had not really responded to any of the traditional treatments, and his outlook had been pretty bleak."

"Then why wouldn't people seek her out so that they can be healed?"

"People have tried before, and I have been told that it doesn't work. It is as if she has to find you and have something revealed to her that needs to be prayed about."

"Man, that is incredible. Does that mean that something significant is definitely going to happen to me?"

Daniel shook his head and said, "Apparently not. I am told that there are people that she prayed for years ago that do not really report any earth-shattering events or miracles, at least not yet."

"I don't know whether to be disappointed or relieved by that."

Daniel laughed and said, "Changing the subject, I got to visit with your brother some on the way here. Tell me a little about you."

"Well, let's see. Where would I start?"

"I'm kind of a gypsy of sorts, I guess you would say. I feel like I have done about everything and accomplished very little."

"What do you mean by that?"

"I am forty years old and don't really have much to show for any of the things I have done. The closest I have come to any kind of business success was a bike shop in San Diego. It was going well, or so I thought, and it turned out my partner wasn't paying the bills but pocketing that money. It didn't take long to figure it out, but the damage was done and the business couldn't recover. I am going to use part of the money from this trip to pay back some people that he shorted."

"That is a commendable thing to do considering you could probably just blame your former partner and walk away. Unfortunately, that's the way most people would handle it nowadays."

"Daniel, if there is one thing I can say that I have inherited from my father, it is integrity. I will not lie nor will I take something that doesn't belong to me."

"I don't mean to sound nosey, but have you thought much about what you're going to do after this trip?"

"I have actually been thinking off and on for a while about that, even back before our father passed away. It may sound strange to you, but I have felt an occasional tug toward the ministry. But I'm not sure about that, and I would not know in what capacity. I will say that I am a little interested in the kind of work you are doing here. Who knows, maybe foreign missions could be in my future wanderings."

Daniel replied, "Don't count it out. The Lord has used a lot of gypsies over the centuries. And I will say that in the brief time that I have observed you this afternoon, you seem to have a comfort level interacting with people. Couple that with a head start on the Spanish language and who knows."

"Well, don't sign me up yet. This is my first trip here, you know. A lot of thinking would have to go into that decision."

Daniel laughed. "I was kidding, of course. But I do have to recruit when I can. Another gringo might be helpful around here. On another note, what are some of the things you like to do? What are some of your interests?"

"Oh, I've done about everything you can do in the outdoors: sky diving, scuba diving, rock climbing, biking, hiking, and a few others I can't recall right now."

"You are pretty athletic then?"

"Yeah, I guess you could say that. I did pretty well in most sports coming up. It was kinda expected by my father that I would get a scholarship in football, but I was really not interested in college. I'm not sure that he wasn't disappointed in that even though he never came out and said it. I don't dwell a lot on it, but if I do have a regret, it's that I should have used my God-given talent to its full potential. And of course, a college education never looks bad on an application."

"You and Matt both seem to have some feelings that you didn't measure up to your father's expectations. I had a lot of conversations with Dr. Martin over the last few years, and I never picked up on any of that. I might add that he did talk about y'all a lot."

"I don't know about Matt, but I could tell that my father was disappointed when I started declining in football my senior year. I'm not sure that the whole community wasn't feeling somewhat let down. I don't think I cared much then, but it bothers me some now. If I get honest with myself, I think it was fear that caused some of that."

"I'm not sure I understand what you are talking about. Fear of what?"

"Fear of failing on the big stage. I don't know if it gets any bigger in college football than being the quarterback at LSU. People from that program had already started talking to me during my junior year. As I look back on it, my talent was in a way somewhat of a curse. In what other area of life can you go from hero to bum as fast as in the sports world especially if you are the quarterback?"

Samuel continued, "I'm not sure that all of my adventurous escapades haven't been attempts to make up for those feelings. Maybe prove to myself and everybody else that I am actually fearless."

Daniel laughed, "I know I haven't known you and Matt long, but I think you two both think pretty deep about all of this."

"Well, if we have anything in common, it may be that we are both analysts."

Both men laughed and stood up as Daniel said it was about time for him to head back to Managua. He said that he sure hated to miss one of Isabella's meals, but he had some family obligations and had to get on back. He told them he would see them around half past eight in the morning for breakfast. He also said that they might go zip lining tomorrow.

*****

Matt lay in his bed reflecting on the events of the day and the past months.

He was pleasantly surprised at how good the food was, and he immediately liked Isabella. She was outgoing and reminded him a little of Ruth. She had already put up a fuss over Anna and even had her in an apron helping wash the dishes. Anna seemed happy with the attention, and Matt was pleased at that. He felt like she needed some positive things in her life right now.

Even though Matt had only been in the country a day, he got a sense that the Nicaraguan people were very relationship oriented. He already felt close to Dr. Romero and knew he was going to hit it off well with Isabella. He was looking forward to meeting and working with others as he knew they would do in the upcoming weeks.

And of course, there was Daniel. What a nice guy and how comfortable it was to talk with him. Matt had never shared any of those feelings with anyone and now felt like Daniel knew his life history. He was actually looking forward to having some spiritual discussions with him as he had never felt that he had the time or desire to talk with his pastor in Atlanta. Matt did not blame his pastor and realized that it was his own fault.

His thoughts turned to his mother. She had been having a hard time lately. Matt could tell it when he talked to her, and Anna would fill him in from time to time. She simply was having a hard time being single. Said she had lost a good friend and couldn't get used to it. They had also had to put her father in a nursing home and that was hard on her. And of course, she could never do enough to please her mother. Matt wished that relationship was better.

As Matt felt sleep approaching, he did something he hadn't done in a long time; he said a prayer. He felt like his conversation with Daniel may have lit a small spark, and he simply thanked God for the day, for safe travel, and asked that he help him make progress with his relationship with his brother.

*****

Breakfast was as good as dinner the night before.

They cooked the bacon different in that they cut it into short pieces and deep fried it. It was an immediate hit. There also were eggs, cereal, fresh fruits, toast, and pancakes. It all seemed to taste better than in the states, or maybe the vacation mindset made it seem so. And of course, the Nicaraguan coffee was as good as ever.

Matt had made it to the kitchen first, followed shortly by Anna, and Samuel, as usual, was later than the other two. Matt suppressed the urge to make some comment about it.

Anna said, "How did you sleep, Matt?"

"Pretty good. I thought I might be too hot but with the fan blowing on me, I actually felt a little cool at times."

She looked at Samuel and asked, "How about you?"

"You know me, sister. I can sleep anywhere, anytime, through any conditions. The accommodations here are first class compared to some of the places I've been in."

Anna replied, "Oh, yeah, Margaritaville and all that. Always the adventurer, huh, brother? When you gonna settle down?"

She was teasing him, but he didn't seem to be in the mood for it.

"Not sure. Besides, what makes you think that settling down is the answer? Matthew, there is the poster boy for settled, and I'm not sure he is the essence of happiness and serenity. What do you think, Matt?"

Matt replied, "Starting a little early this morning, aren't we?" Matt muttered to himself, *So much for answered prayer.*

Samuel continued, "I'm just saying you got plenty of money, a trophy wife, perfect kids—what else could it possibly take to be happy?"

Matt's face reddened and he shot back, "Say whatever you think you need to about me, but I would recommend leaving my family out of it."

Samuel felt like he had said enough and resumed eating breakfast. He didn't look at Matt or acknowledge his last statement.

Anna got up and walked out the door. When she sat down in one of the chairs on the porch, Daniel was walking up the steps that led up from the driveway. She was worried that her being upset would be obvious. It was.

Daniel walked up to her and grasped her hand, "Are you all right, Anna?"

"I don't want to get into it, Daniel. Suffice it to say that I could kill those brothers of mine, and I don't think I would have any remorse."

"Bad start this morning?"

"Yeah, you could say that."

"Well, we have some fun things to do today. Maybe that will help."

"You don't understand. This has been going on between them for as long as I can remember. I can't see how a trip like this can change that."

"Well, the Lord moves in mysterious ways, and maybe your father moved in his own mysterious way."

Anna looked at Daniel with a curious expression, "Do you think that this conflict between them is the whole reason for this trip?"

"Probably not, but I would bet that it is a big part of it."

"Daniel, you seem to have some insight into our situation."

"Well, I spent a lot of time with your father over the last four years, and he talked a great deal about his family. I couldn't help but learn something about y'all."

Anna's face reddened and she asked, "What all did he tell you for Pete's sake?"

Daniel held out his hand as if he were stopping traffic and said, "Whoa, Anna, he really didn't get into anybody's personal issues, and I guarantee you that I have nothing that I can blackmail any of you with."

Anna smiled at his comment and said she was sorry for overreacting. She guessed she was just sensitive.

Daniel went on to say, "Your father knew that I have two brothers, and we would talk some about the conflicts that can arise from time to time. I don't have any long-term issues with either of my brothers, so I am not sure I was much help."

Anna said, "I don't know what to think anymore. It is almost like a feud that has been going on for so long that nobody even knows what started it."

Daniel patted her on the back and told her that nothing was unfixable, and nobody could predict the future. He assured her that he would do everything within his power to help. He reassured her that conflicts between brothers are fairly common, and with God's help, this one could be taken care of.

His confidence was some comfort to Anna, and she thanked him for his concern. She stood up and said she was going to help Isabella with the dishes.

Daniel sat on the porch for a while and pondered the next couple of weeks. He had known Dr. Martin fairly well and thought he had a good idea why he planned this trip for his children. But he didn't know if he was looking forward to getting in the middle of all of their issues. He had known Matt and Samuel a very short time and could already tell that they both had a lot of problems, not just with each other but also their late father. He couldn't help but agree with Anna that it was going to be tough to fix all that by simply coming on a trip like this. And then there were some issues with Anna, and where would that go? "Oh, well," he said to himself, "they are paying customers, and the Lord has dropped them on my doorstep." Daniel said a quick prayer and went into the kitchen.

*****

When Daniel walked in, he found Samuel sitting at the table, nursing a cup of coffee. He looked up and nodded at Daniel.

"Good morning, Samuel. *Como estas?*" (How are you?)

Samuel managed a slight smile and replied, "*Un poco cansado.*" (A little tired.)

Daniel asked, "Did you not sleep good last night?"

"I did okay. I guess I've just got a little jet lag."

"Well, we're going to go zip lining today. I don't think it will be too demanding on you."

"I suppose not," he seemed disinterested. Daniel decided not to pursue any more conversation at that time.

Chapter 11

Zip Lining

The ride that morning was not in Daniel's old van but in a newer one that was quite a bit bigger. Daniel was not driving but Michael was. He was a Nicaraguan that, according to Daniel, did a lot of the driving for the NMO. Whenever mission teams would come, their transportation was in vans like these. Daniel explained that the cost that the teams payed covered the rental of the vans, and most groups would need two to three.

It didn't take long to observe that Michael drove quite a bit faster than Daniel, but they were reassured that his safety record was good. He also was very outgoing, and was always joking and laughing. He played music ranging from Latin style to many songs that were popular in the United States. Daniel told them that one group had named his van the "party van." The group this morning was not in the party spirit, so Michael was a bit more subdued than usual.

They were traveling the same route that they had come yesterday, only in the opposite direction. Daniel told them that they would be going back to Managua to a zip line that was located there. As they passed back through Diriamba, it seemed to be as busy as it was the day before. All the various modes of transportation missed each other by inches at times and that seemed to be the norm. Horns were used more than they are in the United States, but it was more as a warning than a reprimand. They saw many of the same sites they had seen the day before, and some new ones. Matt noticed the people more than he had the day before. Everybody seemed to be going somewhere, and they all looked busy.

Matt and Daniel sat in the bench seat behind the driver, and Samuel and Anna were behind them. Their moods were somber, and nobody was saying much.

After a long period of silence, Samuel leaned forward and asked, "Hey, Daniel, why do you think our dad wanted us to go zip-lining?"

"He didn't. I called an audible. Made the decision on this one myself."

"I don't understand. I can go zip lining in Gatlinburg!"

"Not with Hernando, you can't."

Almost in unison, Matt, Anna, and Samuel asked, "Who is Hernando?"

Michael heard them, and began fist pumping and exclaiming the name Hernando over and over again, along with some other expressions, all in Spanish.

When Michael's reaction died down, Daniel replied, "Hernando is someone I wanted y'all to meet. Let me hold off on telling you about him because I want you to see for yourself."

After what turned out being a quiet ride, they made it to Managua and turned into an old military base. They drove on till they reached a small parking lot. They were walking toward the building where you make arrangements for the zip line, when a medium-build Nicaraguan man in a wheelchair came speeding toward them. The three Martins all took evasive action to avoid being run over, but Daniel stood where he was. The wheelchair stopped suddenly, only inches in front of him.

Daniel said, "I'll declare, Hernando, someday you ain't gonna stop in time, and I won't be happy."

"Not good grammar, Danielson. You come learn karate?"

"Oh my god, he's been watching old movies again."

"Matt, Samuel, and Anna, may I present to you Hernando, zip line guide and Bible scholar without equal."

All three were a little shocked about the zip-line-guide part because Hernando had both legs amputated above the knee.

Hernando said, "Okay, if Matt is short for Matthew, then we have two names from the New Testament and one from the Old."

Daniel asked, "There is an Anna in the New Testament?"

"Oh, Danielson, look in the book written by the physician."

"Don't any of you ever try to outdo Hernando when it comes to biblical knowledge," Daniel said with a joking tone in his voice. "Can we get down to any kind of zip line business somewhere in our future?"

Hernando laughed and went on to say, "Please forgive my brief lapse of professionalism. I am very pleased to meet the three of you, and I am sure that if you are not already having a good day, we can do something about that. I have learned that you can be as happy as you want to be. If Jesus is in your heart, your day already started off good."

All three Martins reflected on the way their day started.

Daniel said, "In case y'all didn't pick up on it, he's also a lay minister."

Everybody laughed and Hernando said, "Everybody follow me, and we'll get you buckled up for the zip line."

They entered the thatched enclosure where they had to check in and be fitted with the harnesses for the zip line. There were three Nicaraguan men there, two young and one older.

The older man said, "Hernando, you are going to run our customers away some day by running them over."

Hernando replied, "It is just my enthusiasm coming through, and besides, Daniel is the only one I play the game of chicken with. He loves us too much to be run off."

Daniel was quick to reply, "Don't count on it. There are other zip lines in Nicaragua, you know."

Hernando was just as quick with his reply, "But there is only one Hernando!"

Daniel rolled his eyes, "Walked into that one, didn't I?"

Hernando began to look over his customers to get them fitted with the harnesses for the zip line. He started with Matt.

"You are the oldest, Matt?"

"I am."

"I thought so. You appear to be the cautious type."

"I would have to say that is accurate."

"More than likely, you have not been on a zip line before, unless it was with your kids. I see that you have a wedding ring, and I am assuming you have children."

Matt was having fun with this and replied, "I have not been on a zip line before, and I have two."

Hernando then said, "A little afraid of heights?"

"How did you know?"

"Hernando knows these things, and let me say that it is an honor for me to guide you on your first zip line experience."

Matt replied with, "The pleasure is all mine." He bowed slightly.

Hernando turned to Samuel and said, "You are in the middle between Matt and Anna, and I see no wedding ring."

"That is correct. Never married."

Hernando smiled a big smile and shook his head, "Many hearts have been broken then?"

Everybody laughed, and Samuel replied, "I am not sure how to answer that one."

Hernando said, "The obvious requires no answer."

Samuel had a sheepish grin on his face and turned a little red.

Hernando continued, "I would suspect that you have ridden the zip line before and even in some countries besides the US."

Samuel nodded in the affirmative.

"I would also say that you have also ridden the winds of adventure many times and done many things more dangerous, and that you have no fear of heights."

"*Es verdad.*" (That is correct.)

"So you speak the language!" Hernando said with enthusiasm.

Samuel simply said, "*Sí*"

Hernando exclaimed, "The day is getting better and better!"

He then turned to Anna and said, "I see no wedding ring, and it is because there is no one yet worthy of such a creation of God as you."

Anna smiled and said, "Hernando, you are embarrassing me."

"My apologies, and I fear that before the day is over, my heart will be broken."

Daniel said, "He is on a roll today. I don't know if we are dealing with Sherlock Holmes or Romeo."

Hernando replied, "Ah, Daniel, you are just jealous. Okay, we better get this show on the road."

They were all fitted with the necessary harnesses and made their way over to the stairs leading to the first platform. Hernando left his wheelchair and maneuvered himself onto the second step. By facing backward and using his arms and the side rail, he was able to push himself up to the platform one step at a time. The strength in his arms became obvious during this exercise.

When on the platform, they could see the layout which consisted of three fairly long lines, all over water as there was a small lake below them.

Anna said that she was going first and was not going by herself. Hernando indicated that he would be her guide and promptly grabbed a rope hanging next to the wooden structure holding the line. He hoisted himself up, seemingly without a lot of effort, and hooked his harness to the top cable. The two other guides helped Anna and Hernando hooked her to the line.

Hernando said, "My sweet señorita, are you ready?"

Anna replied, "I guess so." There was some reservation in her voice.

Hernando then exclaimed, "Then leave the driving to me!"

Off they went, and Hernando was heard singing "I'll Fly Away" as they made their way toward the other platform. Anna was squealing.

Everybody was laughing, and Daniel said, "Like I said, he is on a roll today."

One of the other guides said, "It is no different from any other day."

Daniel said, "Since I am responsible for these folks, let me go next and make sure Anna survived the first leg, and also survived Hernando."

Matt said to Samuel, "Let me go after Daniel. I think I'll go with a guide the first time and maybe solo after that."

Samuel replied, "Be my guest."

After Matt reached the next platform, Samuel went and the other guide came last.

This routine was repeated twice more with the difference being that Matt went without a guide on the second and third line. Hernando had entertained everybody with his antics and his singing. Each time he went, he would sing a familiar song, usually at the top of his lungs. He did not seem to be slowed down any by his handicap.

Samuel, of course, was at ease on the zip line and even got a little acrobatic at times. He was surrounded by the guides, and they were all laughing and talking in Spanish. Matt could not help feeling jealous.

When they were all resting at the end, Daniel said, "Well, Hernando, have you fallen in love with your client?"

Hernando got real serious and said, "The beautiful señorita has swept me off my feet."

He immediately got a goofy look on his face, his eyes got real big, and he slowly looked downward as if looking for his feet.

Everybody laughed so hard that they were doubling over and tears were streaming down their faces. Samuel could barely catch his breath, and Matt had to lean against a tree. It took several minutes for the commotion to die down, and even then, sporadic laughter would erupt off and on.

Hernando tried to act indignant and said, "I am not believing that you would laugh at a poor, unfortunate Nicaraguan such as the humble Hernando."

Laughter broke out again, almost as much as the first time.

When they gained control again, Daniel said, "Well, I can guarantee you that Matt and Samuel Martin are not going to stand by and see their sister run off with the first slick-talking zip line guide she meets."

Hernando's expression changed in an instant, and he turned toward Daniel with a look of surprise combined with slight shock and said, "Daniel, is there something you failed to tell me about your guests when you introduced them. Maybe something as insignificant as their last name."

Daniel said, "I don't know where you could be going with your question."

"Don't try to act innocent. I know that Dr. Martin had three children, and I don't think that it would be mere coincidence that you have showed up with three people who just happen to have the last name Martin. Oh, and to add to the mystery and drama, I know that he had two sons and a daughter."

"Drama would be right up your alley."

"Do not try to get out of your guilt of allowing me to spend so much time with these honored guests and not know their true identity."

Daniel acted like someone who had won some points in a game and said, "I was waiting to see how long it would take the 'Hernando who knows all' to figure it out. It took a big hint for you to get it by the way."

"I will allow you this one small victory, but the hint should have come much earlier. I will say that it becomes obvious now that I know. There is some resemblance to the doctor in each of them, especially Anna."

Anna said, "I have always been told that I was a perfect blend of my mother and father. I will take your observation as a compliment."

"It is meant as one."

Matt then asked, "Hernando, how did you know our father?"

"Señor Matt, the answer should be obvious to you. He cut off my legs."

Matt, Anna, and Samuel were shocked by the bluntness of his answer and were all speechless.

Daniel sensed that it was an awkward moment and said, "Hey, let's all go get some lunch and maybe Hernando will tell us his story."

They went to a restaurant not far from the zip line that was one of Daniel's favorites. It was a buffet that had a wide variety of selections and especially had good fish.

There was the usual small talk that goes with a meal, and as they were close to finishing, Daniel said, "Hernando, I am sure that the Martins would like to hear your story about what happened to you."

Everybody nodded in agreement.

Hernando said, "I am happy to tell the story because it has become my testimony, and I believe that God would have us all to share that when called on to do so. It is especially an honor to tell these here today because their father played such a role in the story."

He began, "Growing up, I lived with my father, mother, and a sister in a remote area of our country near Waslala. We had what you might call a small farm, raised some crops, and had some livestock. I would emphasize that it was small, but it provided us plenty to eat. And at times, we could sell some things.

"When I was sixteen, one day, I was working near a small building you would call a barn in your country. My father had told me to clean out an area where a lot of things had built up like old lumber and wire and other trash. There was some old barbed wire tangled up in the pile, and I became tangled in it. The more I tried to get out of it, the more it seemed to hold on to my legs. Eventually, my father came to check on me and had to help me get out of it. I had some cuts on both legs, but nothing seemed serious. There were no doctors around so we took care of it like we always do.

"After a few days, the cuts became red and were draining, and I started to have fever. There was a local pastor who had some medical knowledge, and he said that I better be taken to a doctor as soon as possible. This, of course, meant a long trip, and my family did not have transportation. My father knew someone with a truck and paid him to take me to Jinotepe. We decided to go to the hospital there because my father had some relatives in the area. I know now that God sent me there because of the fact that your father was visiting and doing some work in that hospital.

"To try not to make the story too long, I became much worse, and the medicine I was given was not taking care of the infection. I became delirious and did not remember meeting your father before I was taken to surgery. You, of course, know the outcome of that sur-

JAMES McWHORTER AND JON McWHORTER

gery which turned out to be lifesaving as I would have died without the amputations.

"I wish I could say that I had acted grateful for what your father had done, but my response at first was far from that. I am ashamed to say that I actually cursed at him when I was told that he was the surgeon that had removed my legs. He took it without anger and simply told me he would continue to pray for me. I told him that there was no God that cared for me so don't bother. He wrote something on a piece of paper and placed it on the table by my bed. When he left, I put it in the trash without looking at it.

Dr. Martin kept coming by on his rounds, and I would not talk to him. Before he left the room, he would write something on a piece of paper and leave it on the table. My curiosity finally took over, and I looked at it. It was Romans 8:28, and for some reason, I did not throw it away that time. Incidentally, I have it in my Bible to this day and would not take many dollars for it."

Matt asked, "For those of us who are not too well versed in the Bible, what does this verse say?"

"Basically, it says, 'All things work together for the good for those who love the Lord and are called according to His purpose.'"

Matt nodded and said, "Does sound appropriate considering the circumstances."

Hernando continued, "On the last day that your father was there before going back home to the United States, he pulled a chair up beside my bed and sat down. I would not look at him, but he spoke anyway and said some words that I now know got me started in the right direction.

"He told me, first of all, that he was not going to say that he knew how I felt because he had never suffered that type of loss, and that some of what he was going to tell me came from observing people over the years. He said that he never liked the word 'disability' but preferred to think of it as I had lost some abilities, but with time and God's help, I would gain new abilities. He went on to say that my happiness in life ultimately had nothing to do with whether I had legs or not. He said that I had no choice about the loss of my legs, but I did have a choice about the loss of my spirit. And he stated that he believed that God put us all here for a purpose, and he intended for each of us to work every day and do the job he laid out for us. He concluded by telling me again that the choice was mine. He patted me on the shoulder and walked out of the room.

"Even though I was bitter and resentful at the time, I can remember that he made an impression on me because he seemed to be sincere and seemed to really care. He could have easily left without ever talking to me that day. I later learned that your father had left a significant sum of money with Dr. Romero to help with my father's expenses. I learned about that much later because he insisted on giving it anonymously. The road of recovery for me has been a long one, and I was fortunate to be able to see your father a few years later. I apologized for my rude behavior, and he said that it wasn't necessary. He understood."

Hernando concluded, "Two years after my surgery, I rededicated my life to Christ, and what you see today is what you get."

Matt said, "That is an incredible story, Hernando, and I must say that you do seem to be happy."

Hernando replied, "It is as your father said years ago. It has nothing to do with my legs or the lack of them. Any time my happiness is based on anything but Jesus, I will be happy sometimes and not at other times. Consistency can only come through Christ. I had to learn it the hard way.

"And remember, the word we should use is 'joy.' That is what you can never take away from me under any circumstances."

Samuel then said, "I don't know how to ask this, but what we saw today was not just an act that you put on for the gringo zip liners? Something you see as part of the job?"

Hernando said, "I take no offense at the question, and it is a fair one. I do feel like my personality and the things I do help people to have a better experience when they come here. But let me say that I want people to see a man that is displaying happiness and joy because he has Jesus in his heart and not because of any circumstances or job he finds himself in. I feel that this is my work that God gives me to do every day."

Anna said, "And you would have to be a good example, especially to young people, about overcoming obstacles in life."

Hernando replied, "I would hope so."

*****

Back at the compound, they were all sitting around on the porch winding down from the day. The breeze felt good.

Samuel broke the silence and said, "Good call, Daniel. That Hernando is a character. I really enjoyed all of that."

Daniel replied, "I am glad you did. I will say that Hernando has never once let me down. He entertains and inspires every group I take there. I also want to say that I hope the three of you do not think that I took you there just to meet another person in this country that admired your father. My true purpose was for us to have a good time and for you to meet a man that 'walks the walk' and doesn't just give lip service to the scriptures. Pun intended by the way."

Everybody laughed.

"I say that to Hernando when I need to get him stirred up. That need does not arise very often."

Anna asked, "Is he married?"

Daniel replied with a chuckle in his voice, "Sorry, Anna, he is."

Her brothers were acting like they were disappointed, and Anna said, "Okay, you two, I wasn't asking for myself. I was just curious."

Matt and Samuel both said with sarcasm, "Yeah, sure you were."

"Well, if you all will excuse me, I am going to help Isabella in the kitchen. I know she loves me. Not sure I can say that about my heathen brothers."

Matt and Samuel both rolled their eyes and shook their heads.

Samuel went inside, and Daniel and Matt were sitting on the porch by themselves. Neither one was saying anything and Matt broke the silence after a few minutes. "Daniel, I cannot for the life of me see how someone like Hernando gets to the level he is spiritually. My God, look at what he has working against him."

"Well, Matt, I can guarantee you one thing—it did not happen overnight. He had to get to a point of sheer determination and decide that he was not going to live a life of misery. He had some hard times to get through, and as he indicated today, it was a long struggle. He would be the first to tell you that he has some tough days even now, but he is able to get through them. And he basically summed up his theology when he said that he believed that God has a certain amount of work planned out for him each day and that is what he is supposed to do. He never sees it as a choice, and he feels that God equips him to do what he is called on to do. That is how, as he explains it, he does not now see himself as handicapped."

"But, Daniel, isn't that making it a little too simple? Remember, I'm an analyst."

"Well, Jesus himself kept it kinda simple. He said if we do the will of the Father, then the world will know that we are his disciples. He also said that we must come with the faith of a child, not an analyst as you put it."

"But there are all kinds of spiritual principles. Then there is the whole thing about prayer, and some are answered and some aren't. I don't know how you can get it down to simply telling me to go to work for the Lord every day. By the way, I did pray last night that Samuel and I would get along better, and he basically spit in my face this morning. I am sure Anna filled you in on that."

"She did."

"I guess I am reaping what I have sown. I did not treat him well at all at our father's funeral."

"If you want to change y'all's relationship, it may take more than one prayer."

"Yeah."

Chapter 12

Maggie and Ruth

Maggie and Ruth were having their morning coffee at Maggie's kitchen table as had become their routine. Maggie was crying, and Ruth handed her another tissue.

Ruth said, "I'll declare I think you must have stock in the tissue company."

"Ruth, you have the compassion of a fence post."

"I'm just trying to cheer you up. I remember when Jack died, I cried for a year. You just kept handing me another tissue."

Maggie replied, "Well, I'm not going to cry for a year. Right now, I'm just worried about the kids in Nicaragua."

"What are you worried about? Have you heard from them?"

"Anna called upset and said that Matt and Samuel were as bad as ever, but that is not what is bothering me right now."

"I'm having a little trouble following you, Maggie. What are you talking about?"

"I've got a nagging feeling that some big old skeletons in the closet are getting ready to come out, Ruth. My initial thoughts about this trip were that Joseph's intent was for Matt and Samuel to learn to get along better and for Anna to grow up a little, but the more I think about it, the more I'm thinking that Joseph wanted them to know something that he couldn't tell them. He knew that they would find it out on a trip like this. I have about convinced myself of it."

"I don't understand. Couldn't tell them something. Why?"

"You have to understand Joseph before you could understand what I am talking about, but I'm not sure he would have been able to explain it himself."

"You're still not making sense to me, Maggie."

"Blame it on a verbal contract. He was honoring a request made of him, and you know his integrity. Nothing, and I mean nothing could make him break a promise. Of course, he felt that if I told them, it would be the same as him telling it since we were married. I was okay with that because I was just hoping they might never know. It did bother him though because I think he felt like in a way, he was living a lie. That is why I think he wanted the kids to know, even if it has to be after his death."

"Maggie, you are talking in some other language. I am having a hard time following you. Anyway, since Joseph's gone, why don't you go ahead and just tell them whatever it is you are talking about."

"I don't know. I don't want to for one thing. Maybe I'm holding out hope that they don't ever find out."

"You told me a little bit about the trouble you and Joseph had before Jack and I moved here, but I sure don't know much about it. I remember it had something to do with him drinking too much. Is that what you are talking about?"

"It is in part. Joseph and I definitely had trouble, and it had a lot to do with him drinking a lot. I don't know if you would classify him as an alcoholic or not, but he did go through a period of heavy drinking. After he stopped, he never touched another drop. In other words, he never was a social drinker."

"Did something in his past cause that?"

"I think it did. I always assumed that Joseph's brother died some mysterious, accidental death, but he actually committed suicide. The two of them were very close, and Joseph was the last to talk to him. I am convinced that Joseph went to his grave blaming himself, thinking he could have done something to stop it. He would never talk about it, and I only knew about it because it came out when we were in counseling.

"I guess if you combine growing up with an alcoholic father and the guilt of his brother's death, he was a setup for it. But he never would have made excuses or blamed anyone."

Maggie continued after a several-second pause, "It took a lot of time and a great deal of effort to get through that. The months that the kids and I were away from him were a time of a lot of soul searching and prayer."

"Was that before Anna was born?"

Maggie acted as if the question startled her. She did not answer and started crying again.

Ruth said, "We don't have to talk about this if it is going to upset you."

"Oh, Ruth, if it were only an issue with the drinking I don't think any of the kids would worry about it that much, but there is so much more to the story."

"What on earth are you talking about?"

Maggie acted as if she didn't hear the question.

"But, Maggie, you've got good kids. I can't imagine that they couldn't deal with a skeleton or two."

Maggie let out a sigh, "The boys maybe. Anna's gonna have a real hard time. I wouldn't be surprised if I didn't have to go back to Nicaragua."

"Go back? I didn't know you ever went."

"Once."

They sat in silence for a while, and Ruth sensed that Maggie did not want to talk about it anymore. She told her she would call her about doing something for lunch later and went home.

Maggie got up, went in her bedroom, and walked to her dresser. There was a small lockbox in the bottom drawer, and she took it out. She opened it and began looking through the contents. She wanted to make sure that she had not misplaced any of her old documents. She felt sure that she was going to need one of them.

Chapter 13

Rain

It was the second day of steady rain and the Martins had mostly spent their time fighting boredom. Samuel's routine was one of reading in his Bible, writing, and the occasional nap. Matt would do a lot of pacing on the porch and would do some work on his computer. There would be the occasional phone call to his wife or his partner. Anna enjoyed an ongoing relationship with Isabella and was learning a lot working in the kitchen. Isabella said she had the makings of a good cook if she stuck with it.

Matt and Anna did learn something about Samuel, and it was purely by accident. As he would sit on the porch and do his writing, he would have papers and a notebook or two. Matt found a loose piece of paper lying on the deck of the porch, and he correctly assumed that Samuel had dropped it. He picked it up, and it was a poem. He was surprised to see that Samuel was the author.

"Hey, Anna, come take a look at this."

Anna came out of the kitchen, and they read the poem together.

"Hands of a Surgeon"
A tribute to Joseph Ewell Martin, MD

He lay there ever so still, hands folded on
his chest.
Hands that shook the hands of friends,

Hands that healed many over the years,
Hands that held other hands and taught
other hands,
Hands that were strong and gave comfort
to many.

He is gone now and so are these hands.

But many still live because of the skill in
these hands,
And many still heal who were taught by
these hands.
Few will ever forget the strength in these
hands.

—Samuel Martin

Matt said, "Go find Samuel and give this back to him. Tell him
that I think it is good."

"Why don't you tell him yourself?"

"Time is not right, yet."

"You think it ever will be?"

"If you just tell him what I said, maybe that will begin to thaw
things out a little."

"Y'all are so bullheaded."

"Anna, just go and give it to him!"

She found Samuel lounging in one of the love seats in the great
room and handed him the paper.

"Matt found this on the porch and wanted me to tell you that
he likes it. I do too."

Samuel sat up and took the paper from Anna. "I wasn't ready to
come out of the closet as a poet yet, but thank you."

"You gonna go thank Matt?"

"Nah."

"I swear, Samuel, that stubborn streak of yours is gonna get the
better of you one day."

"Don't wear me out with it, Anna. Have you noticed how he has treated me over the years? One thing that younger brothers want is the approval of the older brother, and I have never gotten anything close. And to make it worse, I have just gotten criticism and his self-righteous judgement. Am I supposed to ignore that? Well, guess what. I have tried and it doesn't work. This token compliment is too little, too late."

"You don't think it's a start."

"Let him come tell me himself."

Anna shook her head and went in the kitchen to help Isabella. She was getting lunch ready. It was a chicken dish that had a cheese sauce with it, and a potato casserole with some type of gravy. Isabella was also slicing plantains and frying them. The result was a chip that was great for dipping.

Anna asked Isabella if she had any brothers, and she said that she didn't. She had one sister. She said that she didn't live close by, so she didn't get to see her very often.

Anna said, "In my next life, I'm not having brothers."

Isabella said, "They're fine boys. They just got to come to grips with some things."

"Well, they are about to drive me crazy, so I wish they would hurry up. I'm not really seeing the fine boy part. Samuel spends so much time in the Word, but I can't tell it's doing him any good."

"You just got to realize the pride part of it. As long as the pride's in there, the devil will use that to keep the Word from having a good effect. I think pride may be our worst enemy. You got to humble yourself before the Lord and let him work on you."

"I guess you're right. You never told me how many kids you have, Isabella."

"I have two, three if I count you."

"Why haven't we met them?"

"Right now, they are staying in Costa Rica with their dad. We actually live there now. I just come up here when I'm cooking for groups."

"Girls or boys?"

"One of each—a girl, twenty-nine and a boy, twenty-five."

"Any grandchildren?"

"Yes, my daughter is married and has two girls, one five and one seven."

"I guess that is why I hear you humming lullabies all the time. You must be thinking about them."

"Thinking about a lot more than them. I can't count the number of babies I have rocked over the years. Didn't have much of a singing voice, so I hummed. Who knows, maybe I rocked you."

Anna felt like that was an obvious joke, but found it odd that Isabella's eyes had teared up a little; and she had quickly turned away, presumably so Anna wouldn't notice. She decided on a little humor and said, "I don't think so. I'm pretty sure I'd remembered."

They both laughed, and Isabella swatted Anna with a dishtowel.

"You haven't told me what you gonna do with your life when you get back home from this trip, except find a husband, of course."

Anna rolled her eyes and said, "I don't know for sure. I was in nursing school, but I'm not sure I'm going back."

Isabella said with excitement, "Child, you gotta go back. That is in your blood!"

"I'm not sure what you mean. My father was a doctor, not a nurse."

"I meant your mother."

"I'm not sure I know what you're talking about. My mother was a stay-at-home mom with a degree in elementary education."

Isabella said, "Oh." She let it drop.

*****

Daniel showed up in time for lunch and started carrying on about the chicken. Said it was his favorite dish. When he asked Isabella her secret, she said she wasn't going to tell because then, he wouldn't need her to come cook anymore.

She cut her eyes over to Anna and said, "And don't you go giving out my recipes to Daniel. I don't trust him. He'll do anything to save the money."

Daniel said, "Isabella, you know we couldn't get along without you around here."

'I don't know about that. How do you Americans say it? You will take me out in the pasture."

"Awe, Isabella, you are not old enough for that yet, and it's supposed to be, 'put me out to pasture.'"

"Sometimes I feel old enough, and don't correct me. My English is better than your Spanish!"

They were all seated around the table, eating, and Anna said, "Hey, Daniel, we have a poet in our midst."

"Oh yeah, who?"

"Samuel Jackson Martin. I said his name that way because I think it will look good on the cover of the book when he gets published."

Daniel said, "I had no idea. What kind of poems do you write?"

"Well, to tell you the truth, I haven't written many. They are kind of personal, and at this time, I have no ambition of becoming a published poet. Matt and Anna discovered one by accident, and as you know, Anna can be prone to some exaggeration."

Matt said, "Well, I am not an expert on the subject of literature, but I thought it was pretty good. It is unique."

Samuel looked at him and said, "Thank you."

Anna was thrilled. Although a small thing, she had witnessed civility between her brothers. She felt a glimmer of hope, however small, and she would take her victories when she could get them. She smiled at Daniel, and he smiled back. He understood what she was feeling.

Daniel said, "I'd love to read it. By the way, the rain is supposed to let up this afternoon, and we can go back to Managua to a market that is on our to-do list. My wife will be there doing some work that I think you'll find interesting. It will give you a chance to meet her as well as seeing another perspective on Nicaragua."

Matt asked, "What did your wife do before moving down here?"

"Coincidentally, she was an elementary school teacher. I remember Dr. Martin telling me that your mother's background was in that."

Anna said, "That is true. Isabella somehow had in her mind that she was a nurse."

Daniel had a puzzled look on his face and started to say something but changed his mind.

*****

The van ride to Managua was uneventful, not much different from previous trips. There was an occasional shower, but overall, it looked like the rain was stopping. Some of the landmarks were becoming more familiar to them.

As they entered the Sunshine market, people were milling around everywhere. Daniel told them not to wander off but to stay with him. After passing several shops, they caught up with Sharon and Olivia. Daniel made all the introductions. Sharon walked over to Samuel, put her arm around his waist, and said, "Honey, where did you find this one? I might want one." Sharon, with her outgoing, never-met-a-stranger personality, was an instant hit.

Samuel had a smile on his face and turned beet red.

Daniel said, "Don't mind her. She is not in her right mind. Gringos are few and far between around here."

She let him go and said, "I guess if I took him home, I'd have to feed him. Better leave him be."

Everybody laughed, and Matt said under his breath, "Yeah, the golden boy."

Sharon said, "I am pleased to meet all of you. Daniel has been talking about y'all a lot over the last few days. Let me introduce Olivia, a good friend of mine."

Everybody shook her hand, and she said that she was pleased to meet them. She said that she had heard a lot about Anna and was hoping that she could work some with Sharon and herself. Anna said she would love to.

Sharon and Olivia explained what they were trying to accomplish in their work with the ladies in the brothels. Sharon explained that she spent a great deal of her time teaching them English.

Matt asked, "I thought y'all said that you were trying to get them jobs that would be an alternative to what they are doing now?"

Sharon answered, "We are, but jobs are mighty scarce around here. We are looking into creating some. But nothing is easy, and it all requires money."

"I've heard through some of my business associates that it is hard to do business in Nicaragua."

"That is true, but we are not trying to start some international business, just something local that could employ several of these ladies."

"Maybe my business background could be of help."

Samuel did not wait for Sharon to respond, but said, "Maybe some of your money would help."

He said it in a sarcastic manner, and Matt ignored it.

Anna and Daniel looked at each other and shook their heads.

Daniel noticed three men walking toward them, and he did not like their look or body language. He had seen them before but did not know them. Olivia did and told Daniel that she did not like the fact that they were approaching. Daniel stepped toward them a few steps and greeted them in Spanish. The one who appeared to be the leader had a sarcastic grin and said, "*Hola, amigo.* I see you bring several gringos with you today."

"They are my guests and wanted to see some of the sights in your country."

"We are not used to having tourists in this market. Maybe we can do some business though, now that they are here."

Olivia became agitated and said in a loud voice, "You need to leave us alone. We have no business with you or your friends."

The group spokesman grinned and said, "Gringos usually have many dollars, and we have to charge them to make sure they are safe while they are here. The cute señorita there may be especially at risk since many here may want to spend some time with her." He gestured toward Anna as he said it.

Daniel was getting more concerned as was everybody. One of the three men walked over toward Anna and was smiling at her.

Samuel walked toward him, and the other two started toward Samuel.

Daniel was worried that the situation was getting dangerous.

About this time, Ramon was walking toward them. Daniel's heart was pounding in his chest, and he wondered how bad it was going to get; but Ramon walked over to the leader of the three Nicaraguans and said sternly, "Leave them alone."

"But, Ramon, we were just having some fun."

Ramon's expression never changed, and he said, "Go have fun somewhere else."

It appeared that none of them wanted to challenge Ramon, and they slowly backed away and left.

Daniel did not understand since Ramon's reputation was not good, but he was extremely grateful. He extended his hand that was shaking to Ramon and said, "Thank you."

Ramon returned his handshake and said, "You're welcome. Are these the children of Dr. Martin?"

"They are."

"I heard that Dr. Martin's children were here, and I had something I wanted to say to Anna. It is because of something her mother did for my family many years ago. I mean her no harm, only I did not get to thank her mother because she died when Anna was born."

Ramon was speaking Spanish, but Anna had heard her name mentioned twice and asked Daniel what it was all about.

"I don't know. I am thinking he has you mixed up with someone else."

Daniel asked Ramon, "Are you sure that you have the right person?"

"I am. Her mother was a nurse who worked in the hospital in Jinotepe. She took good care of my grandmother during the last part of her life. She did many things beyond her duty."

Daniel said, "Anna, he is convinced that your mother was the nurse that took care of his grandmother years ago. He wants to thank you. It may be best just to go along with it."

"That is twice in one day that someone has referred to our mother as a nurse. Why is he singling me out? I have two brothers. Surely he knows that."

"I don't know why, but since he just saved our lives, is it okay if he talks to you?"

Anna said, "I don't really have a problem with it."

Daniel told Ramon that it was all right. He talked directly to Anna and Daniel translated. She shook his hand when he was through, and he turned and walked away.

Anna thought it all must be a problem stemming from the language barrier. She just shrugged it off. Matt did not. As soon as he could, he took Daniel aside and asked him if he knew what was going on. Daniel said that they would try to talk later.

*****

After they finished their visit in the market, and after saying their goodbyes to Olivia, they headed toward Daniel's house.

Daniel said, "I gave Isabella the night off, so we'll have pizza at my place. Y'all need to see where I live and a good old American meal will do you good."

Samuel said, "I thought pizza was Italian."

"It used to be, but now it's American."

The ride to Daniel's house took them through parts of Managua that they hadn't seen. The traffic was busy and literally bumper-to-bumper at times. One would think there would be more accidents than there were. Matt was liking Nicaragua more and more, and was still surprised at that. There was something about the people that impressed him. He thought it must be that they always looked busy. He thought more about the exchange between Daniel, Anna, and Ramon in the market, and knew that he and Daniel needed to have a talk.

They turned off the highway and at the top of a street were let into a neighborhood by a man working a gate. The houses were nice and very diverse in their architecture. After passing several, they came to Daniel's. It was a large, ranch-style house painted bright yellow. They all got out and went in.

The kids were there, and Matt commented that Bo had that surfer look like Samuel. Hair slightly long, cool demeanor. Daniel said that the girls in his school were paying him a lot of attention. Bo acted embarrassed and denied it.

Sharon came in with several pizzas, and everybody was happy to see that. She was a great hostess and made them all feel at home.

After they had eaten their fill, Daniel asked Matt to join him on the back porch. It was open and long, extending the length of the house. Several strategically placed ceiling fans kept the air circulating. There was not as much of a breeze as was always present on the porch at the compound.

The two men sat down, and Daniel spoke first, "Matt I feel like we need to talk about Anna. Isabella recently told me that she is adopted. I am assuming you know that."

"I do."

"I was also told that Anna doesn't know."

"That is correct. My parents were very adamant about it."

"It's really not much of my business, Matt, but I am pretty sure that Isabella is going to tell her. She as much as told me she was when we talked about it. She said that she knew that your father would want her to know, but he could never tell her."

Matt said, "I find it odd that my father couldn't tell her."

"Isabella said that it was a promise made to her mother. You don't know anything about that?"

"No, I was never told anything about her birth. I was never told where she was born. I wonder how Isabella knows so much about it."

"I asked her that very question, and she got real emotional and never answered me. I let it drop."

Matt was massaging his temples and finally said, "Daniel, I don't know what to do. Part of me feels like it should be me that tells her, but I sure don't want to. I'm not sure what it's going to do to her. She is so emotional after the death of our father and stays upset with Samuel and me. I don't know what to do. Do you feel sure that Isabella is going to tell her?"

"I'd bet money on it. I think she almost did this morning."

"That sure is odd that Isabella and that man in the market—"

"Ramon."

"Yeah, Ramon. Both of them said that Anna's mother was a nurse, so I guess she was working in Nicaragua at the time Anna was born. We also know that she died when Anna was born, or at least that is what Ramon said. I wonder if she worked with my father, and maybe that is how he and my mother ended up adopting her daughter."

"Sounds reasonable."

"Daniel, there is another person to consider and that is my mother. There is no doubt that Anna will call her immediately, and it sure is a bad time for her."

"No doubt about that."

Matt was shaking his head, "This is a mess. I can only imagine how Anna is going to react to it. What good could possibly come from her finding this out at the age of thirty five?"

Daniel said, "I'll do anything I can to help. I'll tell her if you want me to."

"Thanks, but I would never put that on you. Do you think there is any way Isabella can be talked out of it?"

"I don't think so, Matt. It's almost as if your dad told her to do it. Makes me wonder if he did."

Chapter 14

Cliff Jumping

They got back to the compound fairly late, and Samuel and Anna went inside. Matt sat on the porch and enjoyed the breeze. He could not stop thinking about Anna. He found himself wondering about her birth mother. Was she single? If not, what happened to her husband? He had never thought about it before, but now it was staring him in the face, so to speak. The problem, as he saw it, was that Anna would want to know more information, depending on what Isabella knew and what she told her. He figured that their mother would have to fill in any blanks, and what was that going to be like for her? He doubted that Anna was going to be happy about not being told any of this before, and would she take that out on Maggie? Should he call Maggie? It was too late tonight, and he would put that off.

Matt was tired and figured he'd thought about it enough for now. He couldn't fix anything tonight. They would be leaving after breakfast tomorrow and going on a trip to the northern part of the country. They would be gone for two days, so if Isabella didn't tell Anna in the morning, that would buy some time. He tried to be optimistic.

*****

When Matt came into the kitchen the next morning, Anna was already there, apron on, helping Isabella with breakfast. For a moment, it looked like they were involved in a serious conversation, but soon they were laughing. Matt let out a sigh of relief. Samuel had beat him to breakfast this morning and seemed to be in a pretty good mood. He said good morning, and Matt returned the greeting. They heard a van pull up and soon Daniel came in. He was upbeat and said, "Good morning. Hope everybody is ready to do some riding today."

Matt asked, "Where we heading?"

"Well, as I mentioned to y'all yesterday, we are going to the northern part of the country. We'll end up tomorrow close to the border with Honduras."

Anna asked, "Where will we be staying tonight?"

"We will go as far as Matagalpa today and then on to Somoto tomorrow."

Anna said, "Like I know where that is."

Samuel asked, "That is the Somoto Canyon you are talking about?"

"It is. You know about it?"

"Not much. I had some friends in Puerto Rico who travelled a lot, and they had been there. They said it was a great place."

"It is. You have the Coco River flowing through a fantastic canyon. The tour is great."

Anna said, "Y'all know that I am not the athletic type. How demanding is this tour?"

"Not bad. Most of your time is spent floating in the river. You'll like it. There is a four-hour and a six-hour tour, and we will take the shorter one."

Matt said, "Have I heard something said about cliffs? Remember that Hernando pointed out that I have a small problem with heights."

"Not to worry, Matt. The cliffs are all different heights. We'll find one you like."

"I'm not sure that like is the right word to use there, and you better get the video the first time, if you know what I mean."

Daniel said, "Hey, y'all pack an overnight bag and remember you're gonna get wet on the canyon tour, so pack extra. If you have tennis shoes, pack a pair to wear in the canyon. Oh, and I almost forgot, bring your passports. It is likely that somebody will ask for them on this trip."

They heard voices out on the porch and then Dr. Romero came in. He had been down at his clinic and said he wanted to come by and say hello. "I haven't seen you all in a few days and was wondering how you are doing?"

Matt said, "Ask me in a couple more days and see if I have survived the Somoto Canyon."

Dr. Romero laughed, "I don't think I have ever heard of a fatality from there yet."

Matt replied, "I may die of altitude sickness on one of those cliffs."

Anna said, "Exhaustion and anxiety may get me."

Dr. Romero then said, "What about you, Samuel? What will do you in?"

Samuel looked at him with that level of cool that only he can display and simply said, "Boredom?"

Everybody was laughing, and Anna said, "Oh, yeah, the golden boy, fearless and the master of it all."

Daniel said, "Oh boy, I hope the guide will be able to keep up with him."

The commotion died down. Daniel told everybody to start getting their stuff together, and he asked Dr. Romero if he could talk with him for a minute as he headed back to his clinic. He told everybody to go ahead and put everything in the van, and he walked out with him.

As they walked the short distance to the clinic, Daniel said, "Dr. Romero, I assume that you are aware that Anna is adopted."

"I am. Why do you bring it up?"

"I think I am asking for advice more than anything." He told him about his conversation with Matt, about Isabella and Ramon.

"Daniel, I do agree that Isabella is very likely to tell her that she is adopted. I think Joseph always wanted her to know the truth."

"But how does Isabella know all of this?"

"She worked for a long time in the nursery at the hospital in Jinotepe where Anna was born. She knew Anna's mother very well, and of course, she also got to know Dr. Martin over the years and became close to him."

"I guess you know all the details surrounding her birth and adoption?"

"I do, but it is a story for another day. I will help in any way I can. Why don't you all go on and have a good trip, and we can talk when you get back."

"Thank you, we will."

*****

They all loaded up in the van. Samuel sat in the front seat so he could talk to Michael. They had gotten to know each other fairly well, and aside from Daniel, Samuel was the only one who could speak Spanish. Michael enjoyed the company. Anna sat in the very back seat and sort of stretched out. She said she might doze a little. Matt and Daniel each occupied one of the two middle seats.

The drive would require them to go back to Managua and then on up to Matagalpa. The sites on the highway to Managua had become fairly familiar and then they would travel another two hours or so, on a road they had never been on, north to Matagalpa. Daniel had told them that it was a town known for coffee production and that they would like it. He said that it was in the middle of a mountain range, and the elevation was over two thousand feet. The significance of that was that it was cooler than Managua. The city had been nicknamed the "city of eternal spring."

The drive was uneventful. There was some small talk, but for the most part, everybody was absorbed in their own thoughts. Samuel and Michael would erupt in laughter every now and then. Michael would occasionally high five Samuel and was enjoying a gringo that spoke fairly good Spanish. Matt did a lot of texting back home, trying to keep up with his family and his business. Anna dozed as promised.

Matt was still worried about the issue with Anna. He was a self-proclaimed analyst and had been thinking a lot about it over the last twenty-four hours. He knew nothing about Anna's birth except what he had learned the day before. He wondered what the details of her mother's death were; what was the cause? Was she single, if not, what happened to her husband? If she was single, did anyone know who Anna's father was? These were all questions Anna was going to want answered. Would Isabella tell her all of these things? Who else besides his mom and Isabella know? He felt sure that Dr. Romero would know. Should he talk to him? Matt did not like facing a problem with incomplete information. He still was thinking about calling his mom.

When they got to Matagalpa, they checked into the Hotel San Jose. It had a great staff and the rooms were nice. After they got settled, they all went out, walked around, and enjoyed the sites. The weather was cooler as promised, and the town was nice. Later in the afternoon, they went back to the hotel. Daniel told them that they had a little time to rest and in about an hour would be going to dinner.

At about six o'clock in the evening, they traveled to a restaurant that Daniel had picked called the Toro Bravo. He promised that they were about to have one of the best steaks they had ever eaten.

They were seated on a balcony with a great view, and the weather was perfect. The service was second to none, and when they had all ordered, Matt said, "Daniel, tell us more about Somoto Canyon."

"It is a canyon that has become a go-to place for tourist looking for a great "eco" experience. In some places, the walls are straight up and are over two hundred feet. The river is emerald green and not as cold as most mountain streams."

"What about the cliffs?"

"They are seen in various places throughout the canyon and are part of the rock formations."

"How tall?"

"Many different heights. I'm told that the highest is about twenty meters or sixty feet."

Matt asked Samuel, "You have any experience cliff jumping?"

"Yeah, I was in Jamaica with a group of people, and we all went to a cafe called Rick's. It is a tourist attraction and is known for cliff jumping. It has a thirty-five-foot jump and then there are some platforms that are higher. Most of the tourists go off the thirty-five-foot one."

Anna said, "I am assuming that you made the jump?"

"I did. The thirty-five foot one."

Daniel asked, "How was that?"

"To tell you the truth, it was high enough for me. I heard many stories of injuries and even an occasional death. Part of the problem is that a lot of the jumpers are encouraged by alcohol, and I don't think that is the smartest thing to do. But it's a tourist attraction, and I guess everybody feels like they have to do it."

Matt asked, "So you are not planning to go off the sixty foot one then?"

"No, I wouldn't recommend it. Too dangerous."

Samuel was not being entirely honest. He had gone off one of the higher platforms at Rick's that he had mentioned, and did not feel that he would have a problem with the sixty-foot jump. He said that for Matt and Anna's benefit, really for Matt, because he did not want to pressure him to jump from that high. Too high a risk for injury.

Matt said, "Awe, man. I was looking forward to it."

Daniel said, "Don't worry. We'll find one high enough for you."

Anna said, "Hey, Daniel, let me ask you something. I know that our father planned a lot of what we do on this trip. Is this one he thought of?"

"Yeah, the zip line is the only one I came up with on my own, at least so far. He had been to the canyon and was impressed with it."

"I'm curious about that because he certainly wasn't the hiker type or eco tourist as you call them."

Samuel said, "I agree. He never was the adventurous type. Mom was the one who was fearless and would do about anything."

Daniel replied, "He said those very things when the group was pressuring him to go. I remember him saying that he didn't need to go wading around in some ditch when he could get all of Mother Nature he needed sitting on the porch."

Everybody laughed and Matt said, "That sounds just like him. So what made him go?"

"I think the group just finally wore him down, and if the truth be known, I think he didn't want to be thought of as too old to go."

Anna asked, "When was that?"

"It was a medical trip about four years ago. It was the first year that I was here as a full-time missionary."

Matt said, "Wow, he would have been sixty four or sixty five. I am impressed. But hey, I have to know, did he jump off any cliffs?"

"Went off the sixty."

The table became chaotic and everybody was talking at once. "I'm not believing... You gotta be kidding... The dad I know would never... Come on, Daniel, get serious."

Daniel raised his hands and said, "Okay, okay, just thought I could get a rise out of y'all. He did go off a cliff, but it was a whole lot less than sixty feet. I am not sure exactly, but I know it was below twenty. He only did that one because the nursing students that were on the trip shamed him into it. That was a great day as I look back on it. We had a ball."

Matt the analyst asked, "So what do you think our father had in mind for us on this part of the trip?"

"I am not sure, Matt, but I think he just wanted y'all to see the beauty of that canyon and have a good time. He said over and over that he couldn't see how anybody could see a sight like that and doubt the existence of the Creator."

"I thought that maybe he wanted me to overcome my fear and leap from great heights to plunge into the frigid waters below."

Anna laughed and said, "Matt, as usual, you sure are going deep with this one. Pun intended by the way."

Daniel said, "Wow, Matt, that sounded almost poetic. Maybe we have two in the family."

Samuel said dryly, "I'm not convinced that we have one."

*****

Their steaks came and were fabulous as predicted. It was about as close to a perfect evening as you get. The weather was perfect, the service great, the food was good, and the company was better than they had had in a long time. Anna could not have been happier that her brothers were being civil to one another.

Back at the hotel, Daniel told them all to get a good night's sleep because they did have some hiking and swimming to do tomorrow. Matt lay awake for a while and seemed to be relaxing some. He did have some anxiety about jumping off a cliff but he figured he would survive. His worry about Anna had subsided some, and he figured that he would do whatever he needed to do when the time came. He continued to be pleasantly surprised with how much he was liking Nicaragua. It seemed like every experience and place he visited made him like it more. He noticed also that he talked on his cell phone less the longer he was here. He said a short prayer and drifted off to sleep.

*****

The next morning, they were in the hotel lobby, ready for the day's adventure. Michael showed up with the van. He had spent the night with some friends that he had in the area. He was upbeat as always, and he and Samuel had started in on each other as usual.

Daniel outlined the plan for the day and told them that Michael would drive them to Esteli and then they would take the chicken bus on to Somoto. He explained that Michael could take them all the way to Somoto, but Daniel wanted them to have the bus experience. He went on to say that the bus was his call and not Dr. Martin's.

They made good time and got to Esteli in two and a half hours. Michael let them off at a bus stop and said he would see them this afternoon in Somoto. They did not have time to see many of the sights of Esteli, but Daniel told them that it was a town known pri-·marily for cigar production. He said that maybe they could come back some day and stay there as they had done in Matagalpa.

The bus finally came, and it was everything they thought it would be, big and yellow and brightly painted. There was a Bible verse across the front above the windshield. The bus also was full by the time they climbed up the steps. Anna and Matt found room to sit down beside an elderly gentleman that was traveling with a young girl, presumably his granddaughter. Daniel and Samuel stood as there were no more seats available. It was hot, and even though the windows were open, the air did not seem to circulate very well.

They would stop frequently and pick people up or let others off. The bus capacity did not make any difference. There was always room for more. At times, there were people hanging off the back, one man holding a bicycle.

After an hour and a half, they arrived at the town of Somoto. When they got off the bus, they were met by Juan, their guide for the tour. He spoke no English, so Daniel was the one who talked to him about the details of the tour.

They took a twenty-minute taxi ride to a house where they were able to change clothes and where they could leave their belongings. The hike to the river was about a mile. The view there was as described. The water was a beautiful green, and even at the start of the tour, the rock formations were nice.

They entered the water and found it to be cold. After some time, and some hooping and hollering, they got used to it. They floated along with the current for the most part but would swim some if it was too slow. They did have life jackets on. The scenery was breathtaking with the canyon at times narrowing to around ten feet. The canyon walls at those points would be straight up and over two hundred feet tall.

Occasionally, they would have to hike around short distances where the rapids may be too strong. There were various cliffs of different heights that they would jump off, but none were challenging till they came to one that was supposed to be eight meters or about twenty-four feet. Daniel said that this one should be high enough for them to say they did some cliff jumping and to get the T-shirt.

Anna promptly said that it looked higher than that to her, and since she wasn't trying to prove her manhood, she would watch the boys go. They had put their cell phones in waterproof bags, and she said that somebody had to do the video work anyway. She endured the teasing from Matt and Samuel and remained firm in her decision.

The climb up to the cliff was not too difficult, and the ledge at the top was large enough for Juan, Daniel, Matt, and Samuel to all be there at the same time. The guide said that he would go last to make sure everybody got off safely. Matt said he wasn't going first, and he thought the host, Daniel, should lead the way. He said he would go second if Daniel survived. All agreed.

Daniel stepped to the edge, shook his arms around to loosen up, and jumped off. Matt thought that he dropped forever before hitting the water, and this didn't bolster his courage any. Matt stepped to the edge and looked down. He got that sick feeling in his stomach that he used to get when the roller coaster was getting near the top of the first hill. He just stood there looking down.

He just kept standing there, and Anna began to cheer him on from the pool down below. Samuel sat down and leaned against the rock wall behind the ledge. After a short time, he fell asleep. Matt just kept standing there. The guide sat down and started fidgeting with some rocks.

Daniel was beside Anna, and they were floating around the edge of the pool. He broke the silence after several minutes and asked, "Do you think he is going to go or will he climb back down?"

"Oh, he's going. We might be here this time tomorrow, but he's going."

"Are you sure? I'm not keeping time, but it's been a while."

"I know Matthew Martin, and he will die of starvation before he climbs back down. He realizes that he doesn't have Samuel's athletic ability, but he won't quit."

It seemed like forever, and Daniel thought that the shadows were growing longer. All of a sudden, there was movement from Matt, and he told Anna to get her cell phone ready. Matt stepped up and jumped. He stumbled slightly at the top and that caused him to land slightly sideways. Daniel winced and thought, those ribs might bother him for a few days. He swam over to make sure Matt was okay and noticed a half smile on his face mixed with a slightly pained expression.

"You okay, Matt?"

"Yeah, that landing left something to be desired, but I'm glad I went."

"All joking aside, you really do have a fear of height, huh?"

"I really do."

"Well, I think it is cool whenever anybody can overcome their fear."

"Thank you. And speaking of fear, I think we will now observe one who does not know what the word means."

The guide called down to Daniel and asked if he was ready for Samuel. Daniel indicated he was, and Juan woke him up."

Samuel had that instant of disorientation that comes when you first wake up, and it took a minute for his eyes to get used to the sunlight. He remembered where he was and walked directly to the edge, assumed a position reminiscent of an Olympic diver, and jumped. Immediately, everyone could tell that this was not a regular jump. He went off frontward but arched his back and did a back flip, a perfect gainer. It was one of those times that the gracefulness of the movements made it look like it was in slow motion. The landing lacked what it took to be a ten, but it was close.

Matt recognized immediately that he was feeling admiration and no jealousy. Was he making progress? He swam over to Samuel and said, "Nice one, brother."

"Thank you. Not quite as good as yours."

"I don't understand. You didn't see mine."

"Makes no difference. If you didn't climb down, yours was better than mine. Took more guts."

Samuel swam on ahead and Matt felt good.

*****

Not too far ahead, they came to the infamous sixty-foot jump. There was a group that had been ahead of them and two people had gone off it.

Matt said, "Hey, Samuel, I am wondering why you wouldn't want to try that one."

Anna said, "Yeah, I was wondering that myself."

Samuel replied, "To tell you the truth, I would like to do it, but I had a couple of reservations. One, I did not want to come across as a show off, and two, I did not want anybody else to feel pressured to do it."

Matt said, "Hey, I am satisfied with my accomplishment today, so you can be sure that I feel no pressure whatsoever. I would like to see you do it."

Anna said, "I would hate for somebody like you to miss an opportunity like that. You don't know if you'll ever have it again."

"I would love to do it."

Daniel told Juan that Samuel was going to do the jump, and the guide said that he did it all the time and would go with him. The climb to the cliff took a little while, but they made it without any problems. Juan jumped first and Samuel walked to the edge. He did not go immediately but stood for a minute, building his courage. He stepped off and landed without incident. He did not do anything fancy this time.

The rest of the tour consisted of swimming and floating, and the final part was a boat ride that took them to the exit point. The hike back was not too long but seemed longer because they were worn out. They changed clothes, thanked Juan, and tipped him generously. Michael was there with the van.

The trip back would be strait to Managua and then on to Diriamba. It would take between four and five hours. They were all in their usual places in the van. They were tired, but all knew that it had been a great day. Matt's ribs were aching some, but he was happy about it.

Chapter 15

Isabella

After the group had left for Matagalpa, Dr. Romero walked back down to the compound. He stuck his head in the door and found Isabella washing the dishes.

"Got any coffee left?"

"Come in, doctor. If I don't, for you, I will make some more. Have a seat."

"Thank you. You know, nobody makes coffee as good as you."

"Dr. Romero, charming as usual. I know you must have something on your mind because you would not come down here for the same coffee that is in your office."

"You have always been too perceptive, Isabella. I can never get anything past you. I did want to talk to you about something. Daniel was asking me about Anna this morning. He says you are going to tell her she is adopted."

Isabella put her dishcloth down and leaned on the island.

"Dr. Romero, she is one of the most precious people in the world, and I would not hurt her for anything, but you and I both know that Dr. Martin wanted her to know."

"I know that he did, and I would do anything to honor his wishes as he was closer than a brother to me." He paused and looked like he was thinking about something, then continued, "I guess I can't see what good it will do for Anna now, especially if she knows the whole truth."

Isabella said, "I cannot tell her the whole story. It will be too painful for me, and I do not feel it is my place to."

"I understand what you are saying, but I know that Anna will want to know more than just the fact that she is adopted. She will have questions. I think that Maggie will have to be the one to answer those."

"I agree with you." Isabella paused and wiped her tears. "I hate to be emotional like this, Dr. Romero, but I think Dr. Martin knew that if I ever saw Anna again that I would fall in love with her all over again. He also knew that if he told me to tell her this information that I would do it. Maybe he knew that nobody else would do it. I cannot fully understand it either, but you and I both know that he did not do anything without a good reason. I think his strong sense of honesty was the main reason. He would never have hidden anything from Anna if it were not for his agreement with her mother. You can see why I do not feel that I really have any choice."

Dr. Romero reflected for a moment, "There is one thing that is for sure. When Joseph got something firmly set in his mind, he never wavered from it. Call it stubborn if you want to."

They both sat for a minute without saying anything, and then Dr. Romero said, "Isabella, I am not here to tell you what to do. I just wanted to talk to you about it. We all have to handle things however we think is best."

After Dr. Romero left, Isabella just sat for a while and remembered the months that she helped take care of Anna while they were waiting for all the paperwork to go through for her adoption. She hummed a lullaby.

Chapter 16

Part of the Story

It was Wednesday, and the Martins had the day off. Daniel told them to rest up because they were going to start building a house on Thursday. He told them that it would be hard work, and it would be hot.

After a good breakfast and as soon as the dishes were done, Anna and Isabella rode a moto to the grocery store in Diriamba. Isabella said that they were going to have a girl day and were going to do some shopping and would have lunch downtown. She told Matt and Samuel that there was stuff to make sandwiches with, and they were on their own for lunch.

Samuel said he felt a little under the weather and went to his room to lay down. Matt went out on the porch and enjoyed the usual breeze. He reflected on the trip so far and had a good feeling about it overall. Samuel was not in a good mood this morning, but Matt thought it might have to do with him feeling bad, or at least he hoped so. He could not keep from thinking about Anna, and he had that anxious feeling you get when you have a problem and you don't know what to do. The more he thought about it, he became convinced that Isabella would talk to her on their outing today. What better time would there be? He felt it was a good time to call his mother.

"Hello, Matt, glad you called. Haven't talked to you in a couple of days."

"Yeah, Mom. We were on an adventure to the Somoto canyon."

"I saw pictures from there when your father went a few years ago. The scenery looked beautiful."

"It was. We had a great time. I have never seen anything like that before."

"Y'all are doing okay then?"

"Yes, ma'am. No big problems. Samuel is feeling under the weather today, but nothing major going on. Anna went with Isabella on a trip to town."

"How is Anna doing?"

"She is doing okay." There was a pause and Matt said, "She is actually the reason that I called. I wanted to talk to you about something."

There was a brief silence and Maggie said, "Does it have anything to do with Isabella?"

"It does. How did you know?"

"Well, it's not just a lucky guess. I have been thinking more and more lately that Anna's past was a big part of your father's plans for this trip."

"Funny you should say that. Daniel talked to me, and he is convinced that Isabella is going to tell Anna she is adopted. They have gone on an outing to town, and it wouldn't surprise me if she told her today."

"I thought that might happen."

"Well, I am worried for a couple of reasons. One is I don't know what Anna's reaction is going to be. I don't think she is going to be thrilled about the news. Secondly, she might have a lot of questions, and I don't have the answers."

"It would not be up to you to tell her anyway, Matt. I am the only one who can do that."

"Yeah, but you are there, and we are here."

"That can change."

"What are you saying?"

"I'm pretty sure that I will have to come to Nicaragua."

"That sounds pretty drastic. You don't think that you can talk to her on the phone about it."

"Matt, it is too complicated for me to try to cover on the phone. We will need to have a family discussion as it really affects us all."

"Is there anything that you can tell me to help me deal with Anna?"

"I hate that you are in this position, Matt, but I am going to have to be the one to deal with it."

"I'll have to respect that, but I hate for you to have to come here."

"It's okay. I would like to see Nicaragua again anyway."

"I never knew that you had been here."

"I was there after Anna was born."

"If I ever knew that, I guess I had forgotten it. Anyway, if I my supposition turns out to be right, Anna will probably call you today. You can let me know."

"Okay, Matt, and again, let me say that I'm sorry that you have to deal with this. As you and I know, it is not easy being the oldest."

*****

Anna and Isabella were enjoying downtown Diriamba. They had been to a supermarket that was similar to the ones in the United States, but smaller. Anna was amazed that they had many of the same items that she would see back home, but a lot too was missing. They did not carry her favorite candy bar.

They had also gone to other shops just looking around as ladies do. It was fun for Anna to experience the cultural differences as well as the similarities. She enjoyed watching Isabella bargain with the shop owners if they were considering an item to buy.

At lunchtime, they rode a moto to a restaurant not far from downtown. It was decorated with a lot of bamboo and had sort of a tiki look to it. Isabella said that they had the best food for the prices.

Anna was sipping on a drink that Isabella had recommended. She could not remember the ingredients, but it did have milk in it. It was a local favorite, and Anna enjoyed it. The food was excellent. Anna had a seafood dish that rivaled anything she had eaten in the States.

After they ate, they were relaxing and chatting, when Isabella's mood changed to somber and she said, "I want to talk to you about something, Anna, and I don't know how to do it."

"Just come out with it. What could be so serious?"

"It is something your father wanted you to know but could not tell you himself."

"Well, don't keep me in suspense, just tell me."

"You are adopted."

"What?"

"You were born here in Nicaragua and adopted by Dr. Martin and Maggie, and then taken back to the United States."

"Isabella, is this some weird joke or something?"

"It is not. Do you remember me talking about your mother being a nurse?"

"I do, and there was a man in the market that referred to my mother as a nurse. I thought there was some mistake."

"There was no mistake. Your mother was a nurse working in Nicaragua when you were born. She died from problems associated with your birth, and you were adopted by Dr. Martin and Maggie."

"I don't believe it. Why would I not have been told about this?"

"It was a request that your mother made to Dr. Martin, and being the kind of man he was, he would not go against her wishes. And, of course, Maggie would feel bound by your father's agreement."

"I don't think I understand it, Isabella. My birth mother, I guess that is what I should call her, did not want me to know I was adopted, and my adopted parents honored that request. Is it supposed to be that simple?"

Isabella thought for a minute and then replied, "I guess that is the main part of it."

"I am having a hard time processing this. It doesn't seem real. Why would you be telling me this now?" Did you not feel bound by the request for me not to know?"

"Your father told me to tell you if the opportunity ever came about. In his heart, he wanted you to know."

"Why you?"

With tears in her eyes and her voice shaky, Isabella said, "I do not know for sure, but I was there when you were born and always would think of you as one of my own."

Anna had that look of disbelief and shook her head as if trying to clear something from it, "This is getting stranger as it goes along. So by you telling me after my father's death, he has fulfilled his promise to my birth mother but also has seen to it that I would be told, and that was what he wanted all along. That seems to stretch integrity to its limits."

Isabella answered, "I do not fully understand what you said, but you know your father was an honest man."

"Isabella, I am blown away by this. It brings up so many questions. Where was my mother from? What about her family? Was my birth mother married? What happened to my birth father—if that is what you call him? What requests did he have? Who was he? And I still say, why would my adopted parents honor a request all these years from someone who died?

"It is a complicated story, Anna, and I am not able to answer all of the questions for you. I have told you all I can."

"Does Matt know?"

"I think he knows about your adoption, but I am not sure."

"Well, I am sure that Maggie knows. I guess I should call her Maggie instead of Mom from now on."

An anger was building within Anna, and it was starting to show.

Isabella said, "Maggie is your mother. You shouldn't talk like that."

"I don't know, Isabella. I just found out that something has been kept from me for all these years. How am I supposed to feel and act?"

*****

When Anna and Isabella got back to the compound, Matt was sitting on the porch working on his laptop. As they were walking up the drive, he could tell by the way Anna looked that Isabella told her. When she walked up the steps, Anna gave him a look that made him think that he may be in trouble.

"Do you know that I was adopted?"

"Yes."

"Does Samuel know?"

"No."

"Isabella didn't really tell me a lot of details. I don't guess you can tell me much either."

"I have never been told the details."

"Well, if you will excuse me, I am going to call Maggie."

Matt and Isabella went into the kitchen and left Anna alone on the porch. She took her cell phone out of her purse but didn't dial the number for a while. Matt and Isabella sat in the kitchen and didn't say much. Samuel came in and said he might be feeling a little better and ate a banana. After a while, he went back into the great room to lie down. In about an hour, Anna came in, and it was obvious that she had been crying. She sat down and didn't say anything.

Matt couldn't stand the silence and asked, "What did she say?"

Anna kept looking down and simply said, "She is coming to Nicaragua."

Chapter 17

Construction

T he next morning, everybody made it to the kitchen in a timely manner, anticipating a busy day of construction. Anna and Isabella were busy with breakfast, but there was not the usual talking and laughter going on. Matt spoke to Anna when he came in and barely got any response. He figured he must be on the bad list. Samuel said that he was still a little under the weather but felt good enough to go to work. He did not seem to be in the best of moods.

Matt was disappointed that their situation had taken a turn in the wrong direction. He had been happy with the progress two days ago at the Somoto Canyon, but now he would have to deal with Samuel and Anna's moods all day. He was feeling sorry for himself for the bad luck of Anna finding out about her adoption. Why did it have to be now? Would his mother come to Nicaragua as she said she would? Should he tell Samuel? His thoughts were interrupted by Daniel coming into the kitchen with a man that they had not met before.

"Good morning, everybody. I would like for y'all to meet Elijah. We call him E for short. He will be helping with the construction over the next couple of days. He has built more of these houses than he can count."

Elijah was a tall Nicaraguan that looked to be in his thirties. He spoke good English. He shook everybody's hand and said that he was looking forward to working with them. He and Daniel joined them for breakfast.

There was not much small talk, and Daniel noticed Anna's change in mood. He gestured toward her so Matt could see him, and Matt nodded his head yes. Daniel then knew that Isabella had told her about her adoption. He just shook his head.

*****

The trip to the house site took a while. They traveled quite a distance out of town, down a road that was mostly dirt with a little gravel. Daniel drove the van because Michael was driving the truck carrying the building materials. Samuel rode in the truck since he and Michael had gotten to be good friends.

When they arrived, they were appalled at the house they were replacing. It was put together with sticks and tarp material with some pieces of old tin. The family started tearing it down as soon as they arrived. It didn't take long. Some neighbors joined in to help.

Anna was an immediate hit with the kids in the neighborhood and quickly drew a crowd. They were a happy group, and soon, Anna was laughing and having fun. Her popularity increased greatly when she started giving out cookies she retrieved from her backpack.

The men unloaded the truck and stacked all the materials next to where the house was going to be built. Many of the men from the surrounding area helped with that. Even though it was not yet mid-morning, it was already hot. Not much breeze was stirring. There was also a shortage of shade. Samuel was sweating more than the rest of them and was obviously not feeling that well.

Daniel asked, "Hey, Samuel, you okay?"

"Yeah, I just feel a little fluish. I'll be alright."

"You sure?"

"Yeah, I have just been a little under the weather ever since we got back from Somoto."

"Well, you don't have to be out in this heat working today if you don't feel like it."

"No, man. I'm fine."

*****

The six poles that were the main support structure for the house were placed and set by E. The job now would consist of framing the house with metal beams and then wrapping it in insulation. The tin siding and roof would go on last. A wooden door and two windows were the finishing touches. Although not large, it was so much nicer than what they were replacing.

They had all worked steadily all morning and had all the framing done. Matt and Samuel had done fairly well with not a lot of cross words, but that was about to change. Anna walked over to offer them some water just as they began arguing about how the insulation should be started.

Matt was saying, "That is not right. Daniel said we were supposed to start on the side that goes over the roof."

Samuel replied, "That doesn't make any sense. I distinctly heard E say that he needed it on the other side first where he has to cut the tin at an angle."

Anna said, "Hey, guys, y'all want some water?"

Neither man acknowledged that she had spoken.

"He won't need it there till he gets ready to make those cuts."

"I guess you know when he's ready to start on that."

Matt shook his head and said, "I know what Daniel told me, and he certainly knows more about it than you."

"Always got to be right, huh, Matt?"

Anna was still standing there and spoke again, "How long are you guys planning to keep this up?"

Samuel was hot, tired, and irritable. He looked her way and said, "Why don't you stay out of it. I am sick of your pie-in-the-sky, fairytale ways. Why don't you mind your own business for once?"

Matt hit him…hard!

It happened so fast that Matt had no time to think about it. His fist landed below Samuel's left eye, caught the side of his nose, and cut his upper lip. Samuel stumbled backward but did not fall. Blood was running down his chin and dripping onto his T-shirt.

Matt stood there with his fists in the ready position, more out of instinct than anything else, and did not know what to expect. Samuel never changed his expression and did not move toward Matt or show any sign that he had any intention of hitting him back. He slowly and deliberately took off his T-shirt and wiped his mouth. He dropped his shirt to the ground. For a long minute, he stood looking at Matt. His arm and chest muscles caused Matt more than a little bit of concern, but much to his surprise, Samuel turned, picked up a load of tin, and walked away.

Matt felt sick to his stomach. He felt terrible and could not believe he had done that. How could he act like that? He had that horrible feeling of wanting to take it back but knowing that he couldn't. He knew in his heart that the problems between he and Samuel were primarily his fault. How can jealousy cause someone to act that way toward another human being, especially a brother?

Matt turned toward Anna who was still standing there, and when he tried to say something, the words wouldn't come out. She stood looking at him with a lifeless expression as if all of her emotions had just drained out of her.

"You know, Matt, you never have been a brother to him. Maybe now you never will." She walked over and got in the van.

Matt just stood there, wondering if he had ever felt worse in his life. He suddenly was sick of this trip. All the progress that he felt they had made was gone. How could he ever now have any kind of relationship with his brother? Would Anna ever feel the same again? How long would she resent him for what he had just done? Would his failure to tell her about her adoption be a problem between them into the future? He didn't need this. He began thinking about going home.

Matt sat on one of the sawhorses and just stared at the ground. Daniel walked over and at first didn't say anything. Matt didn't look at him.

"Sorry that happened, Matt."

"Yeah, me too."

"Anything I can do?"

Matt kept looking at the ground and replied, "Nothing anybody can do."

"Maybe with the Lord's help—"

Matt cut him off, "With all due respect, Daniel, I'm not really feeling it right now. Maybe another time."

"Sorry, just trying to help."

"I know you are. Didn't mean to be short with you."

"Did you know your hand was bleeding?"

Matt looked at the back of his right hand, and there was a short but deep cut just above the knuckle of his middle finger. It was oozing some.

Daniel said, "Looks like that might need a stitch or two. You want to go see Dr. Romero?"

"Later. I think I'm going to do some work. Maybe that will get my mind off all of this. You got anything I can wrap around my hand?"

Daniel had a first-aid kit. He worked on Matt's hand and got it bandaged to where it would quit bleeding. They walked back toward the job site where Samuel and E were getting ready to get on the roof to start putting the tin on. Matt told E that he wanted to help with that, so E stayed on the ground and said he would hand the tin up to them. The breeze had picked up, so it wasn't so hot as it had been earlier.

They got into a routine of E and Daniel handing the sheets of tin up, and Matt and Samuel screwing them down. Neither Matt nor Samuel spoke to or looked at one another but worked in silence. The wind had picked up quite a bit, making the tin harder to handle, and Daniel told them that they may need to wait till tomorrow to finish. Matt said that since there was only one more piece to go on that side, they would quit after they got it in place.

Matt took the sheet of tin as E handed it up, and as he was about to put it in place, a gust of wind came up and blew it toward the side. The force of the wind pulled it from the grip of his right hand, and now he was holding it only with his left. The tin began sliding through his left hand, and it's sharp edge was cutting into his palm. He could not let it go because there were people below him. To make matters worse, the force of the wind was blowing the tin like a sail and pulling him toward the side. He was certain he was going over the edge. His heart was pounding, and he did not know what to do. Suddenly, he felt a tight grip on his right arm; and in the same instant, Samuel's other hand grabbed the tin and forced it down to the surface of the roof. He had been on the other end of the roof finishing up, and when he saw what was happening, he made it over to Matt in two to three quick steps.

Matt climbed down the ladder and was visibly shaken. He was white as a sheet, and his hands were trembling. He quickly walked around to the backside of the house and threw up.

E and Samuel started picking up tools and stacking up some of the building materials, and Daniel walked over to check on Matt's hand. The cut in his left palm was fairly deep and still bleeding.

"Looks like you're gonna need stitches in that one too."

"Yeah."

"Matt, I should have kept y'all off the roof today when I saw the wind picking up like that."

"Forget it. The way I feel today, I wouldn't have listened to you anyway. Can you tell me if there are flights out of Managua to the States every day?"

"I'm pretty sure there are, why?"

"I plan to be on the next one."

"You can't be serious."

"Never more serious in my life."

"Because of what happened today?"

"Let's see, where do I begin? Yesterday, my sister found out she is adopted. I'm on the list of those she resents for not telling her, and she is real happy with me for fighting with Samuel this morning. Speaking of Samuel, my relationship with him is at least as bad as it has ever been, and oh, let's not forget that I capped that off pretty good by hitting him in the face this morning, and that not too long before he saved my life! Whatever my father had in mind for this trip ain't working out. I've had enough."

Samuel was close enough to Daniel and Matt to hear their conversation and was shocked to hear about Anna. He wondered how it could be that he didn't know anything about that. He felt worse now for having talked to her the way he did. He understood Matt's reaction a little better.

Daniel said, "Matt, I hope you'll take some time to think about this."

Matt asked, "Can you get me to the airport if I book a flight in the morning?"

"I don't want to, but I can."

*****

Dr. Romero finished putting stitches in the cuts on both of Matt's hands. Samuel and Anna had stayed at the compound. Samuel's lip did not require any stitches. Matt had already called and booked a flight for tomorrow morning. He would have to leave the compound at four o'clock in the morning to get to the airport on time.

Daniel and Dr. Romero left Matt with the nurse, Carolina, to apply bandages to his hands, and walked into Dr. Romero's office. It was at the other end of the clinic, so Matt could not hear their conversation.

"I don't know if you heard, Dr. Romero, but Matt is leaving."

"Leaving? When?"

"First thing in the morning."

"I am sorry to hear that. How did that happen?"

Daniel filled him in on the happenings of the day and then said, "Also, Isabella told Anna about her adoption, and she has not taken it real well."

"How much does she know?"

"I am not sure, but there must be more to tell. Maggie is coming to Nicaragua."

"Really! When is she coming?"

"I don't think we know that yet."

"This is too much information for one day, Daniel. It can't be a good idea for Matt to leave especially if his mother is coming."

"I feel the same way, but he has his father's stubbornness and says his mind is made up."

Just then, they heard Matt coming down the hall, and he walked into the office.

Dr. Romero said, "Well, did Carolina get you fixed up?"

"Yes, sir. Thank you."

"Matt, Daniel tells me you are leaving tomorrow."

"That's correct."

"There is a lot more to be done here. I for one wish you would stay."

"I'm losing ground, Dr. Romero. I need to regroup and fight it another day."

"We don't always get another day."

Matt was not in the mood for much conversation and replied, "I can never adequately express to you, sir, and to you, Daniel, my appreciation for your help and concern. But I have to do it my way."

Chapter 18

Matt, Samuel, and Anna

Samuel and Anna were sitting on the porch, and neither one of them had spoken since they got back from the construction site. Samuel looked at Anna and did not recall ever seeing her like this before. She showed no emotion at all, and he was used to her always being so outgoing and full of energy. He was remorseful about his remarks to her earlier in the day, and had to filter all of this through the new information he had learned concerning the fact that she was adopted. He had not yet processed that. He finally said, "I didn't know you were adopted."

"Neither did I."

"I am so sorry for what I said today. I hope you know how much I love you." Samuel got choked up when he said it.

"That's why it hurts so bad."

"I never in a thousand years would say something like I did. I still don't know why I did it."

"That's not what hurts."

"What do you mean?"

"It is hard to explain it. I guess the fact that I am the youngest in the family, and the fact that I am so much younger than you and Matt gives me special feelings toward y'all. I have been spoiled and pampered by the two of you all my life, and I have loved it. What has gone on between y'all for so long has broken my heart to pieces and what happened today finished it off."

"I guess it's all my fault, then?"

"Who cares whose fault it is?"

After a short pause, Samuel said, "What now?"

"Why don't you tell me, Samuel? With Matt leaving, this is it. There won't be another chance."

"What do you think I can do?"

Anna raised her voice, "For God's sake, Samuel, why don't you put on your big-boy pants and talk to him. Maybe y'all can finish the fight that started this morning and be done with it once and for all! I don't care anymore if y'all kill each other!"

Samuel did not reply because he did not know what to say. Soon, they heard Daniel and Matt walking back from Dr. Romero's office. The two men walked up the steps onto the porch. Daniel sensed the mood and said he needed to get on back to Managua. He told Matt that he would pick him up around four in the morning. Matt sat down. Anna looked over at him, shook her head, got up, and went into the kitchen.

The two brothers sat there for a long time, and neither of them said anything. Samuel kept thinking about what Anna had said. Finally, he spoke up, "Leaving tomorrow?"

"That's the date on the ticket."

"You feel like that's the best plan."

"Yeah."

"Why?"

"A blind man can see it."

"I don't think I get it. You quitting?"

"I know it makes no sense since we're all getting along so well," Matt said it with sarcasm.

"What about Anna?"

"Don't put that one on me, man. I don't need the responsibility. It's not my fault that nobody told her about being adopted. I guess that was another brilliant idea that our father had. Looks like it worked out about as well as this trip."

"So the way you handle that is to run away from it, huh? You don't think she needs your help with it all?"

"I don't need this. I'm done with it. You help her."

Matt started to get up, and Samuel said in a loud and stern voice, "You're not going anywhere till we're through talking about this! Anna's adoption is only part of your problem, and you know it."

"I can't deal with it any more. Today was the final straw."

"I don't think you're leaving. It's not in you to quit. You've never quit on anything in your life. If you leave here tomorrow, you leave knowing you quit on your family. You ain't got that in you."

Matt didn't respond. He stood up, walked toward the door, turned around, and said in a low voice, "I'm as good as on the plane."

*****

The next morning, Samuel woke up earlier than usual. He was running a fever, and he had a headache. It hurt worse behind his eyes. His lip and jaw were sore. He thought about Matt, and he felt sick that he was flying out today. He thought that it would now be near impossible for them to ever have any kind of relationship. He was already having regrets that he had not taken the high road more and tried to do better. He was also worried about Anna and how it was all going to affect her.

He got up, slipped on some shorts and a T-shirt, and walked toward the kitchen. He was surprised to see Daniel asleep on one of the couches in the great room. He wondered what was going on because he knew that he couldn't already be back from taking Matt to the airport. That question was answered when he walked into the kitchen and saw Matt sitting in his usual spot at the table.

Samuel stood looking at him for what seemed like a long time and then sat down. He looked over at the clock on the wall.

Matt said, "That's right. I missed my plane."

Samuel managed a smile and shook his head. "Yeah, I see."

A few minutes went by and Anna came in. When she saw Matt sitting there, she had a curious look on her face. She said nothing.

Matt looked at her and said, "Missed my flight."

She was beginning to get it and managed a smile.

After a while, Samuel looked at Matt and asked, "How are your hands?"

"Not too good. Won't be able to do any manual labor today, maybe even for several days. How's your lip?"

"Not good at all. Hurts when I try to talk."

Matt said, "That's a win/win for me."

Both men laughed, and Matt extended his hand to Samuel. "Go easy with the grip now."

Samuel shook his hand and said, "No problem."

Anna and Isabella stood behind the island, both of them smiling with tears running down their cheeks.

Isabella said, "I told you they were fine boys."

Chapter 19

Dengue Fever

Daniel came into the kitchen about the time everybody was finishing breakfast. He was rubbing the sleep out of his eyes, and his hair definitely needed work.

"Not only am I subjected to sleep deprivation, but I guess y'all would have let me starve too."

Matt said, "Yeah, Daniel, I guess I have to take the credit for the sleep problem. As far as breakfast, we thought you would rather catch up on some of that lost sleep."

Isabella spoke up next, "Daniel knows that I spoil him. Don't let him fool you. He knows I have saved a plate for him."

Daniel replied, "I should have known I could count on you, Isabella. As for the sleep, I could not have been happier when you told me that you weren't leaving."

"Yeah, and I really appreciate you saying that. To say I had a bad day yesterday is an understatement. I have spent the better part of breakfast apologizing to my siblings. I owe you one too."

"I appreciate it, but it's not necessary. All's well that ends well."

Samuel asked, "Do we have any plans for today? Matt can't really do much construction, and this crud I've got has about got me down too."

"We don't really need to worry about the house. I thought I would get E and a friend of his to do what little there is to finish up.

I think I need to get you down to see Dr. Romero. It doesn't look like you're getting any better."

"I hate to bother him. Maybe if I just rest a day or two."

Matt said, "I'm afraid that I have to agree with Daniel. Seems to me that you are getting worse."

Anna said, "That makes it unanimous because I feel the same way. You said yourself that you feel worse."

"Guess I'm outnumbered then. Let me grab a shower first."

*****

Matt and Daniel went out on the porch and enjoyed the sights and sounds of the morning. The compound was not far from a main road, and it stayed busy. You had the usual motos, buses, and the occasional horse-drawn carts. There were a lot of birds around that morning, and their chatter gave the place a more tropical atmosphere. A light breeze and Nicaraguan coffee topped it all off.

"Matt, if you don't mind me asking, what made you stay?"

"I don't mind the question. You'll be happy to know that I feel like it was at least in part an answer to prayer."

"Oh yeah, how so?"

"Well, my emotions were out of control last night, and I was feeling bad about everything that had happened. Samuel told me that I was basically giving up and quitting, and that bothered me. When I went to bed, I started praying. I was mad at God at first, but I basically ended with sort of a fleece. I told God to give me a clear answer when I woke up as to what I should do."

"And you felt like you got your answer?"

"I absolutely do. When I woke up this morning, the first thought I had was that I could not leave. There was no doubt in my mind, whatsoever."

"That is great to hear, Matt."

"Well, I'm not an expert on the power of prayer, but it's a start."

"It sure sounds like you are feeling good about it. You think it will help with you and Samuel?"

"That may be the most incredible part of it. I have a peace about that, and I have never felt anything like that before. Our relationship was part of my prayer."

"It does me good to hear this. Y'all have been a part of my prayers since you got here."

"Well, Daniel, I don't understand exactly how it works. It seems odd to me that I had to hit Samuel in the mouth before I could start liking him, but I've always heard that God moves in mysterious ways."

"Funny you should use that expression. I told Anna that very thing."

"Speaking of Samuel, I'm getting worried about him. You don't think he's got malaria or something like that?"

"No, I don't hear of much malaria. He might have one of the tropical fevers we see down here."

"That sounds like it could be serious to me."

"Can be, but most of the time, it's not. We'll see what Dr. Romero says about him."

*****

Samuel walked out onto the porch followed by Anna and Isabella.

Daniel said, "Everybody ready?"

Samuel said, "Is this some kind of field trip? Everybody's got to go?"

Anna said, "Well, I'm the only sister, so that gives me a right to go."

Isabella said, "I have adopted them, so I am going. Besides, Dr. Romero may need my advice."

Everybody laughed and Matt spoke up, "If everybody is going, I'm not going to be left out."

Samuel shook his head and said, "Well, I'm glad I could provide y'all entertainment for the day. By the way, I hope this does not mean that we are 'calling in the family.' Everybody from the south knows what that means."

Everybody laughed and Matt said, "I think we should at least get a diagnosis before we do that."

They walked the short distance to Dr. Romero's office. When they walked in the waiting room, there were only four patients there. Daniel found Dr. Romero's nurse, Carolina, and explained why they were there. She ushered them all into an exam room and sat Samuel on the edge of the exam table. After a few minutes, Dr. Romero came in and greeted everybody. He examined Matt's hands and said that they looked good. He started picking at Isabella, "Did you bring me a cup of coffee or will I have to walk down to the compound to get one?"

"Dr. Romero, as I have told you before, you and I both know that you have the same coffee here as we have at the compound. And besides, my medical advice to you would be that a little more walking might do you some good."

Dr. Romero laughed, "You know I don't have time for exercise, but expert advise is always welcome. As for expert medical opinions, have you diagnosed our patient here, or do I have to do the work?"

"He has the dengue fever."

"Well, let me have all of you wait in my office while I evaluate the patient, and we'll see if I concur with your assessment."

After everybody left, Dr. Romero asked Samuel to tell him what has been going on.

Samuel said, "I started feeling bad after we got back from our trip to the Somoto canyon. I had a low-grade fever and just felt like I had a virus or a mild case of the flu. I thought I had overdone it on the trip and didn't think much about it. Over the last couple of days, I've felt worse and have developed a headache that is there most of the time."

"Describe the headache for me."

"Yes, sir. I don't remember having one like it before. It feels like it is right behind my eyes."

"Is it severe?"

"I would say that most of the time, it is."

"Anything else that you've noticed?"

"Muscle aches and what seems like bone pain, occasional nausea. And I have seen a rash on my chest, but it is not bad."

Dr. Romero asked Samuel to take his shirt off so he could have a look. He listened to his heart and lungs, and checked his ears and throat, as well as felt of his neck and thyroid. He asked Samuel if he had noticed some swelling in the back of his neck, and Samuel said that he had not.

"Samuel, I'm afraid that Isabella is right. You have one of our most common hemorrhagic fevers. I guess our mosquitos have liked you from the beginning of your stay here."

"So what was the name that Isabella said?"

"Dengue fever."

"You said something about hemorrhage?"

"Yes, it is classified as a hemorrhagic fever, but most people who get it don't develop that problem."

"That is good to know. What do I expect with this?"

"Why don't you put your shirt back on and we'll join the others in my office. I'll explain it to everybody at once if that is all right with you."

"That sounds good."

When they were all seated in Dr. Romero's office, he started his explanation, "As I have told Samuel, Isabella was right, Samuel has dengue fever. The fact that Isabella knew that is a testament to how common it is here. It is a mosquito-borne viral infection, and Samuel must have been bitten fairly early after his arrival here."

Matt asked, "Are there tests you have to do?"

"We'll do some routine lab work including what is called an ELISA test, but I am sure dengue is what he has."

Matt asked the next question, "So you don't really rely on any tests to make the diagnosis? You can be sure just going by the symptoms?"

"That is true for the most part. We will do blood work, but I expect there will be results that will go along with dengue fever."

Anna said, "All this worries me. What are we looking at? What can we expect?"

"Try not to worry. Most of the time, this is a self-limited, viral illness that goes away on its own. It lasts anywhere from one to two weeks. There is no treatment other than supportive, the usual things with a viral illness: Tylenol, fluids, and rest."

Samuel said, "You said when we were in the exam room that this is one of the hemorrhagic fevers. I still don't know what that means."

"That comes from a severe form of dengue that can be associated with bleeding."

Anna did not give Samuel a chance to ask the next question, "What are the chances of something like that happening, and how serious is it?"

"It can be very serious, but fortunately, it is also very rare."

Samuel said, "That's good to know. The rare part, I mean."

Chapter 20

Dr. Romero and Jose Ramirez

J ose Ramirez dropped by Dr. Romero's office late in the afternoon as he was prone to do occasionally. He was about ten years younger, but he and the doctor were close friends as well as cousins. He traveled a lot in his job working for the president, and when he was in Diriamba, he usually stopped for a visit.

"Well, Jose, what brings you out this way?"

"Oh, helping with a dispute with the local government. You know how that goes."

"Not too serious, I hope."

"No, this was an easy one. How are our guests from the U.S. doing?"

"Well, let's see. Matt hit Samuel yesterday, almost fell off the roof while putting on some tin, cut both hands, and almost left Nicaragua this morning. Samuel has dengue fever, and Anna has been told she is adopted."

"Wow, that was a full day. So Matt decided not to go?"

"That is right. He changed his mind at the last minute."

"What about the fight with Samuel. What happened there?"

"I think you are aware of some of the ongoing conflicts that they have had. I think it was all of that coming to a head."

"So Samuel did not hit him back?"

"No, and it's a good thing. I'm not sure Matt would have done too well with an all-out fight. The good news is that they are reconciled now. That is according to Daniel."

"I guess that is a good thing, huh?"

"It is. The conflict has gone on for years, and most of us think that this was at least part of the reason Dr. Martin wanted them to come on this trip."

"What about Anna?"

"What do you mean?"

"How did she take being told about her adoption?"

"Daniel told me that she did not handle it that well. I think the events of the last couple of days have distracted her some, but they're not through with that yet."

"Did Isabella tell her?"

"She did."

"Why do you think she would do that?"

"Jose, Dr. Martin wanted her to do that."

"Doesn't make much sense after all these years."

"I feel the same way, but what's done is done."

"I heard that Mrs. Martin may be coming to Nicaragua."

"That is what she said, but I don't think they know when yet."

"Speaking of Anna's adoption, how long has Ms. Miller been dead."

"She died about eight years ago."

"Boy, I wonder how much money Dr. Martin paid her over the years."

"I guess it would total up to being a pretty large sum."

"You know I told him that I thought I could get him out of that obligation, but he wouldn't budge on it. Said he felt like he should keep that up. Said it was the least he could do. He said that she had suffered a lot and maybe the money helped some."

"Well, you knew him well. He had to have a real good reason to change his mind about something after it was made up."

"On another note, I heard that Ramon had talked to them in the market the other day, and the word now is that he wants to talk to Daniel about making some changes in his life. You know, he is not real bad, but I would not have expected that."

"I have always thought that he had a good streak. I remembered him way back when his grandmother was dying. It really had an effect on him. He was very close to her. He absolutely idolized Anna's mother for what she did for them."

Jose got up to leave and said, "As always, I enjoyed the visit. Keep me informed as the events surrounding the Martins play out. Let me know if there is anything I can do to help. I'll have my people at the airport let me know when Mrs. Martin is coming."

Chapter 21

Maggie had just said goodbye to Ruth after they had finished their morning coffee routine. She was puttering around in the kitchen when her phone rang.

"Hello, Matt, I was wondering when you were going to call."

"Well, I guess I could say the same to you. The last word I got was that you were coming here and then radio silence."

"I know I should have touched base with you, but I didn't know my plans yet. Coincidentally, I was fixing to call to let you know that I will be coming the day after tomorrow. I'll text you with flight details."

"You know we'd all love to see you, but are you sure it is necessary for you to come?"

"I do feel strongly about that, Matt. We need to get done with some unfinished business so we can put that behind us. How is Anna by the way?"

"She is on a bit of a high right now because Samuel and I seem to have reconciled our differences, finally."

There was a pause, and Matt thought he might have heard a sniffle.

"Matt, tell me how that came about."

"Well, let me quote Dad. I remember him saying on many occasions, 'The Lord fixed it.' We got into a fight and I hit him. To his credit, he didn't hit me back. The whole day was so bad that I was going to fly home. I prayed about it all, and by the grace of God, I'm still here. And it looks like our differences are behind us now."

"Matt, I don't think you could have told me anything that could have made me happier than that."

"Been a long time coming."

"Well, sometimes old feuds die hard."

"Can't argue that one with you. By the way, I need to tell you that Samuel has dengue fever. He's been feeling bad for the last few days, and he saw Dr. Romero this morning."

"That is not too serious, is it?"

"Not usually."

"I recall your father having a case of that once, and if I remember correctly, he was well in a couple of weeks."

"That goes along with what Dr. Romero told us this morning. He said that complications are possible but they are rare."

"Well, we will plan on him doing well."

*****

The rest of that day and the next were uneventful, each Martin fighting the boredom in his or her own way. Samuel would have some periods of time that he felt better, but mostly, he rested a lot. He would come out on the porch occasionally but usually didn't stay long. Anna was still not her old, outgoing self, and spent most of her time with Isabella; and Matt had his routine of working on his laptop punctuated by the occasional cell phone conversation. His 'work' had become less over time as he realized that his partner was getting along fine without him.

The trip had done different things for each of them with some similarities. Matt had finally moved on past his old feelings about Samuel and overcome the jealousy that had haunted him for so long. He had been forced to give God credit for that in that he had never been able to accomplish it through his own efforts. He had begun to realize that there was more to life than work and the things that went with it. He had learned to be more concerned with relationships and how important they were.

Samuel had found a new peace in his relationship with his brother that he thought may never come. He had forgiven Matt for the past injustices he had committed. He had no problem giving God the credit and knew that it was an answer to many prayers. He also was thinking more about the possibility of missionary work and had found inspiration in observing Daniel. He would pray more about that in the days and weeks ahead.

Anna had found a great mentor and a second mother in Isabella. Their relationship had helped to develop her confidence. And she would have never thought that one could get so many life lessons in the kitchen. She was thrilled that her brothers appeared to have finally fixed their relationship, and she prayed for that to be permanent. Her excitement about that was clouded some by the information about her adoption and the unanswered questions that she still had to deal with. She did not like the fact that she felt anger and resentment toward her mother, and she had some feelings about her father that she had not ever experienced, and she did not know where that would go.

*****

The next morning, they all loaded up to go to the airport to meet Maggie's flight. Daniel picked them up after breakfast, which would give them plenty of time. She was due to arrive at eleven that morning. Samuel wasn't feeling well but insisted on going. He said he needed to get out of the house.

The trip to Managua was uneventful, and they found the airport to be the same as before with vans, trucks, and various other vehicles coming and going. They took their places among the crowds of people and waited for Maggie to get her luggage and make her way through the double doors that led down the hall and out of the airport. The wait was not long as Maggie was among the first passengers. She was being escorted by Jose Ramirez, and much to their surprise, Ruth Shelby was with them.

Matt, Samuel, and Anna all were laughing and shaking their heads. Matt said that if he would have thought about it, he would have bet anything that Ruth would come. Everybody agreed.

They all hugged and made the appropriate introductions. Maggie said that she could get used to an agent of the president meeting her upon arrival whenever she flew international. Jose bowed slightly and said that he would not be surprised if the president himself paid her a visit some time during her stay.

Ruth wasted no time and started in on Samuel, "I'm sure you have never heard of mosquito spray and how that might be a good idea when visiting a country like this one. I would also bet that you've never even heard of vitamin C and its value when dealing with viral illnesses."

Samuel replied, "You'll see, Ms. Ruth, that it is not practical all the time to be spraying on mosquito repellant. Besides, the bugs just like me, like everybody else does. I can't help that."

Everybody was laughing, and Ruth said, "Well, sick or not, we're going to work on that mop of yours. Must be a shortage of barbers in Nicaragua."

Ruth turned to Daniel and said, "You'll have to excuse me, Daniel, but Samuel has always been a favorite of mine. I have done my best to help raise him right, but he does have a free spirit and has to be watched closer than some."

Daniel replied, "Yes, ma'am. Some of us are like that."

Maggie said, "You'll get used to her, Daniel. It just takes time."

Anna hugged her mother, but Maggie sensed a slight coldness to her daughter's welcome.

"Welcome to Nicaragua, mother." Anna had never said it that way before, always addressing her as 'mom.'

Maggie was experiencing a feeling of resentment toward her late husband. She hadn't felt that way many times during their marriage, but she couldn't help but blame him for what she was going through now. She felt like she had some understanding of his motives, but still it was hard to deal with it. She did know one thing: she was going to get it over with quickly.

Chapter 22

The Rest of the Story

After they got back to the compound, Ruth and Maggie got settled in. Maggie told everyone that she wanted to have a family meeting after dinner. She had asked Dr. Romero, Isabella, and Daniel to join them as they all were so much involved in it all anyway. Of course, Ruth would be there as she was considered family.

Matt walked into the kitchen before dinner and had to smile. Sandwiched in between Isabella and Anna was Ruth. She had her apron on, and it was as if she had been there every day. She and Isabella were talking over some fine culinary point as if there was some universal language of the kitchen. She noticed Matt and said, "Tell everybody that dinner is ready."

"Yes, ma'am."

They all enjoyed a great meal. There was some small talk, but the mood was one of nervous anticipation in that everyone was anxious to hear what Maggie was going to say. There was also that feeling of maybe not wanting to know what they were going to find out. Dr. Romero had joined them as requested, as had Daniel.

After the table was cleared and the dishes done, they all sat back down. Maggie had retrieved a folder from her room and sat in a chair at the head of the long table. Anna was to her immediate left, Samuel was next to Anna, and Matt was on her right. Dr. Romero was beside

Matt, and Daniel was next to him. Ruth and Isabella were to the left of Samuel.

Maggie began, "I have a story to tell that is difficult for me, but I feel that I am the one that has to tell it. I would like to start by saying that I am sorry that you, Anna, had to find out about your adoption this way. Your birth mother did not want you to know the story, and your father has honored that request, at least while he was alive. I hope my children know that he would never have hidden anything from y'all if it were left up to him. I think the fact that you know now, in a way, confirms that."

Maggie paused, cleared her throat, and continued, "I am going to have to tell some things about your father's past that will not be pleasant for you to hear, but we're going to get it all out in the open and be done with it.

"First of all, your father had a drinking problem that started when he was in surgical training and continued into the early years of his practice. He handled it fairly well, and never drank while working. The first few trips here, he would drink, but he hid it well. His first trip to Nicaragua that was not with the church was when he met Anna's mother."

She paused, took a paper out of the folder she brought, and said, "I want to get right to the hardest part of this story." She handed the document to Anna and said, "If you will look at that, you'll see that it is your birth certificate from Nicaragua. I want you to take a minute to look at it."

Anna took the paper from her and began to look at it. She had a puzzled look on her face and said, "This is in Spanish, but I do recognize my father's signature. Does that mean that he delivered me?"

Maggie said, "Look closer at what it says."

Anna was having trouble making sense of it.

Samuel said, "Let me take a look at it." Anna handed it to him, and he looked at it and wouldn't look up for a long minute.

Matt asked with impatience, "What is it, Samuel?"

Samuel said in a quiet voice as if he did not want anybody to hear, "Our father's signature is where the baby's father signs."

154

There was a look of shock mixed with horror on Anna's face, and she gasped.

Matt said, "Are you positive about that?"

"I am."

Matt looked at his mother, "Our father had an affair down here, and Anna is his biological daughter? This is too incredible to be true!"

Maggie said, "I'm afraid that it is true."

No one else in the room said anything. Anna bowed her head and stared at the table. Matt stood up and said, "I've heard all of this that I need to."

Maggie said, "Sit down, Matt. You're gonna hear the rest." She said it like she meant it, and he sat down.

"Your father was in Nicaragua when Anna's birth mother was about eight months pregnant. They were in her car, and your father was driving. They were involved in an accident, a car hitting them from the side, the passenger side. The result was a complication of pregnancy that I learned was called an abruption of the placenta. Basically, this is a separation of the placenta from its attachment to the uterus. It is an emergency and required an immediate cesarean delivery to save Anna's life. Unfortunately, a complication occurred that caused massive bleeding, and Anna's mother did not survive. She did not die immediately, but had time to talk to your father and express her wishes about Anna not knowing all of this."

Matt asked, "Had Dad been drinking at the time of the accident?"

"No, and the accident was ruled by the police not to be his fault. But things are different here, and he was still required by law to compensate Anna's birth mother's family financially. This was because he was driving the car."

Anna looked up and said, "So you are saying that I have family out there that I don't know about. By the way, I would like to know my mother's name."

"Susan Miller, and no, there are no living relatives. Her mother, your grandmother, was a widow that was living here with her and remained here till her death a few years ago. Your father paid her monthly up until she died. She never tried to contact you because of her daughter's request. There is no other family as far as I know. I am told that you already know that your mother was a nurse."

Everybody at the table was looking at Maggie, trying to imagine what was next. Isabella kept wiping her eyes. For once, Ruth was speechless.

Maggie took a deep breath and continued, "Joseph called me and told me what had happened, and as soon as I could get Matt and Samuel settled at my parents, I caught a flight down here. Your father was in bad shape. He was drinking heavily and not eating much. I was worried about him. I don't think I've ever seen anybody that depressed before. I didn't know where to turn, so I called Pat Sanders. He came, took your father back to the states, and with a lot of doing, helped get him straightened out. That took a few months. I credit him with saving your father's life. He never drank a drop of alcohol after that."

Anna looked at her mother and said, "How sweet. You jumped on a plane and rushed down here to save your man." She said it with mean-spirited sarcasm.

That hurt Maggie; and she lowered her head, covered her face with her hand, and started crying. Ruth got up and got her a napkin, patted her on the back in an attempt to offer some comfort. There were tears in Ruth's eyes.

Isabella leaned up to where she could get a better line of sight to Anna and said, "I'm not going to put up with this. Do you know why Maggie didn't go back to the States with your father? Did you know that she stayed in Nicaragua by herself for six months? Do you know why she did that? Well, I will tell you why. She did it for you!" Isabella was upset and couldn't say anything more.

Anna lowered her head and stared at the table.

After Maggie composed herself, Dr. Romero spoke up, "Nicaragua law required that Maggie had to live here for six months before the adoption would go through. This was necessary even though Dr. Martin was Anna's biological father. It doesn't make much sense, but it was the letter of the law at the time."

Matt said, "So you stayed down here six months. I do remember being with our grandparents for a long time and Anna kinda showing up after that."

Samuel asked, "Y'all came home after that?"

Maggie replied, "That is right."

Samuel then asked, "When did you first make the decision that you were going to adopt Anna?"

"When your father called me from Nicaragua and told me about her."

Anna looked up at her and was unable to speak. She started sobbing, and Maggie leaned over and put her arm around her. Anna buried her head in Maggie's shoulder and chest, and said that she was so sorry for what she said. Maggie was patting her on the back and motioned for everybody to leave them alone. They all got up and went out on the porch.

*****

Outside, the breeze was pleasant as it usually was in the evening. They could all hear Anna's sobs form time to time, and emotions were running a little strong. Isabella could not stop crying, and Ruth was trying to comfort her. She was upset for the way she had talked to Anna. Ruth tried to reassure her that it had to be said.

Samuel was sitting with his head in his hands, and Dr. Romero went over to check on him. He felt his forehead and checked his pulse. He told him to go in and lie down for a while. Samuel complied with his instructions, got up, and went inside. Dr. Romero walked over to where Matt and Daniel were sitting at the other end of the porch. Matt said, "Pull up a chair, Dr. Romero, and join us." He pulled a chair over and sat down.

Matt asked, "How do you think Samuel is doing?"

"Okay, but I think he has had a bit too much activity today and not enough rest. I hope he can relax some now and catch up."

Matt said, "Maybe he will. I'll keep an eye on him the rest of the evening. On another note, I cannot thank the two of you enough for all of your help to my family. It has been above and beyond the call of duty."

Dr. Romero spoke first, "I do not exaggerate when I talk of my relationship to your father, so I feel like I am part of the family. I am sorry that you had to learn some things about him in this way, but over time, you will learn to admire him even more as a man who overcame adversity to become what he was. The hard times he endured made him a stronger and more compassionate Christian than I feel he would have been."

"I do not doubt what you say, Dr. Romero, but right now, I am not sure how to sort it all out. The pain that Anna is feeling right now is hard to swallow. Makes me feel an anger and resentment toward him."

Dr. Romero said, "What you heard tonight was not who your father was. None of that would have happened if your father had not had a drinking problem. It was a time that he was dealing with some demons from his past. He was human as we all are, and it is a testimony to God's grace that he made it through it. Also, the strong faith that your mother has is extraordinary and allowed her to forgive your father. He knew he would not have made it without her. That is part of the good that came out of all of this. Your parents' relationship was stronger than it would have been." Dr. Romero paused and then said, "I may be saying too much, Matt, but I just wanted you to see it from a different perspective."

"Yes, sir."

After a few minutes, Matt asked, "Dr. Romero, you said something about demons from my father's past. What exactly are you talking about?"

"I was referring to his past when he was growing up. His father was an alcoholic, and their relationship was never good. He had a brother, and they were very close, but he committed suicide. Your father never got over that, and I think he blamed himself till the day he died. Guilt is a demon that I think many people will try to suppress with alcohol."

"I have never heard anything about this. Why would he have blamed himself?"

"I don't think I know exactly since your father did not talk to me much about it, but I think he was the last one that talked to his brother and knew something was wrong. I guess he felt like he could have, or should have, done something."

Matt reflected a minute and said, "It's amazing how much we don't know sometimes. This is a lot of information to try to absorb."

The three of them sat in silence for several minutes. Daniel spoke next, "For what it's worth, I feel like y'all have turned a big corner here tonight and over the last few days. Time for healing now."

Matt replied, "I will say that it is a big relief to get that conversation over with. I have been worried about it since Anna found out that she is adopted. I can understand why my mother felt like she had to come down and be the one to tell this story. And by the way, do they come any stronger than her?"

Daniel said, "I have known your mother for less than twenty four hours, and I am already a big fan. She reminds me a lot of my own."

"She has always been a doer, Daniel. The fact that she got this done the first night she was here is a testimony to that. She sees the problem and sets the course. She has always been that way."

Dr. Romero said, "That reminds me of something your father always said: 'If I didn't have a good nurse and a good wife, I'd never know what to do next.'"

Daniel said, "You know, I have a good feeling now. We'll get Anna through this and go on with some more activities. Y'all need to experience more of the country in your remaining time here."

Dr. Romero said, "We have to get Samuel well first."

Matt thought he detected a slight degree of worry in his voice.

Chapter 23

Maggie and Matt

D r. Romero and Daniel got up and left, both expressing to Matt their good feeling about how things can now go in a positive direction. Ruth and Isabella had already gone inside earlier, Matt now being by himself on the porch. He had mixed emotions but felt good overall. After a little while, his mother came out and joined him.

"Well, Samuel is tucked in, and I gave Anna to Isabella and Ruth to get settled. So I guess it's just you and me, Matt."

"Yes, ma'am. Seems to end up that way a fair amount of the time."

"I guess it's appropriate. Although I would never admit it, a mother's first born always has a special spot in her heart that no one else can ever get."

Matt laughed, "You are not saying that I'm above the golden boy, are you?"

"I guess you can use that nickname now that the two of you are getting along better. I never really liked it before, you know."

"You won't have to worry about that anymore. How is Anna?"

"Lord, Matt, that child is a bundle of emotions if ever I saw one, but I guess with all she has been through over the last few months, I can understand it."

"You feel like she's going to be okay then?"

"I am sure she will. The main thing that I think she'll have to do is come to grips with the fact that her father at one time had some serious problems. She's only known the reborn one."

Matt said, "That's for sure. I guess that applies to all three of us. I am sure I was around at the time of some of his drinking, but I don't remember it."

"No, Matt, you wouldn't. He was able to hide it pretty well."

"One thing I can't seem to get no matter how many ways I analyze it is why he would feel so strongly about us knowing all of this after so many years. Maybe I'll have to wait a while to see the good that comes out of it."

"I am not sure that I can answer it for you, but I think it had to do with his strong sense of always trying to do what was right. I think he always felt like he was hiding something from y'all."

"Well, maybe kids aren't supposed to know everything."

"You're right, but this particular situation was unique to say the least."

"I even have problems with him getting Isabella to break it to Anna. That does not really seem right, and does not honor the wishes of her birth mother."

"I agree, but I think it is the best he felt that he could do, and maybe he felt like he was sparing me some heartache by doing that. I don't know for sure."

"Well, I sure am glad you came down here. I one hundred percent agree that you had to be the one to tell this story."

"On a lighter note, Matt, I did notice the bruise on Samuels face and the cut on his lip. I got to thinking about it, and I don't remember y'all ever fighting like that."

"Thank God that it was one sided and he didn't beat me like he could have, and maybe should have."

"If you don't mind me asking, what happened?"

"Well, we were at the construction site working, and he and I got into an argument. Anna said something and Samuel snapped at her. He was pretty ugly to her, and I just lost it. I hit him before I knew what happened. I don't know if I have ever felt that bad before."

"Samuel didn't do anything?"

"No, ma'am. He just stood there looking at me. I was more than a little worried that he was going to do something."

"Is that how you cut your hands?"

"The right one. The left one on a piece of tin. Not long after I hit him, Samuel basically saved me from falling off the roof. That only added to how bad I felt."

"You really feeling good about you and Samuel now?"

"I am. I have never felt the peace about it that I do now. It is like the jealousy that I felt before is gone."

"I can't get over it. That is great news." Maggie paused briefly and then said, "What about this dengue fever? Dr. Romero doesn't seemed to be worried much about it."

"As I understand it, everybody gets over it in a couple of weeks."

"So you don't think we need to take him back to the States?"

"I don't guess we do. I would have to think that Dr. Romero has treated more cases of this than the doctors back home. Besides, there is no treatment for it anyway since it's a virus. Dr. Romero says that serious complications are rare."

"I trust him. I just have to worry. It's my job as a mother."

"I understand that better now that I have children. Hey, how about Ruth coming down with you? When did she decide to make the trip?"

"You know Ruth. I think she started packing the first time I mentioned that I might come."

"Boy, don't you know she is going to hover over Samuel. I was happy to hear her admit that he is her favorite. It has always been so obvious."

"I would have to agree with you there, Matt. I can remember when he was growing up, he would go over and visit her. Sometimes, he would stay for hours. I have to think that those two must have something in common that the rest of us don't know about. Soul mates, maybe."

"You may be right."

"It sure is nice out here, Matt. I can see why your father carried on about it so much."

"Yes, ma'am. I picked up on that immediately after I got here. I love to come out here and just sit and do nothing."

"It has been great visiting with you, Matt, and I hate to leave good company, but I am worn out. Think I'll turn in."

"You have certainly had a long day."

Matt sat for a while by himself, thinking about how far they had all come in a short period of time. He wondered what was next.

Chapter 24

Fever

Everybody was gathered around the breakfast table the next morning. Ruth, Isabella, and Anna were in there usual positions in the kitchen, all talking at once. Samuel had not made it yet, and Matt asked, "Anybody seen Samuel this morning?"

Ruth said, "I looked in on him earlier, and he said his fever had been up and he hadn't slept that well. I gave him two Tylenol and encouraged him to try to drink some." She started toward the great room and said, "I'll go check on him."

She found him lethargic, and he told her that he was nauseated and he did not feel like he could drink anything right now. She felt his head, and she was sure that he had fever. Ruth went back into the kitchen and reported Samuel's condition. Matt got up and started for the door. He said, "I'll go down and see if Dr. Romero has made it to his office yet."

When Matt had walked the short distance to the office, he found that no one was there. He called Dr. Romero on his cell phone, "Good morning, Dr. Romero. I'm sorry to bother you so early but Samuel is not doing well. His fever is up, and he says he can't drink anything this morning."

"Has he had any Tylenol?"

"Yes, sir. Ruth gave him some about an hour ago."

"I am not far from there, Matt. I'll stop by in a minute."

"Thank you."

When Dr. Romero arrived, he asked which room Samuel was in. He, Maggie, Ruth, Matt, and Anna all went to check on him. After he had examined Samuel, they went back to the kitchen. Isabella handed Dr. Romero a cup of coffee, and they all sat down. Everybody had worried looks on their faces, and Dr. Romero said, "He is okay, just dehydrated. That is not uncommon with this problem. We'll give him some IV fluids, and that'll help."

He called Carolina on his cell phone, and she had made it to the office. He gave her instructions on what to bring to the compound, and it wasn't long before she came in. She started an IV on Samuel and ran the fluids rapidly for the first bag, and then started a second bag at a slower rate. She left to go to the clinic after a short discussion with Dr. Romero.

Maggie said, "Dr. Romero, is it time for me to start worrying?"

"No, all of this is expected with dengue fever. I see no signs of any serious complications at this point."

Anna said, "But this has been going on for several days. Wouldn't you expect it to be getting better by now?"

"Not usually. Most cases will last close to two weeks, so we may still have symptoms for a while longer."

Matt asked, "How would we know if he had complications?"

Dr. Romero smiled and said, "That's what you pay me for." Everybody laughed, and Dr. Romero got up to leave and said, "There is a physician in the States that is on staff at Tulane that is a tropical medicine specialist. His name is Dr. Mike Simmons. One of our doctors from here trained with him and knows him well. Dr. Martin also knew him because they all trained at about the same time. I do not have his number, but I feel sure that Dr. Sanders knows how to reach him. Maggie or Matt, one of you may want to call him and get his opinion on things. It may help you feel better."

Maggie said, "Lord, I hope you don't think that we are doubting you or don't trust you completely."

Matt said, "Yeah, I hope we aren't coming across that way."

Dr. Romero smiled, "No, not at all. I just think that getting another perspective on it from someone else might make you feel better." He left and walked down to his office.

*****

Maggie went out on the porch and dialed Pat Sander's number. "Hello, Maggie. I heard you were in Nicaragua."

"That is right, Pat. I guess things go full circle because I have a problem, and of course, when I called you from here thirty-five years ago, I had a problem."

"Well, Maggie, what in the world is going on? I guess if you only call with a problem once every thirty-five years, I can handle that."

Maggie laughed and said, "Well, the problem is that Samuel has dengue fever, and Dr. Romero thought that you might be able to put me in touch with Dr. Mike Simmons."

"I am sure I can, Maggie, but isn't dengue fever fairly straight-forward, not much to do for it?"

"You're right, Pat. But I am a mother, and it is my job to worry, so Dr. Romero thought it might help for me to talk to Dr. Simmons. By the way, do you know him?"

"I do, Maggie. We all trained at Charity at about the same time. Even though he was on the Tulane service and we were LSU, we were all still friends. Joseph knew him well."

Maggie then said, "Dr. Romero says that he is an expert in all of this."

"That is true. He is now the head of the tropical medicine department at Tulane. He has a good reputation."

"That sounds good, Pat. I think I would like to talk to him."

"Let me see if I can get him, Maggie, and I'll give him you're number. And be sure to keep me posted about Samuel."

"Thank you, Pat."

Maggie was pleasantly surprised when her phone rang in just a few minutes.

"This is Maggie Martin."

"Maggie, this is Mike Simmons."

"Thank you for calling me, Dr. Simmons."

"You are welcome, and there is no need to be formal. I was a friend of your husband and let me tell you how sorry I am for your loss."

"Thank you for saying so."

Dr. Simmons then said, "Pat Sanders filled me in some and said that your son has dengue fever. Samuel, isn't it?"

"That is right."

"Maggie, let me say first of all that I know Carlos Romero well, and you are in good hands."

"I do not doubt that, Mike, but it was actually him that suggested I call you."

"I don't mind helping in whatever way I can."

"Thank you, and I guess I just need reassurance that he is going to do well."

"Maggie, as you know, there are no guarantees with any medical problem, but this is usually a self-limited illness followed by a full recovery."

"Are complications that can occur serious?"

"They can be but they are rare."

"What happens if he develops complications?"

"The worse thing is bleeding, and all the things that can go with it. There can also be some cardiac problems."

"Can it be fatal?"

"It can."

"Mike, if this were your son, would you go ahead and bring him back to the States?"

"That is a tough one, Maggie. The doctors there have seen more cases than we have in the United States, making them more qualified to deal with it than we are."

"You think Carlos has seen this a lot?"

"Absolutely, and I am sure that he would bring in other doctors to help him if needed. One of the best authorities on tropical fevers lives in Nicaragua. His name is Hugo Ortega. He did some training with me, and comes back here occasionally and lectures at the med school. I think highly of him. I'm pretty sure your husband met him."

"Thank you for calling me. Talking to you has been helpful."

"You are welcome. Keep us informed as how Samuel is progressing. I will help in any way I can."

*****

Maggie walked back into the kitchen and Matt spoke first, "Were you able to talk to Dr. Simmons?"

"I was, and I found him to be nice. He knew your father back when they were in training."

Ruth spoke up, "For Pete's sake, Maggie, what did he say about Samuel?"

"I was getting to that. He really didn't add much to what Dr. Romero has told us, but reassured me that we were in good hands."

Ruth said, "I knew that because he is in the Lord's hands. It can't get better than that. By the way, I called Dr. Johnson and got him added to the prayer list."

Maggie said, "Thank you, Ruth." She continued, "When I asked him about taking Samuel back to the States, he said the doctors here are more qualified to treat him, so he doesn't recommend it."

Matt said, "That is interesting."

They heard a vehicle pull up, and Daniel walked in followed by Michael.

Daniel introduced Michael to Maggie, and Ruth and told them that he and Samuel were good friends. Daniel asked, "Where is Samuel by the way?"

Matt explained to him Samuel's current condition, and Daniel told Michael in Spanish. Michael asked if he could go in and see him, and Matt said, "Of course." It wasn't long before there was a lot of loud talking in Spanish and laughter to go with it.

Matt said, "I guess the IV did him some good."

Ruth said, "I'm not sure he needs to be carrying on like that."

Maggie said, "Oh, leave him alone, Ruth. You know what they say: laughter is the best medicine."

Chapter 25

Dr. Romero and Maggie

D r. Romero came in as they were about finished with supper, and Isabella insisted on him letting her fix him a plate. He went in to check on Samuel and then joined them at the table. "Looks like Samuel is feeling better this evening."

Ruth said, "I gave him some Tylenol and made sure he drank some juice. I also made him get plenty of rest."

Dr. Romero smiled and said, "Ms. Ruth, I may be able to use you if you ever want to move to Nicaragua."

"Well, I do know a little about doctoring, and it's a good thing. I'm not sure the Martin family has a clue."

Everybody laughed, and Dr. Romero said, "Between you and Isabella, I may not be needed."

Isabella chimed in, "I am glad it is finally recognized. Just remember doctor that I was the first to diagnose Samuel with the dengue fever."

"I have learned to value your opinion, Isabella."

Maggie said, "I talked to Dr. Simmons as you suggested. I like him."

"Good, Maggie. Did you learn anything?"

"Not really, your explanations were pretty complete. He did mention a doctor here. I believe his name is Ortega."

"Yes, that is Hugo Ortega."

Maggie said, "He said that he is an expert in all of this and that you know him."

Dr. Romero replied, "He is one of the leading authorities in the world on tropical fevers. He and I are good friends and he knew Joseph also."

Anna asked, "What would he do that you are not doing?"

"There is nothing he would add now. He would be called if any complications develop."

After the table was cleared, Dr. Romero said to Maggie, "Would you join me on the porch for after-dinner coffee?"

"Carlos, I would love to." She bowed slightly.

Matt raised his eyebrows and looked at Anna. Neither one of them had ever heard Dr. Romero's first name before, and was there a slight hint of romanticism in the invitation?

*****

As Maggie and Dr. Romero enjoyed the breeze out on the porch, Dr. Romero said, "Maggie, you have had more than your share of difficulties over the last few months. You seem to be holding up well."

"Thank you. I have a lot of support at home with my church group and good neighbors. I don't think I would have made it without Ruth."

Dr. Romero laughed and said, "She sure is a character, but I don't think I have ever seen anybody work harder than her. And she sure seems to dote on Samuel."

"We were talking about that earlier. She and Samuel have always been close. She helped spoil him when he was growing up. She never had children and just sort of adopted him."

"I remember Joseph talking about her and Mr. Slocum. He would joke that between those two, he never had to worry about the neighborhood."

"Boy, that is true. Billy Slocum became an uncompensated grounds keeper and maintenance man over the years and still is."

"Sounds like a good one to have around."

They sat in silence for a short time and Maggie asked, "Carlos, how long has Maria been gone?"

"It has been seven years, but seems like yesterday."

"Do you ever get over it? I know Joseph has only been gone a few months, but I thought I would be further along than I am with the process."

"I don't think you ever get completely over it, Maggie, but it does get better."

"What about your boys? We didn't have time to catch up on things when you were there for Joseph's funeral."

"Both are doing well. The oldest, Juan David, is working in the northern part of the country in the coffee business. He says that he will own a big plantation someday. Joseph is in medical school and is planning to be a surgeon. Wouldn't your Joseph have liked that?"

"My Joseph could not have been prouder when you named your youngest after him, so you know, he would be especially proud to have him following in his footsteps."

"What a joy it would have been for him to be able to operate with Dr. Martin."

"Yes, Carlos, we are going to miss out on a lot, but we just have to be thankful for the times we had."

"I agree, great memories."

"I guess the medical mission trip will carry on okay without him."

"It will, Maggie, but it will definitely be different. He will be missed."

Maggie stood up and said, "I think I'm going to turn in and read a little. I thank you again for taking care of Samuel."

Dr. Romero took her hand and kissed it. They stood looking at each other for a few seconds. He let go of her hand and said, "I'll be back first thing in the morning."

Chapter 26

Dr. Ortega

Everybody was in the kitchen the next morning, including Samuel. He said that he didn't think Ruth would let him sleep in, no matter how bad he felt. She countered that by pointing out that he would never get well if he didn't eat something. She said it as she was handing him two large vitamin C tablets.

Samuel said, "My god, Ruth, what veterinarian did you get these from? They've got to be for a horse."

She replied, "We don't need any comments. If I had been on the case sooner, you would have been well by now."

Samuel said under his breath, "Or half dead."

"I heard that."

"Well, Ruth, you give me these horse pills, you make me rub on these oils that I might point out, don't always have the nicest aroma, and of course, I have to drink more fluids and hideous juices than any three people."

"I feel confident that you will someday appreciate your good care."

Matt and Anna were both rolling their eyes and shaking their heads.

Anna said, "Changing the subject, Mrs. Martin, what time did you get in last night?" She cocked her head and gave her mother the inquisitive look.

Matt said, "Yeah, I was wondering that myself."

Samuel said, "What are y'all talking about?"

Anna said, "Oh, you didn't know that your mother went out with Dr. Romero last night? Oh, wait, I believe she called him Carlos."

Everybody was looking at Maggie with nosy looks on their faces.

Maggie had the demeanor of someone who was ready for the inquiry and replied, "Well, I am not sure it is any of y'all's business, but I will have to say that I never knew how romantic Latinos are."

Anna got animated and said, "Mom, I can't believe you said that!"

"Well, you asked."

Matt said, "Seriously, what did y'all do?"

"I can't believe that y'all are asking me this. I think I'll decline to answer and leave y'all wondering."

Samuel said, "We just need to know so we will know how to deal with the rumors back home. We don't need a scandal in the family."

"Well, all I will say is that there is nothing between Car—I mean Dr. Romero and me."

Dr. Romero walked in as everyone was laughing. As that died down, he walked over to Maggie and said, "Good morning, Maggie." As he said it, he took her hand in his and held it for a few seconds.

Anna said, "Yeah, we can see that."

Maggie said, "Talk about timing."

Everybody laughed, and Dr. Romero said, "I'm afraid I'm at a loss."

Maggie said, "Believe me, you don't want to know."

Dr. Romero had that feeling of being the only one in the room that didn't get the joke. Isabella was laughing and handed him a cup of coffee, "Doctor, sometimes you don't seem to be all there."

Matt said, "You got in on the conversation late. We were talking about your and mom's 'date' last night."

Dr. Romero quickly caught up with it all and acted concerned. He said with exaggerated seriousness, "Maggie, I hope you didn't tell everything!"

There was another round of laughter, and when it died down, Maggie said, "Never."

Dr. Romero said, "That is a relief. On another note, this is supposed to be a house call. Samuel, how are you feeling this morning?"

"About the same, I think. I will have times that I feel better, and then my fever will go up and that headache will come back. I will feel like everything is drained out of me."

"You feel like you're keeping enough fluids down."

Samuel looked at Ruth and said, "You don't have to worry about that."

Dr. Romero felt his pulse and said, "We'll keep doing what we're doing. No need to change anything at this time. I'll look in on you again this afternoon."

*****

Back in his office, Dr. Romero sat at his desk, leaned back, put his hands behind his head, and was lost in thought. Carolina walked in and stood looking at him. She said, "You are worried about him, aren't you?"

Dr. Romero felt like his poker face was working pretty well with the Martins, but he knew that he could not fool his nurse. She had been with him too long for that to work. He gave it a try anyway. "What makes you think that? I might have been thinking about something else."

"But you were not, were you?"

"No, I was not." After a short pause, he said, "I cannot put my finger on it, Carolina. I just have a gut feeling about it."

"Has something changed to make you feel that way?"

"No, I can't explain it. I have a nagging worry that I can't seem to shake."

"When is the last time that we had a patient with complications of the dengue fever?"

"I don't even know. It has been several years."

"Is Samuel showing any signs of that?"

"No, none now."

"Do you think that you are too close to the family?"

Dr. Romero was surprised by the question and said, "You know how close I am to them, but I don't know why that matters." He was noncommittal when he said it.

"It makes you worry more and that can affect your treatment."

"Carolina, you are talking like a wise old doctor advising a young colleague."

"Maybe you need some advice even if I am not a wise old doctor."

"Go ahead. I have a feeling you are going to offer it anyway."

"Have someone else see him and give their opinion."

Dr. Romero thought for a minute and said, "Don't you think that doing that may scare them?"

"It will be worse if something happens and you blame yourself."

"I don't know, Carolina. I am probably overreacting. Nothing has come up to make me think this is anything but a simple case of dengue fever just like we see all the time."

"Well, I have given you my opinion even if you didn't exactly ask for it. I've got to get to work." She left his office to go tend to patients.

Dr. Romero sat at his desk and continued thinking about the situation. Treating Samuel was like treating his own family, and no doctor liked to do that. It was too easy for one's judgment to be clouded by those close feelings. He wondered if part of his reluctance to consult someone else was due to pride and the fear that he would be viewed as not good enough to handle the problem. He didn't think so because he had always held to the premise that there was no place for pride in the practice of medicine. Too much at stake. He made a decision, picked up the phone, and dialed Dr. Ortega's number.

Dr. Ortega answered after two rings and said, "Carlos Romero, how are you, old friend?"

"I am doing good, but I'm afraid that I have a favor to ask you."

"Of course, go right ahead."

"You may have heard that Joseph Martin's family is here staying at the compound for a couple of weeks."

"As a matter of fact, I have, and I heard that one of his sons has dengue fever."

"Boy, news does get around."

"I can explain. I ran into your cousin, Jose, and he filled me in. As you know, he knows everything."

"I can't argue with that." Dr. Romero went on to say, "Hugo, I would like to get you to take a look at him if you have time to come out."

"I'll be glad to, but let me ask you, is he having anything unusual that you are worried about?"

"That's just it, he isn't, but I just have a feeling about it that is bothering me. It may be that I'm just too close to this one."

"I understand that, Carlos. I have some time later this afternoon if that fits your schedule."

"I would really appreciate that."

*****

Late that afternoon, the Martins were all out on the porch. Ruth and Isabella were in the kitchen working on dinner. Ruth had Samuel in one chair with his feet propped in another one and a small bedspread over his legs. There was the ever-present glass of something liquid sitting on the arm of the chair. Maggie and Matt sat close by, and they all were talking. Samuel would rub his eyes from time to time and would occasionally be detached from the conversation.

Maggie said, "Samuel, I believe that bruise on your face is about to fade away completely."

Matt said, "Mom, I wish you wouldn't mention that. Some of us are trying to forget."

Samuel said, "Well, we're going to have to put on the gloves if I ever get over this fever."

Anna quickly said, "Oh, no, y'all aren't!"

Matt said, "I sure hope you are kidding about that."

Maggie said, "Well, I am still y'all's mother, and we'll have no more fighting."

Matt said, "Yeah, Samuel, we have to respect our mother's authority."

"I guess you're right."

Matt noticed Dr. Romero walking from the direction of his clinic with someone he didn't know. "I wonder who that is with Dr. Romero?"

Maggie said, "I'm sure I don't know, but I think we'll soon find out."

They walked up the steps to the porch, and Dr. Romero said, "I would like to introduce to all of you Dr. Hugo Ortega."

Each one of the Martins shook his hand and introduced themselves as they did.

Dr. Ortega said, "I am so pleased to meet all of you. I did not get to work with Dr. Martin much when he was here, but I knew him and certainly knew his reputation."

Dr. Romero said, "I have asked Dr. Ortega to come out this afternoon, take a look at Samuel, and give us his opinion."

Anna was the first to respond with what everybody was thinking, "Dr. Romero, I thought you would only bring in Dr. Ortega if there were complications. This worries me."

"Anna, I cannot be anything but completely honest. I will not be able to hide my true feelings anyway. As a doctor, I have to be completely objective. It is not entirely possible to be that way when you are dealing with family or close friends. I worry about Samuel exactly the same way that you, Matt, and Maggie do. I have to be absolutely certain that my judgment is not affected by that. I don't know how to explain it any better."

Maggie said, "Carlos, I understand it fully. I have heard Joseph talk about that many times during his years of practice."

Matt said, "I appreciate your explanation, Dr. Romero, and I appreciate your coming, Dr. Ortega. Your reputation has preceded you." Dr. Ortega nodded.

Anna said, "I understand." She wiped her eyes.

Samuel said, "I'm okay with as many opinions as y'all want to get. This will make four if you include Isabella and Ruth."

Everybody laughed, and Dr. Ortega spoke next, "If it is alright with everybody, I will check Samuel here on the porch where the light is good. That is doing it Nicaraguan style. We can get back together and talk when I am finished."

They all went inside as requested.

In the kitchen, everybody was seated around the table except for Ruth and Isabella who continued working on dinner. Ruth asked, "Who is that you brought with you, Dr. Romero?"

"That is Dr. Ortega. He came out to take a look at Samuel and give us his opinion as to how he's doing."

Isabella spoke up, "Oh, I know who that is. He is a big expert on the fevers around here."

Dr. Romero replied, "That is true."

Ruth stopped her work on the vegetables and asked, "Why is he here now? Is something going on I need to know about?"

Maggie said, "We had this conversation on the porch a few minutes ago. Dr. Romero is simply getting another opinion to be doubly sure nothing is missed. It is standard medical procedure."

Ruth nodded her head and went back to the work she had been doing. There was the usual small talk with occasional references to tropical fevers with various other questions that the Martins had. After a while, Dr. Ortega and Samuel walked into the kitchen. Attempts to read Dr. Ortega's face yielded nothing. He was very stoic. Samuel handed his glass to Ruth and got the usual disgusted look since it was not empty. She shook her head and poured it out.

Dr. Ortega knew everybody wanted to hear from him, so he wasted no time, "First of all, I feel like we are on the right track. There is nothing that I would have recommended in addition to what has been done. As you all know, this is a viral illness, and there is no treatment other than supportive. I reviewed all the lab that Dr. Romero did, and I have nothing to add at this time. I do recommend repeating a blood count tomorrow. The reason for that is to mainly check on the platelet count. It is one of the components of the blood that has to do with clotting."

Anna asked, "Are you worried about something, or is that just routine?"

Dr. Ortega replied, "I am not worried, but I did see some petechiae on my exam today, and they can be associated with a problem with the platelets."

Before anyone else had a chance to speak, Anna said, "Dr. Ortega, what are these things you are talking about, and what are they a sign of?"

"They are minute collections of blood under the skin. They usually mean nothing but can, as I said, be the first sign of a problem with the platelets."

Matt said, "Dr. Ortega, from the beginning, I did not like this illness because they call it a hemorrhagic fever. Is it all or none, or can you get a smaller hemorrhage that is not too serious?

"You can get all degrees of problems. Complications are not always of a serious nature."

Dr. Romero added, "The appearance of the petechiae simply mean that we should follow the platelet count."

Matt said, "Pardon my impatience but it doesn't seem like things are going in the right direction."

Dr. Ortega replied, "I understand how you all feel and how frustrating it can be. We simply have no way of predicting what will happen. That is why we check on Samuel daily."

Samuel said, "Hey, I need for all of you guys to remember that I am sitting here. Maybe we can be a little more positive."

Ruth said, "At least Samuel realizes that he is in the Lord's hands, and it can't get any more positive than that."

There were no more questions, and Dr. Ortega said his good-byes. Everybody thanked him and he assured them that he would be back. They all sat down for dinner, and Samuel excused himself and said that he wasn't hungry. Ruth was not happy but did not argue this time.

Chapter 27

The Visitor

The next morning, everybody was sitting around the table in their usual places. The breakfast dishes had been cleared, and Carolina had been by to draw Samuel's blood for the repeat blood count as recommended by Dr. Ortega. Samuel's fever was high again, and he commented that this problem had just about exceeded his attention span. Ruth handed him a glass of juice, and he got up and went into the great room to lie down on one of the couches.

Isabella was looking out the window as she was doing the dishes and said, "There are some more. They are getting to be more every day."

What had been happening was people had been coming by every day and spending a short time by the porch, most bowing their heads and having a prayer. Many would leave items such as papers with verses on them or small portions of food, and various small gifts. None of them knocked on the door or tried to talk to anyone; they would just have their silent time and prayers.

One visitor showed up, however, that changed all of that, the silent part in particular. A familiar van drove up with Michael driving. Daniel got out, came around, and opened the sliding side door. Immediately, everybody heard loud singing with a somewhat off-key version of "I Saw the Light" coming out of the van. Matt and Anna recognized the singer and in unison said, "Hernando."

Michael and Daniel lifted Hernando's wheelchair up onto the porch, and Matt and Anna were coming out to meet him. Anna ran over and hugged his neck, "How are you, Hernando?"

"I am fine if you tell me that you are still single since I saw you last."

"Still an old maid, Hernando."

"There is life in my heart as long as you are free."

Matt walked over and shook his hand, "Hernando, it is great to see you. I see your singing voice has not changed much."

"I will have to say the song sounds better in my heart before it gets to my lips."

Everybody was laughing, and Maggie and Ruth came out onto the porch.

Matt said, "Mom and Ruth, let me introduce Hernando, our zip line guide a week or so ago."

They exchanged greetings, and Hernando said, "Mrs. Martin, it is a special honor to meet the wife of Dr. Martin, without whom you would not be seeing me here today. And, Mrs. Ruth, any friend of the Martins is a friend of mine. I have come today to visit the coolest gringo in the world. I understand that he recently has warmed up some. I also want the record to show that the Hernando who knows all knew about his illness before Daniel told me."

Maggie and Ruth seemed confused by his last statement, and Matt said, "Hernando is somewhat of a Sherlock Holmes type and did pretty good with us when we went zip lining. Hernando, why don't you tell us about my mother and Mrs. Ruth, and we will see how good you are."

"Oh, this is too easy, Matt. First, I will start with Mrs. Martin. I know that you were a good wife and were in charge of the house. You were active with your children and popular with their friends. You are fearless and not afraid to do whatever has to be done."

There was an applause, and Hernando bowed and said, "Now, Mrs. Ruth, you are a little harder but I have some observations. You are a good and loyal friend to Mrs. Martin and have seen her through recent difficulties. You are a hard worker and do the work while others talk about it. You treat Mrs. Martin's children as your own, and one last thing, you speak your mind without reservations."

There was another round of applause, more enthusiastic than the first, and Matt said, "Hernando, you are just lucky."

"It is hard to be lucky five times in a row. I will add to this by reminding you that I knew that you had a fear of heights. I will now tell you that you have recently overcome that fear again as you did on the zip line the day we met."

"Who told you that I jumped off the cliff at Somoto Canyon? It would have to be Daniel or Michael."

Daniel said, "I didn't tell him." He turned to Michael and asked him if he had told him anything about that trip, and he shook his head no.

Matt said, "I guess you got me then."

"Daniel will tell you that it is hard to get ahead of Hernando."

Daniel said, "That may be true, but I'll never stop trying."

At that time, Samuel was coming out of the kitchen door. Hernando eyes lit up, and he said, "Look at this. How do you Americans say it? Look what the cat is dragging."

Matt said, "That's close."

Hernando yelled, "Hey, amigo. *Como estas?*"

"*Estoy enfermo, me siento malo.*"

Daniel translated, "Hernando asked how he was, and Samuel said he is sick and feels bad."

Michael walked over, shook Samuel's hand, and spoke to him, also in Spanish.

Hernando shifted to English, "I am sorry to hear that, and I am here to visit but also to pray for you to be healed and to have comfort."

"Thank you. I need it."

Hernando requested that Samuel sit in a chair, and they all gathered around and laid hands on him. He voiced a moving prayer, mostly in English, with an occasional Spanish phrase. There were some tears, and everyone thanked him. Hernando said that Jesus had heard the prayer, and Samuel would be healed.

Samuel's fever was up, and he made his apologies to Hernando and thanked him for coming. He went back in to lie down. Everybody else stayed on the porch, visiting. Matt told his mother and Ruth that Hernando had a fascinating testimony, and they both wanted to hear it. Ruth was very interested. She was impressed with him and wasn't sure that he wasn't a prophet of sorts. They listened to the story and agreed that it was very inspirational. Ruth commented that it verifies the fact that we should never discount the importance of planting seeds. She said that Hernando's story showed what the Lord could do with one. Maggie was proud of her husband's role in the story.

Ruth and Anna went inside to help Isabella with lunch, leaving Maggie, Matt, Daniel, Hernando, and Michael out on the porch. Daniel said, "Hernando, do you have time to stay for lunch, or do we have to get you back to work?"

"The work will wait. I cannot pass on an opportunity for one of Isabella's meals. I also know that it will be even better with the help of Ruth and Anna."

Daniel replied, "You better be careful. They may decide that they can do without you."

"Oh, Daniel, you forget how valuable I am to them. They will never replace Hernando."

To that, Daniel said, "The ever humble Hernando who knows all."

"One thing I do know, lunch is almost ready. Hernando also has a good nose."

*****

Dr. Romero was looking at the results of Samuel's blood count. He was experiencing the curse of the equivocal result, neither positive or negative, but values that could go either way. His platelet count was one hundred and seventy thousand, and he would much rather it had been two hundred and seventy thousand. He said under his breath, "Is it going up or going down?"

The white blood cell count was similar in that it was six thousand, and his thought was the same, "Is it going up or down?" Both tests can signal complications if they are decreasing.

Dr. Romero was worried about this, but he did not want to alarm anyone. The only thing to do was repeat the blood count tomorrow, but he still had to explain the results from today. He knew he had to be honest, but it was hard to do without showing too much of his concern. Hard to treat family.

Chapter 28

Worse

It was the first morning in over a week that Samuel did not wake up with fever. Ruth had checked on him early and reported that fact to everyone gathered around the breakfast table. There was a feeling of elation and relief, but it was short lived.

With this good news, everyone was expecting Samuel at the table soon, but he did not show up. After a while, Ruth went to check on him. She came back in a few minutes and said, "I don't understand what is going on with him. He is restless and says his stomach is hurting. His arms feel cold to me, and he said his gums bled when he brushed his teeth. He doesn't look good to me."

Maggie asked, "Does he have fever now?"

"No, I took it again, and it is still normal."

Matt asked, "Could there be something wrong with the thermometer?"

Ruth shook her head and said, "I don't think so. It is pretty new and seems to be working the same this morning."

Anna got up and said, "I'm going to check on him."

Matt was scratching his head and said, "I don't understand this. When you have the flu, you get better when your fever is gone." He said it to no one in particular.

Maggie said, "Well, Dr. Romero should be by any time now. We'll see what he has to say about it."

Anna walked back in the kitchen. She was obviously upset and said, "What could be going on? Samuel acts like he is feeling worse!"

Carolina came in to draw Samuel's blood for a repeat count, and Anna immediately said, "Carolina, something is wrong with Samuel. His fever is down but he looks worse!"

There was a look of concern on Carolina's face, but she quickly recovered and said, "Let's don't get too worried. Dr. Romero will be here soon."

Matt asked, "Is he down at the office?"

Carolina replied, "He just got there."

Matt stood up and said as he walked out the door, "I'm gonna go down and talk to him."

Anna jumped up, "I'm going with you, and spare me the protests because they won't do any good." She followed Matt out the door.

They found Dr. Romero sitting at his desk. He acted surprised to see them and said, "Good morning. I was just about to walk down to the compound and check on you all."

Anna spoke first, "Dr. Romero, something is wrong with Samuel."

"What do you mean?"

Matt spoke up, "His temperature is normal this morning, but he seems to be worse."

"How is he worse?"

Matt related all the things that Ruth had told them to Dr. Romero. His reaction was immediate and obvious. He turned pale to the point that it couldn't be hidden by his dark complexion. He did not say a word but immediately stood up and started for the door, Anna and Matt close behind. Anna was asking him several questions on the short walk to the compound, but he seemed distracted and gave her short, partial answers. They met Carolina coming back from the compound, and he told her that he wanted the test results as fast as he could get them.

When they got to the compound, he barely spoke to anyone and went straight to Samuel's room. Nobody but Maggie went with him. After a long half hour, they walked back into the kitchen. Dr.

Romero had loosened his tie and rolled up his sleeves. He asked if Carolina had come back with the lab report yet. He did not sit down but kept pacing back and forth. Isabella handed him a cup of coffee and said that he needed to sit down, and he did. Carolina came in and handed him the report he was waiting for. He looked at it and would not make eye contact with anyone.

Maggie asked, "Carlos, what is it?"

"It is not a good report. His platelets are fifty-five thousand, his white count is a little over four thousand, and his hematocrit is forty-five. That is the percentage of red cells in the blood, and it is high. That indicates that his blood vessels are leaking fluid out into the tissue and other places. That is why he is having swelling in his legs."

Anna looked like she was going to faint, and Ruth put her arm around her to steady her. She asked Isabella to get her a cool washrag. Dr. Romero asked her to bring him one too.

Matt was trying to keep calm and took some control as he felt he should, being the oldest. He said, "Let's all go out on the porch, and let Dr. Romero fill us in on what all of this means. It is certainly cooler out there."

Everybody agreed, and got up and went outside. When everyone was seated, Dr. Romero pulled a chair to where he would be roughly in the center. He looked like he was more composed and relaxed than he had been. He said, "I am sorry to have a lapse of control like that. Thank you for your patience."

Maggie said, "No need to apologize. We understand that this is hard on you just like it is on us. What is it, Carlos?"

Matt agreed and also asked what it all meant. Anna sat next to Ruth with her head leaning on Ruth's shoulder. She did not say anything.

Dr. Romero began, "First of all, I am going to be completely honest with you. In other words, I am not going to try to hide anything or make light of what is going on. What is happening with Samuel is very serious and has the potential to get worse. The developments over the last twenty-four hours have taken him to the hemorrhagic stage of dengue fever. This does not mean that he is having significant bleeding now, but the potential is there. He is having fluid leakage from his blood vessels manifested by fluid in the tissues and some fluid in the abdominal cavity. The decreased platelets are causing more petechiae and now some larger areas on the skin, and that is why he had bleeding of his gums when he brushed his teeth."

Matt asked, "You mentioned that this could get worse. What happens if it does?"

"What we have to worry about is Dengue Shock Syndrome. That is where everything combines to cause the patient to go into shock. Samuel is not in shock at this time."

Matt asked, "What is the plan now?"

"We have to put him in the hospital. I talked to Maggie briefly about that when I was evaluating Samuel, and I have already called Daniel to come with a van to help transport him."

Matt had become the spokesman for the family and asked, "Where do you plan on taking him?"

"To a hospital in Managua."

Nobody seemed to know what to say. Matt asked, "Dr. Romero, can this problem get real serious?"

"It can." Dr. Romero then said, "If there are no more questions, I'm going to make some calls. Dr. Ortega will be notified, and I'm sure he will be the attending physician and consult others when needed."

Maggie asked, "You will still be his doctor, won't you?"

"Of course."

Dr. Romero excused himself and walked to the other end of the porch to make some phone calls. Carolina walked up the steps with equipment to start an IV and told everyone that she would be praying for Samuel. Anna and Ruth got up to go into the kitchen. Ruth said they would make sandwiches since no one knew when they would get to eat again. She also called Dr. Johnson back home to give him an update. Maggie was putting in a call to Pat Sanders. Matt patted her on the back and told her he was going to go check on Samuel.

Matt walked in Samuel's room just as Carolina was finishing the IV. He pulled a chair over by the bed and sat down, "Man, you'll do anything to get attention, I guess."

"I don't know about that, but it looks like I might be fixing to get more than I want."

"Yeah, it looks like we're all taking a trip to Managua this morning."

"That's what the doctor says."

"Anything I can get for you or anything you need me to pack?"

"Make sure I don't forget Dad's Bible."

"No problem. Anything else?"

"I don't think so, but I reserve the right to be a demanding patient and send y'all all over the place to fulfill my wishes."

Matt laughed and said, "I guess you can get that service for a while."

Samuel managed a smile and said, "Hey, I intend to milk this for all I can."

Matt squeezed his hand and got up to start packing for him.

*****

The familiar van pulled up, and Daniel and Michael quickly got out. Michael opened the side door, and Daniel's wife Sharon stepped out. Michael quickly went in to go and see Samuel. Daniel took Sharon over and introduced her to Maggie.

Maggie said, "Thank you so much for coming. I hope it wasn't too much trouble getting your kids situated. If I remember right, you have two."

"Yes, ma'am, and it is no trouble. They are as at home with the neighbors as they are in their own house. I hope I can be of some help."

"Thank you so much." Maggie turned to Daniel and said, "Y'all sure got here quick."

Daniel let out a sigh and said, "I made the mistake of telling Michael we were in a hurry. That's never a good idea."

Maggie replied, "His reputation has made it to the United States."

Daniel said, "I am not surprised."

Matt came back out on the porch and spoke to Daniel, "Good morning, and it's good to see Sharon again."

"Good morning, Matt. Michael is not getting in the way in there, is he?"

Matt smiled and said, "He absolutely is not. As bad as Samuel is feeling, Michael has got him laughing." Then Matt asked, "Daniel, do you know where we are going yet?"

"No, Dr. Romero hasn't said, but I'm pretty sure it's going to be the hospital that most people go to when they have something serious going on. It is called the Hospital Metropolitano."

"You have experience with it?"

"Yeah, I know a few people who have been there. It has a good reputation."

"You know, Daniel, I haven't thought about insurance or anything like that. It would not surprise me if Samuel didn't have any."

Daniel replied, "I think it will be okay. They may require some kind of deposit, but if they do, I have NMO funds in a bank here. There would be no problem with me letting you borrow from that."

"Thank you. That would be helpful till I can get some money sent down from the States."

"No problem, and the NMO board can help with that transfer since they do it all the time."

*****

It came time to leave, and with Michael under one arm and Daniel under the other, Samuel made his way to the van. Sharon held the IV bag. They had fashioned pillows around on the first bench seat to make the ride more comfortable. Dr. Romero was coming in his car, and Maggie was riding with him. Everybody else loaded into the van with Anna getting in last. Isabella had her arm around her and seemed reluctant to let her go.

She said, "I am going to stay here and keep the house burning, but I will be coming soon to check on this one. I don't trust you all to take good enough care of her."

Daniel said, "I think you mean to say 'keep the home fires burning.'"

"Do not correct me, Daniel. You gringos have too many sayings anyway. I want to hear reports many times during the day. You can start when you get him in the hospital."

"Yes, ma'am."

Chapter 29

Hospital Metropolitano

The trip to Managua had become a familiar one, for Matt, Samuel, and Anna, at least. Time would tell if it was the same for Maggie and Ruth. There was one difference today and that was an accident outside of Managua that slowed traffic to a crawl.

When they finally got to the hospital, they drove around to a covered entrance, and Dr. Romero and Maggie were already there waiting. Two orderlies were waiting with a gurney to take Samuel to his room.

Shortly after everybody unloaded from the van, Jose Ramirez walked out through the double glass doors and came over to where they were standing. He said, "Hope your trip was okay. Arrangements have been made for Samuel to have a room in the intensive care unit. There will be a courtesy room close by for the convenience of the family."

Maggie asked, "Do I have to fill out some forms or sign anything?"

"Maybe later. Nothing is required at this time."

Matt asked next, "What about financial arrangements?"

"There are none. Samuel will be a guest of the president."

Maggie, Ruth, Matt, and Anna all looked at each other with expressions of incredulity on their faces.

Matt then said, "I really thank y'all for that, but it is too much."

Jose responded, "It is already done, Matt, and the president is one that does not change his mind once it is made up. There is one more thing. There is an apartment building close to here, and you will be provided an apartment for your convenience as long as Samuel is here. This also is compliments of the president."

They were all speechless. Maggie finally spoke. "Jose, this is overwhelming. Please tell the president how much we appreciate all this."

"I will, but I feel sure that he will be by here at some time, and you will be able to tell him yourself."

*****

Samuel was wheeled down a long hall and through double doors with Intensive Care Unit written on the wall above. They were met by a Nicaraguan nurse who appeared to be in her early forties. She requested that they wait in the visitors' area till she got Samuel settled in his room. She was very personable and assured everyone that she would come back and get them soon. Matt was impressed with how nice the hospital was and that, coupled with how courteous the nurse was, gave him a good feeling.

Dr. Ortega walked up and spoke to everyone, and then he and Dr. Romero left the group and went to check on Samuel. It was at this point that Maggie started crying, and before long, she was sobbing. Ruth led her over to a chair and tried her best to comfort her. Matt had that typical male feeling of helplessness, but he tried. He kept saying, "Everything is going to be all right."

Maggie said between sobs, "I just can't quit worrying about how bad this can get. It's too much."

Anna had come over and was trying to comfort her mother. "It's gonna be all right. Samuel is in good hands."

Matt was impressed that Anna was holding it together well and was a big help to their mother. Sharon joined in with the other two women and did what she could. Matt walked over and stood by Daniel, who also felt awkward and helpless.

In a few minutes, Maggie composed herself. She said, "I apologize for that. Been a little too much emotion over the last couple of days."

Everybody reassured her that they understood, and Ruth said, "I always say a good cry can be medicinal. It can help your heart feel better."

Everybody was nodding their head in agreement, and Maggie said, "I do have to say that I think it helped, but I hope I don't make a habit of it."

They all sat around, engaged in the usual hospital waiting room conversation; and soon, Dr. Ortega and Dr. Romero walked up. Dr. Ortega spoke to everyone again and told them that he had evaluated Samuel and would share his thoughts.

Everybody gathered around, and he began, "Samuel is stable at this time, so we would not classify him with shock syndrome now. From his blood count that Dr. Romero got this morning, we know that there are some problems, especially with the low platelets. There is also an indication that his blood vessels are leaky. What I mean by that is they are allowing the fluid part of the blood, the plasma, to leak into the tissues, and this will cause swelling in the tissues as well as fluid in other places. I have ordered some X-ray studies, but I suspect that he has fluid in the abdominal cavity as well as the chest cavity."

He paused briefly and then asked, "Does anyone have any questions?"

As usual, Anna was the first to ask, "How do we know which way this will go?"

"It usually will get worse before it gets better, but timing is something we don't know."

Matt asked, "You said that you ordered some tests. I assume they haven't had time to be run yet."

"That is correct. It will take an hour or so. I really can't tell you much till I get them back."

Another doctor walked up to where they were standing. He was younger than Dr. Ortega, wore the traditional white coat, and had a stethoscope hanging around his neck. He was nice looking and had a natural smile. Dr. Ortega said, "Let me introduce everyone to Dr. Emilio Calamuños. He is from Columbia and is one of the critical-care doctors here. He follows the cases of all of the patients in the ICU and will help us with the fluid balance and other things as needed."

Dr. Calamuños greeted everyone and assured them that he would do his best for Samuel. He said that he had not met Dr. Martin, but had heard many good things about him. He had an air of confidence about him that made everybody feel better.

No one had any more questions, and Drs. Ortega and Calamuños excused themselves and walked back into the ICU.

Dr. Romero stayed behind with the family and said. "Let me reassure everybody that Samuel will receive the best of care. Dr. Calamuños is very good at what he does. He has taken care of numerous patients of mine and does well."

Maggie said, "Carlos, I am not sure I fully understand what role he plays."

"ICU patients require much more precise fluid and electrolyte balance than patients that are not as sick. He helps with that, primarily."

Matt said, "I feel good about this hospital and the care he is getting, but I would like to hear your assessment of Samuel at this point."

"He is sick. His condition can literally change by the hour. We'll see what all the latest tests show."

They all stood around in silence, no one knowing what else to ask. Dr. Romero said he would be back to get them in a little while and went into the ICU.

Daniel broke the silence and said, "I feel like we oughta have a prayer."

Everybody agreed, and they formed a circle and joined hands, "Father, we come to you today with anxious hearts striving to have the faith that you so want us to have. We have gratitude, Father, for all the good gifts you have given us, yet we long for more. Our brother Samuel lies ill, and we are troubled by that. We know that by the stripes of your Son, he is healed, but we do not know your timing, Father, and we strive to understand and be at peace with it. We do know, Father, that you are the great physician, and you will be the guiding light for those on earth that you have appointed to take care of him. And, Father, for them, we are also grateful. Father, we thank you for hearing our prayer for this one that you have made my brother—" Daniel got choked up and could not continue.

Sharon finished the prayer, "Father, again we thank you for bringing us together and allowing us to talk to you today. We know that you hear our prayers and answer them. Go with us through this journey and give us the strength, courage, and peace that we need. In Jesus's name. Amen."

*****

Samuel's nurse walked up at that time and told them that they could come in and visit him now. She led them through the double doors that opened into the intensive care unit. The rooms were arranged around a square area, and the nurses' station was in the middle. It had an open atmosphere. There was a lot of activity and, of course, the smell of alcohol so familiar in any medical facility. They were led to Samuel's room, number 122.

The room was more spacious than they expected, and it had more seating than hospital rooms in the States, with a love seat and three chairs. The love seat could be pulled out and converted to a small bed. There was also the usual battery of monitors displaying vital signs, heart rate, and other things that are normal for a critical care area.

Samuel looked reasonably comfortable amid the numerous wires attached and the IV tubing. He managed a smile and said, "Pretty nice accommodations. They tell me this is where all the movers and shakers in Nicaragua come when they need medical care."

Matt said, "Nothing is too good for a brother of mine."

Samuel said, "I kinda thought this may have more to do with the connections of another Martin, one who may have been a little more well known than present company."

Matt said, "Oh, well, I can dream, can't I?"

Ruth stepped forward, took a small hairbrush out of her purse, and wagged it in front of Samuel. "Do you know what one of these is?"

"Mrs. Ruth, I just got here, and I assure you we're not gonna be running a beauty contest from here anyway!"

"Don't get smart with me, Samuel Martin. I've told you all your life that your hair was a blessing and a curse. We are gonna keep it combed or cut it off!"

"Yes, ma'am."

Ruth muttered under her breath, "I hope these high-priced doctors are not forgetting the vitamin C."

The way Ruth interacted with Samuel was her way of keeping her emotions in check. She felt that part of her role was to remain strong for everyone else. She was finding that to be harder and harder to do.

Samuel said, "Hey, have y'all been properly introduced to my nurse?"

Everybody indicated that they had not.

Samuel said, "May I present Charlie." Everybody looked puzzled, and Samuel continued, "I know what you are thinking. Charlie is not a Spanish name nor is it a girl's name." He looked at Charlie and asked, "Can you tell them the story?"

She nodded, "Sure, the story is a short one. My father had a good friend from the United States with that name, and always said that he was going to name a son after him. Well, my father had four daughters, and I am the youngest."

They all laughed, and Maggie commented that she always liked boy's names for girls.

Everybody liked Samuel's nurse.

Dr. Romero and Dr. Ortega walked into the room and reported on the tests that they had run. Dr. Ortega did most of the talking, "We are looking stable at this time. The platelets are fifty thousand, which is essentially the same as they were this morning. All of his blood work, including his electrolytes, kidney, and liver function is normal. His chest x-ray does show a small amount of fluid in the chest cavity, but it is not causing any problems at this time. His EKG is perfectly normal. I am very pleased with these results."

Maggie asked, "What does all of that mean to you at this point, Dr. Ortega?"

"Stability. We are not seeing a rapid progression of the problem, and that is good."

Samuel spoke next, "I feel better than I did this morning. Does that mean anything?"

"Not too much. Your fluid balance is better, and that makes a difference."

Anna asked, "No way to make any predictions on anything at this point?"

"No, Anna. I'm sorry."

Chapter 30

The NMO Board

The NMO board is a nine-member board made up of men from diverse walks of life. Three are pastors, one is a physician, five are businessmen, two of whom are retired. The board president is one of the retired businessmen named Jeff Woods. The sole purpose of the board is to promote the spread of the Gospel in Nicaragua. They were having their regular meeting, and the only one that knew about Samuel's illness was the president, having received a call from Daniel that morning.

Jeff had gotten to the point that he dreaded the meetings because of the attitude of one member, Jack Turner, a very successful businessman from Shreveport. He did not embody many of the Christian virtues one might expect from a member of this type of board. He was negative and always tried to dominate the meetings. The board had never voted a member off before, but Jeff wondered if that may be necessary before too long.

Jeff called the meeting to order and opened with a prayer. Two of the pastors were absent, but everyone else was present. He asked if there were any corrections needed to the minutes of the last meeting. He gave a brief financial report and asked if there was any old business that anyone wanted to discuss.

Jack Turner had some, as Jeff knew he would. "I have not gotten an adequate answer to my question concerning the money that this board laundered for Dr. Martin all of those years. I want to know what action has been taken since our last meeting."

Jeff replied, "The chair respectfully requests that the member refrain from using the term launder as it implies illegal activity."

"I'm not real concerned about what something sounds like. I view it as this board helping a man with his hush money so he could write it off."

Every board member was aware that Jack Turner was jealous of the late Joseph Martin. It became apparent when he joined the board two years ago. He had tried and failed to establish a presence in Nicaragua. Most of the translators and other workers there felt like he just came for the photo-op. None of them cared for his overbearing personality.

Jeff replied, "The problems that Dr. Martin had thirty-five years ago are not going to be discussed by this board, since to do so serves no purpose. Additionally, I reported last month that our records clearly indicate that taxes were paid on the funds sent to Mrs. Miller, and this board was simply a means to get the money to Nicaragua. I might add that the board does the same service for others from time to time who need money transferred. It makes sense since we are set up to do that. The board dealt with all of this before you ever joined and sees no reason to go over it again."

"Well, I have never seen the records, and I feel that I am responsible as a board member of a tax-exempt organization to be sure that the law was followed to the letter."

Jeff was doing all he could not to lose his temper, "As I reported to the board last month, during our discussion of this matter, the records are in storage. I will be happy to provide the key to any concerned board member who wants to go through them."

"I may have my tax attorney contact you, and we'll do just that."

"I am certain it would be a good way for you to spend some of your money." Jeff was losing his patience. "Any other business before we adjourn?"

As expected, Jack Turner spoke up again, "While we are on the subject of the Martins, I would like to state my objections to them staying on our property and using our missionary while they are there. We are not in the hotel business, and I don't think our contributors would think highly of their money going to somebody's vacation."

Frank Austin, one of the other board members spoke. "I was not aware of the use of NMO funds by anyone."

Jack Turner then said, "I can't wait till the IRS gets wind of it. I'm sure that's going to help us maintain our tax-exempt status."

There was a lot of murmuring among the board members, and Jeff hurried to restore order. He said, "First of all, not a penny of NMO funds will be spent on the Martins. Daniel is keeping good records, as he always does, and the bill will be paid in full through the late Dr. Martin's attorney in Monroe. As a matter of fact, as you can see on the financial report, they have already paid a large deposit and may even get a refund when they return home."

Jack said with sarcasm, "Private use of our property by VIPs is not what we are about, and I still think there could be problems with the IRS. What about teams that couldn't come during that time?"

Jeff replied, "Jack, your concern for others is heartwarming. I'm going to go over this once and then I will not talk about it again. Through the years, many people, so called VIPs, have stayed at the compound. It is never allowed if a team is booked during the same time. You yourself have stayed there, Jack, but I guess it is okay for select VIPs. The issue with the IRS is a moot point. I personally worked with Dr. Martin and his attorney when he was setting this up. The Martins are paying us just like a mission team does, and as I have already stated, no NMO funds are being used by anybody. Even if we made money off of them, it would not be a problem because it would simply stay in the organization just like any contribution does."

Jack Turner wouldn't quit. "I still say it's a slippery slope, and we should establish a policy against people staying at the compound except when they are with mission teams. We can start by calling the Martins and recommending they move to a nice hotel. I'm sure they can afford it."

Jeff couldn't stand it any longer. "I'm going to tell you what I'm going to do, you pompous blowhard. I'm going to recommend your removal from this board, and I bet I'll get a unanimous vote. You care nothing for anybody but yourself, and you're here so you can try to control something and so you can put it on your resume. And one more thing, the next time I hear the name Martin come out of that mouth of yours, it better be in a prayer because Samuel Martin was admitted to a hospital in Managua this morning with complications of dengue fever. He is seriously ill."

Jeff made his apologies to the board members for losing his temper and adjourned the meeting.

Jack Turner said nothing else.

Chapter 31

Dr. Romero and Dr. Ortega

Carlos Romero and Hugo Ortega left Samuel's room and walked down to the break room to get a cup of coffee. They sat down, and Dr. Ortega could sense that Dr. Romero had a lot on his mind and maybe needed some doctor talk away from the patient and his family.

"Are you all right, Carlos?"

"I am. I just wish this was all going in another direction."

"I know what you mean. My feeling is that the next twenty-four to forty-eight hours will be the critical time."

"I agree. I don't know if I have adequately prepared the family for what may be ahead. You and I both know that this is more likely to get worse than it is better. And we both know that if it gets bad, it carries a high mortality rate."

Dr. Ortega had long admired Carlos Romero and could not help but feel compassion for him now. He was a good man who had always put others before himself. Hugo had watched him go through a long ordeal when his wife died with breast cancer. Dr. Martin's death had also been hard on him, and now all Dr. Romero could see in front of him was the possibility of the death of one of Dr. Martin's sons. Every doctor knows the feeling that somehow they should be able to fix everything and the helplessness of knowing they can't. Dr. Ortega felt like he should help Dr. Romero with all of this.

He said, "You and I have to deal with that reality, Carlos, but they don't right now. They have to be prepared more slowly."

"You are right, but I wonder if I am doing everything the way I should."

"You are second-guessing yourself, and you know that is not good for you or the patient."

"I know that, but I do not know what to do about it."

"You have to give me the responsibility. You cannot bear that burden on your shoulders. We both know that you know more about dengue fever than me, but I am the so-called expert. I have to have the final say so that you never feel in the future that you should have done something different."

Dr. Romero stared at his coffee cup as if it may somehow help him, and then said, "I know you are right, Hugo. Thank you."

Chapter 32

The Apartment

It was late afternoon and Daniel suggested that they all get settled in the apartment that Jose Ramirez told them about. They could get dinner and then go to the local mall and see about getting outfitted for their stay in Managua. He pointed out that they had plenty of funds in their account with the NMO, so it would be no problem buying what they needed. Matt pointed out that he had plenty of plastic in his pocket if that was needed. Anna said that she was going to stay with Samuel. She told her mother that she was sure that she could pick up some things for her, and she was not leaving the hospital right now. Maggie told her to make a list, and nobody argued with her except for Samuel. It did him no good.

Daniel found the man who was in charge of security at the hospital. Jose had given him the keys to the apartment, and he was going to walk with them the short distance from the hospital to the apartment building. Daniel would then have Michael pick them up and take them to the mall.

It was late evening when they left the hospital, but it was still hot. There was no breeze. As they walked the short distance to the apartment, they passed several buildings; but in the middle of the block, there was a church. It was not a large structure, but it was nice looking. It was constructed out of the building blocks that are so common in Nicaragua and was painted white. There was a large wooden cross mounted above the door. The church seemed to be a little out of place.

Matt commented to Daniel, "Hey, that is a nice-looking church. Are you familiar with it at all?"

Daniel replied, "No, I never noticed it before, but I don't get by this way very often."

*****

The apartment was way more than what they expected. The door opened into a big living room that was nicely furnished. There was a large island off to one side with a spacious kitchen behind it. The appliances were stainless steel and up-to-date. To add a special touch, there was a bouquet of flowers on the island. A kitchen table was off to one side and a larger dining table was not far from that. There were three bedrooms, all large, and very nicely furnished. Each had its own bathroom.

Matt said, "I sure didn't expect something this nice."

Maggie added, "I didn't either. I feel a little like 'country comes to town.'"

Ruth said, "I guess I'll have my work cut out for me with the upkeep on this place."

They all laughed and didn't notice that someone was at the door. It was a young Nicaraguan lady that was dressed in a uniform. She introduced herself. "I am Consuela. I will come by every day to do the cleaning and washing. I will not come too early in the morning so I do not disturb your sleep. There is a lady that is available to prepare meals if needed. You can let me know any time you want her to come."

They all raised their eyebrows with surprised looks, and Matt said, "Well, Mrs. Ruth, I guess you can sit this one out."

Ruth replied indignantly, "Well, I hope y'all don't get too used to this. The Lord does not intend for someone else to do our work for us."

Maggie said, "That may be true, Ruth, but I think I'll enjoy it while I can."

Matt said, "Yeah, I could for sure get used to this. I am real impressed with the president. He doesn't seem to do things half way."

Daniel said, "I guess he keeps places like this to accommodate visiting dignitaries, and y'all must qualify."

Matt added, "I need to look up the president's brother that my dad operated on and thank him for getting sick when he did. Without him, we may not be enjoying all this."

They all laughed, and Daniel said, "I think that he may no longer be with us."

*****

Michael picked them up in the van and reported that he had visited Samuel before coming. He said that he was feeling pretty good. They went to a restaurant that was known for its great hamburgers, and they enjoyed it. The food was excellent, and the service was very good. Who'd have thought that you could get a great hamburger in Nicaragua.

The mall was a spacious, two-story building that looked very much like the malls in the United States. Sharon told them that it was nicknamed the Gringo Mall. It had numerous shops and stores, many of them the same as in the States.

Michael, Matt, and Daniel branched off to shop for Matt, and the girls went in another direction. Maggie asked Sharon to shop for Anna since they were closer in age. The plan was to buy a couple of outfits apiece and get Isabella to pack up their things at the compound and bring them in a day or two.

Guys generally shop faster than girls, and Matt was no exception. After he was done, they found the girls in a nice department store. They didn't seem to be very far along in their shopping.

Matt said, "Y'all better hurry up. This place won't be open all night, you know."

Nobody paid him any attention. They went on with their shopping as if the men weren't there. Sharon was holding up a dress and saying, "I think Anna would like this one. It is nice but still has that casual feel that she'll appreciate."

Maggie said, "I like that one. What do you think Ruth?"

Ruth said, "Do they have that in blue. You know Anna is partial to blue."

Daniel rolled his eyes and said to Michael and Matt, "Can you believe this? You would think we're going to the prom or something."

Sharon said, "I heard that."

After what seemed like an eternity that included trips to two more stores, the ladies finally finished shopping. They all loaded into the van and headed back toward the apartment. Matt told Michael to let him off at the hospital and he would have a short visit with Samuel. That would allow him to take the things to Anna that they had picked up for her. He said he would walk back to the apartment when he was done.

*****

Matt walked into Samuel's room and found him asleep, and Anna curled up on the love seat, reading. She smiled when she saw him, and he handed her the bags of things they had bought for her.

He said, "Judging from the time your colleagues spent picking this stuff out, I think you'll be in high cotton."

Anna laughed, "I bet you that Sharon has a good eye for fashion, and Mom and Ruth know what I like. I'm sure I'll be in good shape."

Matt nodded toward Samuel and asked, "How is he?"

"He started having a hard time with some bone pain and that dreaded headache. Charlie gave him something in his IV and that is why he is out of it."

Matt said, "I sure do like her. I wish she could be his private nurse."

"I talked to her about that, Matt, and she said that she would be assigned to him when she is here on her regular shift, but she would also do some extra duty if we wanted her to."

"That is fantastic. I intend to pay her very well for that. Now what about you, baby sister?"

"What do you mean? I don't charge for my shifts."

Matt laughed. "I guess there is no sense in me trying to talk you into coming to the apartment?"

"No, Matt. I'd rather be here."

"Well, I can't help but worry about you."

"Matt, I know I overreact and I have been a mess over the last few months, but right now, I just feel like I need to be here, If not so much for Samuel as for myself. As much as Dr. Romero tries to hide it, I know how serious this can be. This is how I have to deal with it."

Matt gave her a big hug and told her he'd be back in the morning. She said to herself as he walked out the door, "I do love my brothers."

*****

Matt enjoyed the short walk back to the apartment. He paused in front of the church that had caught his eye earlier and was once again struck with the thought that it was out of place in this metropolitan area. He shrugged his shoulders and walked on down the street.

When he entered the apartment, Ruth and Maggie were sitting at the table in the kitchen. He walked over and sat down.

Maggie asked, "How is Samuel?"

"He was sleeping. Anna said that he had some pain, and Charlie gave him something."

Ruth asked, "Did he seem comfortable?"

"Oh yeah. I may want a little of what he was having."

Ruth said, "That is terrible, Matt."

Maggie agreed and then asked, "So you talked to Anna?"

"I did."

"How do you think she is doing?"

"Looks like she has it together better than I've seen her in a long time."

"Really, how so?"

"She was not emotional. Simply stated that staying with Samuel was her way of dealing with all of this."

"Do you think she realizes how serious this can be?"

"Yes, ma'am. She said as much."

Ruth said, "It will be good for her not to be so upset all the time."

Maggie agreed and said, "Maybe she's turned a corner."

*****

Matt couldn't sleep. All of the events of the last several days kept swimming around in his mind. He was trying to say a prayer, but he couldn't stay focused. He still was having difficulty with the whole issue of prayer and how it worked. No matter how much he analyzed it, he couldn't understand. He kept going back to that familiar quote: God moves in mysterious ways.

He said out loud, "But how mysterious?"

He simply could not come to grips with all that had happened and how to make sense out of all of it especially if Samuel didn't make it. What would be the good that could come from that? He couldn't let himself think about that possibility. If he had time, he was going to talk to Daniel more about it.

His thoughts began to drift again, and he was thinking about the day they arrived in Nicaragua. He remembered all of the people who showed up at the compound. He thought about the old woman's prayer for Samuel. He remembered that one of the things she said was, "Samuel would not leave Nicaragua." He sat straight up in the bed and broke out in a sweat.

Chapter 33

Daniel and Sharon

Daniel and Sharon made it home later that evening. They retrieved their kids from the neighbors and got them settled in bed. Sharon was putting some things away in the kitchen, and Daniel sank down into his easy chair. Sharon finished up and joined him in the living room.

Daniel was checking his emails on his laptop and said, "Wow, wonders never cease."

"What are you looking at?"

"Do you remember meeting Jack Turner when he was here?"

"I do remember him. I didn't care much for his personality."

"That is being nice."

"Why are you asking about him?"

"I got an email from him that surprises me. He says that he heard that Samuel Martin is seriously ill, and he wants to help. He goes on to say that he will cover any extra expenses they incur because of that, and the kicker is, he wants to remain anonymous."

"You're kidding."

"No, it is right here in writing."

"That sure is a change from the Jack Turner I met."

"Well, you are the one that always says never give up on anybody. This supports that position."

"I guess it does. On another note, how is my favorite missionary holding up?"

"I'm doing okay. A little tired, but that comes with the territory."

"I think the Martin family has sort of adopted you, or maybe it's the other way around."

"I've enjoyed them. I guess Matt and Samuel have become brothers of sorts, and I like them all, including Mrs. Ruth."

Sharon laughed, "She is one you want with you in the trenches when the going gets tough."

"Yeah, Matt told me about all that she did when Dr. Martin died, and how they didn't have to do anything. I do worry a little about her, though. Samuel is like her own."

"What about you?"

"I don't know what you're asking me."

"How are you going to deal with all of this if things don't go well?"

"I'm going to count on Samuel doing well, but if the Lord allows it to go another way, I probably won't do too good. Why?"

"Honest about it anyway."

"Well, no need to have that, 'you're getting too close to them' talk with me. That has already happened. And besides, I know the missionary's wife. It won't be long before she is also adopted."

"You think so?"

"No, I know so."

"We'll see. What's your take on how everything is going with Samuel?"

"You know me, baby. I'm the eternal optimist."

"That's really not an answer."

"I know. Sorry. It seems to me from all I have heard about this problem, and from what the doctors are telling us, it is likely to get worse. I just don't know how to predict how much worse. Dr. Romero seems worried, but part of that, I'm sure, is how close he is to them."

"This has got to be hard on him."

"No doubt."

"Maggie sure does come across as a pretty strong woman."

"Yeah, think about that for a minute. She loses her husband and not long after that has to come and deal with the issue of Anna's adoption, and now her middle child is seriously ill. It's a lot in a short period of time."

"What about her and Dr. Romero? You think anything might develop there?"

Chapter 34

Stable

Early morning in the ICU found Samuel feeling about the same. He was not much better, but at least, no worse. He did report that his head was not hurting as bad. He felt good enough to sit in a chair. Charlie had arrived and was going about what an ICU nurse does, adjusting wires and IV rates and making sure that the monitors were all functioning as they were supposed to. Dr. Calamuños came by early and made some minor adjustments to the orders and said he would be by later and check on the labs drawn this morning.

Anna came in and kissed Samuel on the forehead. She had showered and dressed in the courtesy room that was right down the hall from the ICU. Charlie complimented her on the dress she was wearing, which was the new blue one Matt had brought her the night before. They engaged in a fashion discussion for a few minutes and then Charlie asked Samuel, "How was your night?"

"Not bad. Whatever you gave me really helped with the pain. I was able to sleep fairly well." Samuel was feeling mischievous and said, "Hey, Charlie, in my delirium of being admitted to the hospital yesterday, I didn't really appreciate how good looking you are."

Anna exclaimed, "Romeo, you better behave yourself! Am I going to have to speak with your mother about this?"

Charlie, being a veteran, took it in stride, "Mr. Martin, I appreciate the compliment, but our relationship must remain strictly professional."

Samuel replied, "I am sorry to hear that. I bet I could talk one of these doctors into giving me a pass, and you and I could go out."

Charlie maintained her nurse demeanor and said, "Not likely."

She stuck a thermometer in Samuel's mouth, and Anna said, "That's better."

Charlie shook her head.

Samuel grinned.

*****

The entourage from the apartment filed in and everybody went on and on about how good Anna looked in her new dress. Maggie commented on how she looked rested, and how that was a good thing since she spent the night in the hospital.

Matt shook hands with Samuel and said, "I'll pay a little attention to the patient. How are you this morning?"

"Holding up pretty well. I guess I have lost the golden child status for sure. Even my nurse was going on about Anna's dress and hardly paid me any attention at all this morning."

Anna said, "I don't know about that, but I do know how much attention you paid to your nurse."

Everybody looked at Samuel with eyebrows raised, and he said, "Anna the exaggerator. I was just flirting a little."

Matt said, "Well, you are quite an eligible bachelor, and you're not getting any younger."

Samuel couldn't resist that opening and said, "Yeah, and I'm not sure how much older I'm gonna get, either."

Ruth said immediately, "Samuel Martin, don't you talk like that! You know that the scriptures say that you become what you think! You better stop saying things like that."

"Sorry, Mrs. Ruth, but I couldn't resist it. The timing was too perfect."

Maggie said, "I don't care what your tests show, I will go ahead and pronounce you better today."

Samuel said, "Gotta laugh, can't sit around here and mope. Another thing, it may be the drugs. One good thing about all of this is you can take some good stuff, and legally, I might add."

Anna said, "Boy is he on a roll today."

Everybody nodded their heads in agreement.

Dr. Romero walked in and was in an upbeat mood. He looked around and could tell that everyone was in good spirits, including Samuel.

He said, "Good morning. You all are looking good this morning."

Anna said, "Oh, if you only knew. Samuel is ready to pull out the lines and run off with Charlie."

Maggie said, "Anna, I have to agree with Samuel. I think you might be exaggerating just a little."

Matt said, "Sounds like we may need to restrict some of the drugs he's getting."

Dr. Romero laughed and said, "I'll have to look into that. Samuel, you must be feeling better this morning?"

"I do feel some better. That blasted headache is not as bad today. I think that is making a difference. I don't think I am ready to leap tall buildings as my sister might have led you to think."

"Maybe in a day or two. The lab from this morning is not back yet. Dr. Ortega will be by later to give you that report. I am going to have to go to my clinic in Diriamba for a while today, and I'll be back tonight."

He looked over at Maggie and said, "Maggie, would you like to join me in the hospital cafeteria for breakfast?"

"I'd love to."

*****

Later in the morning, Dr. Ortega came by. He was pleased that Samuel was feeling better.

"Good to see everybody this morning, and the news for today is that everything seems stable. All of the lab is so close to yesterday's values that we can say they are unchanged."

Dr. Calamuños came in at that time and joined the conversation. "I see no problems this morning with his fluids and electrolytes. No problems with kidney function at this time."

Anna asked, "Can we tell anything about the prognosis from any of this?"

Dr. Ortega smiled and replied, "I like that medical term you used, Anna, prognosis, but I have to say that the prognosis is not really changed by anything in today's results. I am cautiously encouraged though."

Maggie asked, "Will you do any more lab today?"

"I do not plan to. If any problems arise, I will."

Anna asked, "Dr. Calamuños, I see you in and out of the intensive care unit all through the day and night. If I have a question, is it okay for me to ask it if you are not too busy?"

He smiled that large smile of his, and replied, "I will consider it an honor to be of service at any time, and please, call me Emilio." He bowed slightly.

Anna had a large smile also, and Matt looked at Samuel and grinned.

*****

It was early afternoon, and Matt was walking around in front of the hospital, talking to his wife on the phone. He liked to get away from the hospital room once in a while, and he liked the sights and sounds of the city. He had gotten into the habit of walking down toward the church that was between the hospital and the apartment building where they were staying. He was somewhat fascinated by it and felt an odd pull to go inside, but he hadn't done that yet.

The usual traffic flow of the day was interrupted by the appearance of a long sleek black limousine. It had flags on each side of the front, mounted to the fenders. There was a black, official-looking vehicle in front of it and one behind. Matt's first thought that it looked like a presidential motorcade, and he was surprised when it turned into the drive in front of the hospital. It stopped by the main entrance.

Matt felt some excitement and started walking back toward the hospital entrance. The driver got out of the limousine, and three other men got out and looked like they could be secret service agents. More got out of the other two vehicles and formed a perimeter around the limousine. Another man was helped out of the car by the driver. He was dressed in a white suit that had some type of insignia on the left side of the chest. He was tall and had dark hair with gray on the sides. Matt was sure that this had to be the president. Most of them went into the hospital, leaving a few to watch the vehicles.

Matt followed at a safe distance so as not to attract attention. He was allowed entrance into the hospital after a brief stop by one of the president's men. His excitement grew as it became obvious that they were heading in the direction of the ICU. He was hoping that this was the visit from the president that Jose Ramirez said might happen.

The presidential party, or whatever it was, continued through the double doors leading into the ICU. Matt followed, not too far behind, and his excitement grew when he saw them heading toward Samuel's room. Jose Ramirez was there also, and Matt assumed that he must have come in the other ICU entrance. He was just outside of Samuel's door, and when he saw Matt, he motioned for him to come over. The president had gone in, and Jose and Matt came in right behind him.

Jose said, "May I present to all of you, the president of Nicaragua, the honorable Manuel Lorenzo. Your Excellency, this is Maggie, Matt, and Anna Martin. Also Mrs. Ruth Shelby, and the patient, as you know, is Samuel Martin."

The president had a nice smile, and he looked very distinguished, especially with the official insignia on his suit coat. He shook each person's hand and said that it was his honor to meet them. He shook Samuel's hand last and said that he knew that he would soon be well.

Matt was the first of the Martins to speak, "Mr. President, it is an honor to meet you and have you take time out of your schedule to come for a visit. You have been too generous in providing for our needs during this time. We appreciate it."

Maggie added, "I agree with Matt, and I cannot thank you enough for all of this."

The president said, "I am the one who is honored by having all of you visit my country. I am sure you have heard the praises of many for Dr. Joseph Martin, and I will add mine now. As you know, he saved my brother with the skill in his hands and the compassion in his heart. So many others in this country benefited from the skills that God gave him. I tried many times to pay him for operating on my brother, and I tried to reward him for the services to my country. He refused to accept any of it and sent word to me that he was already overpaid."

He paused, and Matt started to speak. The president raised his hand and said, "Please let me finish. What I am doing for you is my way of repaying him now. As he served my family, I will serve his. The difference is that now, he cannot argue with me about it."

There was scattered laughter in the room. He went on, "One thing I learned about Dr. Martin is that arguing with him would go nowhere."

He turned to Maggie and said, "It is good to have you come back. I am sorry it took you so long, and I guess I could say the same to you, Anna."

Maggie said, "I thought about coming many times, but those trips became an escape for Joseph. I felt like he would rather come by himself."

Anna said, "I didn't know till recently that I had roots here. There is no doubt that I will be back. I have become an assistant to Isabella, and I hope to enjoy doing that more in the future."

"She is a good one to learn from. What about you, Matt? Have you enjoyed visiting Nicaragua?"

"I have. I had no idea what to expect, but I have really liked your country."

"And Mrs. Shelby, I will count on you supporting my tourism industry again in the future."

"I'm sure I will, Mr. President. The Martins don't always do well when I'm not around."

The president smiled and said, "Samuel, I hope next time we can avoid the fever problem, and I do apologize for the behavior of my mosquitos. I am confident that when I see you again, you will be well."

Samuel replied, "Thank you for your concern and help. I have got to get well so I can enjoy some more of your country."

The president said his goodbyes, bowed slightly, and he and his entourage left.

Jose Ramirez stayed behind and asked Maggie if there were any problems with the accommodations or anything else.

Maggie said they had more than they needed and thanked him again.

Chapter 35

Special Visitors

The day did not start off well. Samuel was complaining of stomach pain and was having some vomiting, and it was bloody. His platelets were low and so was his blood pressure. He did not look good, with bloody splotches under his skin from the low platelets, and he had more swelling in his legs.

Dr. Ortega came in and began his report to Anna and Samuel. The rest of the family had not made it in from the apartment yet. "I am not pleased with the developments this morning. Further drop in the platelets has caused the bleeding from the stomach, and we are seeing more swelling which makes balancing the fluids harder. Dr. Calamuños is working now on some changes to help with that."

Anna asked, "I have heard of people getting platelets before. Are we going to do that?"

"We are. The problem with platelets is that they don't stay in the system long, so they only have a short-term effect."

"What then?"

"You just have to work with the numbers and do the best you can."

Dr. Calamuños came in, and it was obvious that he was concerned. Dr. Ortega said, "Emilio, help me explain some of what we are looking at this morning."

"Yes, sir. We have a problem that is difficult to deal with in that Samuel has what we call intravascular volume depletion, but at the same time, he has fluid overload. The fluid is just not in the right place. His blood count is not too low yet, so I am not going to give him any blood. I am going to go with some fresh frozen plasma to see if we can get some of the fluid in the tissues to come back into the bloodstream."

Samuel asked, "Why is my blood pressure low now."

Dr. Calamuños answered, "It is the combination of blood loss and leaking into the tissues."

"So you can't give me blood?"

"As I said, your blood count is not low enough for us to do that yet. We will if we need to."

Both doctors excused themselves and left the room. Anna could tell that Samuel felt bad, and his spirits were low.

"Can I get you something?"

"Yeah, I would appreciate it if you would hand me Dad's Bible."

Charlie came in carrying a small bag and hung it up on the IV pole. She said that it was platelets, and she was counting on them stopping the bleeding in his stomach. She reported that his blood pressure was up slightly.

Samuel's sense of humor was still intact even though he was feeling bad. He told Charlie, "I guess you missed your chance. I don't really feel up to going out today."

She never missed a beat. She continued working with the IV and said, "I guess there is a silver lining to every cloud."

Samuel started laughing and then started groaning, "I wish you wouldn't make me laugh when I am in this condition."

She replied, "You brought it on yourself."

Maggie, Matt, and Ruth came in, and Maggie had that worried-mother look on her face. So did Ruth. Matt was his usual self and immediately shook hands with Samuel and asked how he was doing.

"Not too good. Ask Anna. I think she can explain it all better."

Anna went over all the developments and the explanations given by the doctors. Nobody had any questions. Ruth got up and started straightening things around the room.

Maggie got a call, and it was Dr. Romero. He said that he had gotten an update from Dr. Ortega, and he wanted to let them know that he wouldn't be coming till later in the evening. He told her that Dr. Ortega would let him know if there were any changes in Samuel's condition.

*****

It didn't take long for Matt to get restless and go for his usual walk in front of the hospital. He would go as far as the church and then walk back toward the hospital. It had become a pattern for him now. He always stood in front of the church for a few minutes and looked at it. He felt that attraction to go inside but resisted it. He wondered if he was afraid of something, but what? And why were there never any people around?

His phone rang, and it was Daniel, "Hey, Matt, sorry I've been out of touch. How are y'all doing?"

"Not that great. Samuel has some issues going on this morning."

"Sorry to hear that. They got him under control?"

"Yeah, Anna said they were going to give him some platelets to stop a bleeding issue."

"That's a bummer. I'll pray for him again this morning."

"Thanks, man. We appreciate that."

"I should be by not long after lunch. I've got to pick some people up at the airport and then I'll head that way."

"We'll look forward to seeing you."

Daniel added, "Oh, I almost forgot. I went by the compound yesterday, and Isabella sent some stuff that she had packed up. I'll bring that with me."

"That's great. How is she doing?"

"Doing great. I had to endure a chewing because I have not called her to give her a report often enough."

"Sounds just like her."

*****

Back in Samuel's room, everybody was fiddling around and passing the time the best way they knew how. Samuel was dozing as Charlie had given him more pain medicine. Anna was curled up on the love seat, napping. That spot had become her nest. Maggie was doing some needlepoint work as this had become her way of dealing with the waiting, and Ruth was checking the messages on her phone as she had amassed a large group of people back home that she kept informed of Samuel's progress.

Ruth said, "Dr. Johnson says that he thinks that Samuel may be on every prayer list in Louisiana. Says his emails and texts are full every day of people saying that they are praying for him."

Maggie said, "That is great, Ruth. We need every one of them."

Matt was fidgeting and got up to go and talk to Charlie. She was at the nurses' station working on the computer.

"Can't get away from those no matter what we do."

"You are right, Matt. It is hard to be a nurse when you also have to be a computer expert. I hate this thing."

"I have been meaning to tell you, Charlie, how much we all appreciate everything you are doing for Samuel."

"You all are so welcome. He is a special person, and your family is also special. Anna has become like another sister to me."

"Well, we are lucky to have you, and we especially appreciate you doing extra shifts."

"No problem."

"Charlie, I know you can't tell me much, but what is your feeling about Samuel's current condition?"

"You are right. I can't say much, but I am hoping for some better results on his afternoon lab."

"Thanks again."

*****

Maggie, Ruth, Matt, and Anna decided to have lunch in the hospital cafeteria since the doctors wouldn't let Samuel eat till they were sure that he wasn't going to have any more issues with his stomach. Maggie said that it used to irritate Dr. Martin when patient's family members ate in front of the patient when they couldn't eat. Thought it was inconsiderate.

Maggie said, "Anna, you seem to be adapting well to hospital living,"

"It's not that bad. The courtesy room is nice, and all the people are nice."

Matt asked, "Where do you sleep?"

"In Samuel's room."

Ruth asked, "Isn't it cramped on that love seat?"

"No, it's actually pretty comfortable. Don't forget, I'm pretty short."

Matt said, "Daniel said that he was picking up somebody from the airport. Anybody expecting anybody?"

They all shook their heads no, and Anna said, "I am sure he picks up people all the time."

Matt said, "I guess that's right. He said he would be by after lunch"

All of the sudden, Matt sat up straight in his chair and said, "Well, here he is, and look at this! I can't believe it! Look who's here!"

Matt stood up, and when everybody looked around, they saw Daniel walking into the cafeteria with Dr. Pat Sanders and another man of about the same age that they didn't know.

Maggie's face lit up. She put her hands to her face and exclaimed, "I am not believing this! Matt, did you know?"

"No, ma'am."

Everybody stood up and greeted the new arrivals. Maggie gave Pat Sanders a hug and said, "Pat, leave it to you to show up unannounced!"

"You know me, Maggie, always have had a flair for drama."

"It's the surgeon in you coming out." She added, "Great to see you. I'm glad you're here."

"I know you don't need a surgeon, but I imagine you could use an extra friend."

Maggie smiled and nodded.

Dr. Sanders hugged Ruth and Anna, and shook hands with Matt.

Matt said, "Thank you for coming. Hope it wasn't too hard for you to get away."

"No, I needed a vacation. And besides, it gives the younger ones a chance to do a little work."

They all laughed, and Dr. Sanders said, "Let me introduce Dr. Mike Simmons to y'all. I picked him up on the way."

They all shook hands, and Maggie said, "I met you on the phone a few days ago. Thank you for coming."

"You are welcome. I was surprised to hear that all of this was going on."

Maggie said, "Yes, us too."

Matt asked, "Dr. Simmons, do I remember correctly, you trained with my father only on the Tulane side?"

"That's right. We were all at Charity Hospital at the same time."

"No problems with the LSU/Tulane rivalry?"

"Wasn't much a problem in those days. All in good fun."

Dr. Sanders said, "Mike is still at Tulane. He chairs the tropical medicine department."

Matt asked, "So you have a lot of experience with this type of problem?"

"I guess you could say that. I've been at it for a while."

Anna asked, "You will be helping Dr. Ortega, then?"

"I'll be available to help in any way I can. I'll be another opinion in the mix, so to speak."

Dr. Sanders asked, "Is Carlos Romero around?"

Maggie answered, "No, he is working in his clinic, said he'd be back later this evening."

"I'm looking forward to seeing him again. I didn't have enough time to visit with him when he was there for the funeral."

Matt said to Anna, "Sister, why don't you go and see if Samuel is awake."

"I will. Be back in a minute."

Dr. Sanders asked, "Do they limit the number of visitors that can come in at one time?"

Matt answered, "No, sir. They are pretty open with that here."

Dr. Simmons asked, "Does Dr. Ortega have set times that he makes rounds."

Matt said, "He seems to be in and out at different times throughout the day."

Anna walked back in and said, as if she was a press secretary, "Samuel is awake and says he's accepting visitors at this time."

They all laughed, left the cafeteria, and walked back toward the ICU. There was the usual small talk, and Dr. Sanders commented on how nice the hospital was. Dr. Simmons agreed.

Dr. Sanders turned toward Matt and said, "Oh, by the way, I hear rumors that we are not the first high-class visitors Samuel has had."

Maggie said, "That is correct. Pat. I might add that not everybody rates a presidential visit."

When they got to the room, Dr. Sanders shook Samuel's hand and said, "How are you doing, you ole burnt-out quarterback."

"Burning out for sure. Good to see you, sir."

"Still doing anything it takes to get attention, I see."

"I admit I'm a showman, but I tell you, this ain't the way to do it."

"Samuel, meet Dr. Mike Simmons. He knew your dad and knows a little bit about these tropical fevers."

Dr. Simmons said, "Nice to meet you. How is my friend Dr. Ortega treating you?"

Samuel smiled and said, "I guess he's doing the best he can with what he's got to work with."

At that time, Dr. Ortega walked in. Samuel said, "Speak of the devil."

Dr. Simmons walked over and shook his hand, "Good to see you, Hugo. Hope you are doing well."

"Good to see you, doctor. Maybe you can help me with this one."

"Giving you some trouble, huh?"

"I was okay till he decided to have some low platelets and bleeding this morning."

"I see you have some platelets hanging."

"Yes, sir. I decided to go ahead with some today."

"You'll have to catch me up on everything later. Oh, and pardon my rudeness, let me introduce you to Dr. Pat Sanders."

The two men shook hands, and Dr. Sanders said, "Nice to meet you. Joseph spoke about you often."

"Nice to meet you. Dr. Martin also spoke of you often."

"Didn't tell too much, I hope."

"Maybe a few stories, but we don't have to repeat them in present company."

Dr. Sanders laughed, "I agree. Thank you."

Charlie came in and looked around at the crowd that had gathered. She had that look on her face that the Martins had seen before. It was a friendly but firm expression of authority. She said, "I am afraid that I am going to have to ask you all to consider going to the courtesy room. It is time for Samuel to get some rest."

Ruth said, "I'm glad you said that, Charlie. I thought I was going to have to."

Everybody was suddenly in that mode of having had the obvious pointed out to them, and they began filing out of the room. Anna stayed.

As they were walking down the hall, Matt said to Daniel, "Why don't you and I take the stuff that Isabella sent and put it in the apartment?"

Daniel answered, "That sounds good. It's in the van right outside in the parking lot."

As they walked toward the apartment building, Matt said, "Daniel, what is your take on all of this?"

"What do you mean?"

"I think I am trying to somehow see how all of this fits with the great scheme of things. How does God work in all of this?"

"That's a real broad question, Matt. You may have to narrow it down some."

"Well, if Samuel doesn't make it, I am having a hard time putting it all together."

"Are you that worried about him?"

"I am. One thing I learned from my father is this: doctors never tell you everything that they are thinking. It's not really being dishonest as much as it's not dealing with all the possibilities till you need to. It's a skill that all of the good ones have."

"Is it the bleeding that happened this morning that has you more concerned?"

"Yeah. Everything I have read about this problem says that is a bad sign."

"You googled it?"

"Of course."

Daniel laughed, "Matt the analyst."

"Well, going back to what I was saying earlier, I can't see the reason for it all. If the worst happens, what was the purpose of this trip?"

"The scripture tells us to 'lean not on our own understanding,' but to trust God with it."

Matt shook his head and said, "It just seems like that is one of those verses we use to try to explain things when they don't make any sense."

Daniel replied, "Well, another one is 'God's ways are not our ways.'"

"That makes it too simple, Daniel, and we haven't even mentioned prayer and all the ins and outs of that. I prayed for Samuel and I to get along, and it was answered, but I don't feel that my prayers for his health are having any effect."

"To quote Anna, 'You are going deep with this one.'"

"Well, Daniel, you have the misfortune of being my default spiritual advisor."

"I'm afraid that there are a lot of things that happen that our finite minds will never understand. Why did Jesus have to suffer and die so I could be saved? Try to explain that one. And the basic question that always comes up: why do bad things happen to good people? And don't forget faith. It has to come in there somewhere. You have to pray believing that your prayer is answered."

"I guess I have to see the answer."

"We don't always get that, Matt. We might not understand a lot of things this side of the grave. That doesn't mean there was no answer. The key is to never give up. No matter what happens, continue to trust that God is going to take care of you. Trust is the key."

"I guess for now, I'll just have to take your word for it."

"Remember, Matt, you can't fix everything."

As the two men became more focused on their conversation, they had stopped walking, and Matt noticed that they were standing in front of the small church that always attracted his attention.

Daniel's phone rang, and he was talking to someone in Spanish. He hung up and said, "That was Michael. He's heading this way, and you'll never guess who is with him."

Matt smiled and said, "Got to be Isabella."

Chapter 36

Samuel's Doctors

Dr. Romero came in later that evening. After all the greetings were completed, Dr. Ortega suggested that all the doctors meet together and discuss Samuel's case. They went to a physician's lounge not far from the ICU. Dr. Calamuños was also part of the meeting.

Dr. Ortega spoke first, "If you all don't mind, I'll get us started. First, I would like to say that I feel that Carlos Romero is the most qualified of all of us to take care of Samuel, but he and I agreed that it would be better for me to have the primary responsibility because of his closeness to the family. Would you have anything to add to that, Dr. Romero?"

Dr. Romero said, "I appreciate the compliment, Hugo. I don't know if I agree with the qualification part, but I do agree that it would be better if I did not have the final say on difficult decisions."

Dr. Ortega replied, "I will be the designated attending physician, but I will call on all of you for advice and also feel free to give it any time, even if not asked. I am glad to have Dr. Simmons here with all of his knowledge on this subject."

Dr. Simmons said, "Thank you, Hugo. Hope I can be some help."

Dr. Ortega continued, "It's good to have our intensivist with us, Dr. Emilio Calamuños. He is the best I've seen with fluid and electrolyte issues and balancing all of those type problems."

Dr. Sanders spoke up, "I know I'm just the surgeon in the room, but I would love to get an update on Samuel."

Dr. Ortega said, "Let me go over some things and get everybody's thoughts. My main concern now is the GI bleeding that he had this morning. It was not massive, but it can get that way. His platelets were 30,000, so I decided to give him some. My decision to do that was because of the bleeding. The repeat platelet count this afternoon is 65,000. I am not optimistic that it will stay that high long. His blood pressure is better this afternoon, but Emilio has given him some pressor meds to help that. Of course, you never like to see the need for those, but we didn't want to cause a fluid overload. His chest x-ray shows that his pleural effusion is stable, and we are not seeing any changes to worry about on his EKG. His blood count is high but that, I'm sure, is because of the loss of the plasma component of his blood. That is about it unless Emilio has anything to add."

"You summed it up well. I have nothing more at this time. I am considering giving him some fresh frozen plasma, but I'm saving that for now."

Dr. Simmons asked, "What would you be using that for at this time?"

"It is known to increase the platelet count and will also stop some of the plasma loss into the tissues."

Dr. Sanders asked, "Is there any kind of treatment specific for this, or is it all just supportive measures till he gets over it?"

Dr. Ortega said, "Mike, you want to take that one"

"I'll try. Aggressive fluid resuscitation is the primary treatment and that is being done as reported by Dr. Calamuños. Studies are mixed concerning the use of crystalloids or colloids, but I feel like we all would agree that the use of both is indicated in sick patients. The other thing is corticosteroids, and there has not been any evidence to support their use, but I would defer to Hugo and Carlos on that one. The only other thing that I know of that may help is immunoglobulins. There was a study done in the Philippines that involved children, and there was a definite benefit with it. Since it has few side effects, I would recommend using it. I would like to see an EKG every day since cardiac problems can develop."

Dr. Ortega said, "We do have an EKG ordered every day, and I agree that we should go with the immunoglobulins. I don't feel that steroids do any good. Emilio, do you have anything to add?"

"Not at this time. I do not like to have to use the pressor drugs, so I will probably go with some fresh frozen plasma tomorrow and see if I can get him off that."

Dr. Ortega said, "Carlos, you have more clinical experience than the rest of us with dengue. What are your thoughts?"

"I agree with everything you all have said. I do think that immunoglobulins help. They should be given."

Dr. Ortega asked, "Carlos, you have had a feeling from the beginning that Samuel was not going to do well. What are your thoughts now?"

"You and I discussed this some, Hugo, and I still question my objectivity. That being said, I still think we have some difficult days ahead. We are not really seeing any improvement, just a slow progression for now."

Chapter 37

Isabella and Dinner

Maggie, Ruth, Matt, Anna, and Daniel were in Samuel's room later in the afternoon when Isabella and Michael walked in. Michael went straight to the side of Samuel's bed, grabbed his hand, and said, "*Que pasa, amigo?*" (What's up, friend?)

Samuel replied, "*Me siento mal, hombre.*" (I feel bad, man.)

Michael said, "*Lo siento, vas a estar bien pronto.*" (I'm sorry. You're going to be well soon.)

"*Espero que si.*" (I hope so.)

Isabella was her animated self, and went straight to Anna and gave her a long hug. She said, "I heard that you were staying here at the hospital."

"Yes, ma'am."

"I am sure that you are not eating properly."

"The food here is not bad."

Isabella made a terrible face as if she had suddenly bitten into something sour and said, "It cannot be as good as what you were used to back at the compound."

"I would have to agree with that."

"Isabella will fix that. I will fix the meals at the apartment you all have, and yours can be brought here."

Anna protested, "Isabella, I appreciate, that but it's a lot of trouble."

Maggie said, "I agree, Isabella. That is a lot of work for you."

Isabella raised her hand in protest and said, "I will hear none of this. I am going to do my part to take care of this family the only way I know how." She got a little emotional and wiped her eyes.

Ruth walked over, put her arm around her, and said, "I hope you will let me help. I am tired of twiddling my thumbs with all this royal living."

"I am glad to hear you say that. You and I are like the peas of the pod in the kitchen."

Daniel said to Matt, loud enough for Isabella to hear, "She gets pretty close with some of those old sayings."

Isabella turned and said, "Don't start with me, Daniel. You are still under the dog house for not calling me enough."

Daniel rolled his eyes and said, "As I was saying."

*****

Samuel did not look like he was feeling good and told Anna to tell Charlie to give him something for pain. His stomach was bothering him, and the bone pain had come back with a vengeance.

Charlie came in presently and gave him some pain medicine through his IV. She said, "He will be out soon, so if you all want to tell him your goodbyes for the day, I would recommend that you go ahead."

Maggie suggested that they all get together at the apartment for dinner tonight if Isabella and Ruth thought they could get it together on short notice. They both indicated that there would not be a problem, Ruth pointing out that the kitchen was always well stocked.

They all filed by and spoke to Samuel on the way out. Anna accompanied them as far as the front entrance. She resisted all of the invitations to join them for dinner, and Matt told her that someone would bring her a plate.

Anna walked back to Samuel's room and paused briefly before going in. She could see past an opening in the curtain that covered the glass door and saw Charlie standing by the bed. Samuel was asleep, and Charlie was looking at him. Anna noticed tears running down her cheeks. She waited before going in, knowing that Charlie would be embarrassed.

*****

"I have never in my life cooked in a place like this." Isabella was amazed at how fancy the kitchen in the apartment was.

Ruth replied, "I don't think I have seen anything like it before either. Everything looks like it is brand new. My guess is that guests of the president don't do much cooking."

"That would have to be right."

The two cooks had found the kitchen well stocked and had no problem coming up with dinner. They found some tortillas and prepared a chicken fillet sliced to make a burrito of sorts. They had mixed vegetables and rice with a cheese and pepper gravy.

Maggie had invited all the doctors, and everybody was seated around the generous dining table. Dr. Calamuños was the only one who couldn't be there as he was working the night shift. Sharon had also joined them.

There was the usual dinner talk, and Dr. Sanders asked, "Carlos, when did you first suspect that Samuel had dengue fever?"

Isabella was bringing more rice to the table and overheard the question, "Go ahead and tell him who made the diagnosis."

Dr. Romero smiled and said, "Isabella, of course, knew the diagnosis before me, but I felt he probably had it when he just kept feeling bad after getting back from the canyon."

Dr. Sanders asked, "Isn't it rare for there to be complications like this?"

"Very rare, happens more in young kids or adults that have some other medical issue complicating the process. Usually doesn't happen to someone like Samuel."

Maggie asked, "Is the fact that Samuel was in such good health going to help us get through this?"

Dr. Ortega responded, "I feel like it is a big factor. If he wasn't in such good shape, things could be a lot worse."

Matt said, "Does anybody have a good handle on how Samuel feels about all of this. It's almost like we are always talking behind his back. I wonder if he has any idea how bad this can be."

Dr. Romero responded, "I don't know if Hugo would agree, but I think that responsibility belongs to me. I have to admit that I have dreaded having that conversation. I have assumed that he knows more than we have told him."

Matt said, "I was just wondering about that. I sure don't know what the right thing to do is."

Dr. Romero said, "I'll give it more thought, Matt. May have a talk with him soon."

Matt nodded his head and said, "Oh, by the way, I told Anna that we'd bring her a plate." He yelled over to Ruth and Isabella in the kitchen, "Hey, can you ladies fix Anna a plate and I'll take it to her."

Isabella said, "Matt, you are getting as bad as Daniel on thinking you can get ahead of Isabella. The plate has been prepared, and I was wondering what you are waiting for. She is probably starving by now."

Matt looked at Daniel, and they both shook their heads. He excused himself and said he would be back in a little while. He took the plate and headed out the door.

Dr. Sanders said to Maggie, "He sure seems to think highly of his sister."

"He has always been that way. I think part of it is their age difference. He almost acts like a father would."

"What about he and Samuel?"

"You wouldn't believe it, Pat. They had a reconciliation before Samuel got so sick."

"That is hard to believe, Maggie. Their problems went back so far."

"They sure did."

"How did they finally get past all that?"

"Matt said they had a fight, and I guess that was the beginning of the end. Daniel was there. He can tell it better than me."

Daniel had been listening to the conversation and said, "Yes, sir. It was a bad day. We were doing a construction project and both of them were not in the best of moods. They got into an argument, and Matt hit Samuel in the mouth."

Dr. Sanders exclaimed, "You can't be serious!"

"I couldn't believe it myself."

"What did Samuel do?"

"That may be the most incredible part of the story. He just stood there looking at Matt and then walked off."

"I guess Matt was relieved when Samuel didn't hit him back."

"I don't know. All I can tell you was that Matt was not having a good day."

"How in the world did that lead to them burying the hatchet?"

"I can't say exactly, but I don't think I've ever seen anybody as down as Matt was after that. Maybe he was just sick of the feud."

"Didn't you say that he had thought about leaving and going home?"

"Yes, sir. Bought a ticket for a flight the next day."

Dr. Sanders was shaking his head. "What a story. I wish Joseph could have lived to see it. Their conflict really bothered him. I think he partly blamed himself. Said he gave Samuel too much attention for his accomplishments in sports. He thought that contributed a lot to Matt's jealousy."

Maggie said, "Well, I am very happy to see they're over it, especially considering what is going on with Samuel. Pat, I want to say again how much I appreciate you coming."

"Well, Maggie, I felt like I needed to be here. And besides, like I told you on the phone, if you only need me for a crisis every thirty five years, I can handle that."

*****

Matt walked into Samuel's room, and Anna was not there. The night nurse said that she had gone down to the guest room for a few minutes. Samuel was awake but a little drowsy. Matt said, "How are you, brother?"

"Been better."

"You lose your shadow?"

"Not hardly. She'll be back."

"You hurting anywhere now?"

"I'll tell you this, if I ever get over this, I am not going to miss the headaches and the bone pain."

"Pain medicine helping?"

"It does, but I can't be sleeping all the time."

Matt felt awkward but decided to ask anyway, "I was wondering how you are feeling about all of this?"

"The short answer is…scared."

"Hey, I saw the coolest guy in the world jump off a sixty-foot cliff. You can't be scared, man."

"Cool and cliffs don't come into play much with this problem."

"Sorry, I wasn't trying to make light of it."

Samuel looked at him and said, "I know you weren't. I didn't take it that way."

Matt continued, "I guess what I was trying to get at was how you were doing from an emotional or spiritual standpoint."

"You're wondering if I know how sick I am, or might get."

"Yeah, I guess that's it."

"I've picked up enough to figure it out."

Matt felt uncomfortable and did not know what to say next. After a pause, he said, "I guess you and I have never had any kind of meaningful discussion before, unless arguing counts."

Samuel appreciated where Matt was trying to go, and he laughed a little inside at how hard it was for him. He said, "I guess what you are trying to get across is how much you regret whatever part you played in our bad relationship over the years. And now that time can be so short, you are trying your best to make up for it."

Matt's comeback was quick. "No. I just wanted to tell you that your hair needed combing."

Samuel and Matt were both laughing so hard that they were almost howling. Anna came in followed by the nurse, both of them standing with their arms crossed and disgusted looks on their faces.

Anna said, "Just look at y'all. I guess you two have a good excuse for this kind of behavior."

Samuel was trying to compose himself and said, "Sorry, sister, but Matt was trying to be all serious and then tried to have a sense of humor. I'm not used to it."

Matt was trying to stop laughing and said, "The responsibilities that come with being the oldest don't allow time to develop one's sense of humor."

Samuel said, "You don't hear that one every day."

Anna said, "Well, let me remind the two of you that this is an intensive care unit, and a certain level of decent behavior is expected."

Matt pointed at Anna and said, "Speaking of the lack of a sense of humor."

Both men started laughing again. Matt stood up and walked over to the side of the bed, leaned over, and kissed Samuel on the forehead. He said, "You got to get over this soon. We need some more of this."

"I'm looking forward to it."

Matt said as he was leaving the room, "I'll be sure to tell Ruth to bring the hair brush."

*****

Back in the apartment, Matt found everybody sitting around the living room, with the exception of Ruth and Isabella who were still in the kitchen.

He sat down, and Maggie asked, "How is Samuel?"

"He's okay. Still having some pain, but otherwise doing all right." Matt couldn't help laughing when he thought back to his conversation with Samuel.

Maggie said, "Why are you laughing?"

Matt replied, "I tried to have that serious discussion we talked about earlier, and it deteriorated rapidly. I haven't laughed that hard in a long time."

"What on earth did you say, Matt?"

"You had to be there. I will say this, he knows how serious all this can be. He told me that."

Chapter 38

Samuel and Anna

“What in the world were you and Matt carrying on about?” Anna asked Samuel after Matt left.

“We were talking about all of this, and Matt made a joke. It kinda hit a nerve.”

“What do you mean by ‘all of this.’”

“All the stuff that is going on with me. You know Matt. He analyzed it, and I guess he’s worried.”

“You’re not?”

“Of course, I am. I’m scared stiff.”

“Well, you haven’t said much, so I didn’t know.”

“Not a lot to say. Let me change the subject and ask how you’re feeling?”

“Other than worrying about you, I’m doing okay.”

Samuel shifted in the bed to get into a more comfortable position and said, “Well, it’s not like you haven’t had a bomb dropped on you recently. You never say a word about it.”

“I think about it some, but there really hasn’t been a good time to talk.”

“You and mom okay?”

“We are. I don’t blame her for not telling me about everything before.”

“That’s good.”

"When I realized that she accepted me and took me in as one of her own, and that she did that immediately, I don't know how I could feel anything but good about that part of it."

Samuel said, "The thing that amazes me about it is the fact that she was going through the adoption process and didn't even know if her marriage was going to make it."

"Yeah, I have thought about that a lot. How many people would do that?"

"And it sure speaks well of her that she would come down here and put herself through the difficulty of telling us that story."

Anna was shaking her head and said, "What about that story? I don't know that I have been able to process all of that yet."

"What part you having the most trouble with?"

"I think the fact that our father's pedestal may have a crack or two in it is hard for me to swallow."

"I agree with you, but does that really change how you feel about him?"

"I don't think so, really. Past mistakes don't define who we are."

"I guess we all can be thankful for that."

Anna was lost in thought for a minute and then said, "Another thing is the strange nature of my adoption."

"What do you mean exactly?"

"I'm really only half adopted."

Samuel had a puzzled look on his face, "Is that good or bad?"

"I'm not sure."

Samuel couldn't help but laugh a little, "So do you feel like you have been cheated out of half of your adoption?"

"That's crazy, Samuel."

"Well, I thought that you may feel like a martyr that has been deprived of a part of his martyrdom."

"Let me repeat myself, that's crazy."

"Well, you'll have to explain it to me then."

Anna thought for a minute and said, "It's like I can think of the glass as being half empty or half full."

"Oh, I'm getting it. If being adopted is in some way negative for you, you can think of yourself as not being adopted. Sort of."

"I guess that's close."

"I'm afraid that you might be putting a Matthew Martin style analysis on it."

"Well, half of me is his sister, you know."

Samuel wasn't sure how to respond to that, but he couldn't keep from laughing. He said, "Sister, you may need to get some air. I think you have been cooped up in this hospital too long."

"I think it's just a little too deep for you."

"I guess you're right about that, but to be fair, I've never been half adopted before."

"Very funny."

"I'm sorry. It was kinda humorous the way you said it."

"Well, what about you, Mr. Cool?" Other than being sick, what is your current take on life?"

Samuel smiled, "You'll have to narrow it down. Are you talking about past or future?"

"Let's start with the future. What is out there for Samuel Martin?"

"I've actually been giving some serious thought to that."

"Oh yeah?"

"Seriously, I have."

"I'd love to hear it."

"I am interested in what Daniel is doing here, and I'm thinking that the money I get from this trip will allow me to stay in Nicaragua for a while."

"You're thinking about missionary work?"

"I am."

"Have you talked to Daniel about it?"

"I have, and he says he'd love to have the help especially if he doesn't have to pay me."

"That is great to hear. I hope it works out."

"There's something else that has been on my mind lately."

"What's that?"

"I think my wild, bachelor days are behind me now. I would like to find somebody and settle down."

"You talking about marriage?"

"I am."

Anna became animated, leaned forward toward Samuel, and asked, "Who is the lucky girl?"

Samuel acted a little disgusted by the question and said, "I don't have anybody yet!"

"You just going to pick somebody out?"

"Not sure how I'm going to do it yet."

"Well, I think Charlie might be interested."

"You really surprise me sometimes, Anna. I'm just another patient to her."

Anna got that mischievous look on her face, shrugged her shoulders, and said, "You really think so?"

Samuel yawned and said, "All this philosophy has about worn me out. I might request some pain medicine and pass out for a while."

Anna leaned forward and asked, with anxious concern in her voice, "Are you short of breath?"

"A little."

"Is that something new?"

"Started today."

"You didn't tell anybody?"

"Hasn't been that bad."

Anna got up and said, "I'll go and find Dr. Calamuños and see what he thinks."

She found him at the nurses' station, and he turned in her direction as she walked up. He said, "Good evening, Anna. How are you and how is my patient?"

"I wanted to see if you would come and check on Samuel. He is short of breath and says it started today."

"I was about to come by on my rounds anyway. I'll be right there."

Dr. Calamuños examined Samuel and said, "The breath sounds are slightly decreased in the lower part of the lungs, and there are some sounds consistent with fluid, but it is not severe. Since you are not in any distress, I will wait and see what the EKG and the chest x-ray show in the morning."

Chapter 39

Heart Issues

Anna did not sleep well. She had a new worry with Samuel now being short of breath. She felt like she was listening to him all night, and even though nothing seemed to be wrong with his breathing, she still was hearing something that didn't sound right. Around six in the morning, she finally figured out what it was. His heart rate was higher than it had been since his admission. She had become so accustomed to the sound of all of the monitors and the equipment in his room that she knew that one sound was definitely different. His heart rate was running about one hundred where it usually ran in the sixties. She was glad when the EKG technician came in and was especially happy when Charlie walked in shortly after him.

Anna sat up on the love seat and said, "Good morning, Charlie. Am I glad to see you."

"Hey, Anna, what's going on this morning?"

"Samuel started having shortness of breath yesterday, and this morning, I noticed his heart rate was up."

"Well, we'll get his EKG and see what it shows."

Samuel was stirring while the EKG leads were being applied and said, "Good morning, Charlie."

Charlie said, "How are you feeling?"

"Feels like I ran a race or something."

Charlie noticed that he was visibly short of breath, and he seemed agitated. He did not look as good to her as he did when she left yesterday. The EKG was finished, and Charlie was standing there with it in her hand. She seemed to be studying it.

Anna sensed that she was concerned about something and said, "Tell us what it shows, Charlie."

"I can't read these things. We'll have to wait for Dr. Calamuños."

Anna didn't feel like she was being completely honest, but she didn't want to put her on the spot, so she let it drop. The x-ray technician came in with the portable machine and shot Samuel's chest x-ray.

*****

Dr. Calamuños had Samuel's chest x-ray pulled up on the computer, and the EKG was lying on the desk in front of him. He looked at one and then back at the other, and continued doing that as if something would eventually change. Charlie had seen the look that he had on his face before and knew what he was going to say.

"I don't like this, Charlie. I'm sure you noticed these T-wave changes."

"Yes, sir."

Dr. Calamuños soon had Dr. Ortega on his cell phone, "Hugo, sorry to call you this early, but we've got some things going on with Samuel. I'm looking at his EKG, and he has diffuse T-wave inversions. His chest film shows an increase in his pleural effusion, and there is some pulmonary edema now. He didn't have that yesterday."

Dr. Hugo asked, "How does he look this morning?"

"I haven't been in yet, but Charlie says he's restless and short of breath."

"Emilio, I want you to go ahead and get an echocardiogram ordered, and I'll be in shortly."

*****

Maggie, Matt, Dr. Sanders, and Dr. Simmons were seated around the breakfast table in the apartment. Drs. Sanders and Simmons had come over from their hotel as they had all agreed the night before to have an early breakfast. Ruth and Isabella were busy in the kitchen. Matt's phone rang, and it was Anna, "Matt, Samuel is having some issues with shortness of breath this morning, and Dr. Calamuños says it may be a problem with his heart."

Matt asked, "What could be wrong with his heart? He's strong as an ox."

"I don't know. I'm just telling you what the doctor told me. They are doing another test on him now. An echo, they called it."

"Well, we'll be heading that way shortly."

"Okay."

Dr. Simmons heard Matt mention Samuel's heart and asked, "Did I hear there is a cardiac issue this morning."

"Yes, sir. I'm sure I don't understand what Anna is talking about. I believe she said that they were doing an echo."

Dr. Sanders asked, "What do you make of all that, Mike?"

"Dengue fever can affect the heart and cause myocarditis. That sounds like what Emilio is checking for."

Maggie asked, "Is that serious?"

"Like everything else with dengue, it can get that way."

Dr. Sanders asked, "Does that produce heart failure."

"It does."

There wasn't a lot of conversation over breakfast. When they were through eating, Maggie called Dr. Romero and gave him a report on Samuel. He said that he would not be long in clinic this morning and would come on to the hospital.

Matt called Daniel and filled him in, and he said he would head that way.

*****

When they all walked into Samuel's room, Dr. Ortega and Dr. Calamuños were both there, as were Charlie and Anna.

Dr. Ortega said, "Good morning, everyone. You're just in time. I was just getting ready to talk to Samuel about his tests this morning. His EKG had some changes on it that we hadn't seen before and his chest film shows mild pulmonary edema, and his pleural effusion is slightly worse. We did an echo to further evaluate all of that, and it shows some weakening of the heart muscle with a mild decrease in his ejection fraction."

Dr. Ortega paused, and Maggie said, "You are going to need to simplify all of that for us."

"I will definitely do that. Basically, the dengue infection has effected Samuel's heart and caused some weakness of the pumping ability. He has mild congestive heart failure."

Anna asked, "Does that cause the edema that you mentioned?"

"It does, but remember, there is still the leaky blood vessels that cause some of that also."

Dr. Simmons said, "Hugo, I see that his systolic blood pressure is running around a hundred. Is that holding up okay?"

"It is, and Dr. Calamuños does not have him on any pressor drugs right now."

Dr. Simmons said, "That is good. Emilio, what are you thinking about this morning, in terms of treatment for this?"

"Will start dobutamine if his failure worsens."

Dr. Ortega said, "Samuel, your platelets are sixty thousand this morning. That is really good. Liver and kidney function is normal."

Samuel attempted a smile and said, "I am glad that all of the news is not bad this morning."

Daniel and Michael came in, and Samuel and Michael carried on in Spanish the way they always do. The crowd was quite large, and Charlie told them that they were going to have to clear out for a while. Everybody decided to go to the cafeteria for coffee. Anna stayed in Samuel's room.

*****

After a cup of coffee, Matt excused himself and said that he was going for his usual walk in front of the hospital so he could call home and give his wife a report. He had walked his usual route a couple of times, and when he got off the phone, he was in front of the small church that had become so familiar to him. He stood looking at it and felt the attraction to go in that he had felt before. He walked up to the door and tried it. It was not locked. He looked around, and like always, saw no one. He opened the door and stepped inside.

The sanctuary was not large, but it was nice. There were rows of pews lined up on each side with an isle down the middle. The pews were made of wood and reminded him of those he was used to in the States. The other churches that he had seen in Nicaragua had plastic chairs. There was a stage at the front with a pulpit in the center, also made of wood with carvings on each side. Behind the pulpit, there was a large banner with writing on it in Spanish that Matt couldn't read. Standing in front of the banner was a large wooden cross. The lighting came from skylights, and although not bright, had a nice, warm glow. There was something comfortable about the church that he couldn't put his finger on.

Matt sat down on one of the front pews and without thinking about it began to pray. He was worried more about Samuel this morning because of the heart issue and began asking the Lord to heal him. He prayed out loud but in a whisper because he was afraid someone may come in and hear him. He felt that praying out loud helped him stay focused. He became a little emotional and felt his eyes getting moist. He wasn't used to praying and did not know what to say, but it didn't matter to him. He simply asked over and over again for Samuel to be healed. He found himself repeating the phrase, "Heal my brother whom I have grown to love." That made him emotional, but it felt good for him to do it.

After a time, Matt got up and walked out of the church. He stood in front of it for a few minutes, reflecting on what just happened. He did not remember having that type of prayer experience before and thanked God for putting the church there.

*****

Matt walked back into the cafeteria, and everyone was still there. Daniel said, "Man, I was getting ready to come looking for you."

"Awe, talked to the wife a little longer this morning." Matt did not want to share his experience at the church with anybody. "Y'all solved all the problems while I was out, I'm sure?"

Daniel replied, "Working on them."

Maggie said, "Matt, one thing we have decided is that Ruth and I are going to stay here in the courtesy room. Neither of us feel like leaving the hospital. Isabella is going to continue to go between here and the apartment, and bring things when needed. She will prepare some meals, and we can always eat here in the cafeteria if we need to."

"Yes, ma'am."

Maggie sensed that Matt was not himself and asked, "Is anything wrong?"

Matt tried to appear more upbeat and said, "No, not really. I guess I'm just bothered by what's going on with Samuel this morning."

"Yes, we all are."

*****

Anna was perched on the love seat, as usual, when Charlie came in to adjust something with the IV. "You okay, Anna?"

Anna did not answer, and Charlie saw tears running down her cheeks. She walked over, put her arm around her, and said, "It's going to be all right."

Anna said, "Every day, there's something new, Charlie. It's not all right!"

Samuel was sleeping, or Anna would have left the room for this conversation.

Anna continued, "I can't act this way. I have to be strong for my mom and Matt."

"Tears do not mean you are not strong. And besides, you do not have to carry more than your share of the strength."

"You don't understand, Charlie. I am always the one everybody has to worry about. I want it to be different this time."

Charlie was patting her on the back and said, "I have seen a lot of strength from you. To cry occasionally is not a failure. I do that sometimes myself."

"I know."

Charlie looked surprised and said, "You do?"

"I wasn't trying to spy on you, but I saw you crying the other day."

Charlie's face turned red, "Well, I'm not supposed to do that in my job."

"Why not? To see you show compassion makes me think you are a better nurse."

"Maybe I am worried about some feelings I am not supposed to have."

"Look, if you have special feelings for him, don't worry. Everybody else does too."

Chapter 40

Dengue Shock Syndrome

When there is a serious illness in the family, life definitely changes. Normal, everyday routines are gone as the routines of the hospital, nurses, doctors, and technicians take their place. Families get used to the schedules of the doctors, and they get to know some of the language too. You have to learn to read between the lines and read the facial expressions. The Martins' life had now become that. Samuel was not going to get better soon. They all knew that. As Anna settled into the hospital life early on, now Maggie and Ruth joined her. Matt would continue to sleep at the apartment, but he would spend most of his time at the hospital.

The last couple of days had been filled with some good news, some not so good, and Samuel feeling terrible, then not so terrible. Platelets up, platelets down, blood pressure up, then down, and countless different medications and IV's came and went. The Martins were told that things weren't getting better, but at least they were getting worse at a slow rate. That would change today.

Matt walked into the ICU early in the morning and found Drs. Romero, Ortega, Simmons, Sanders, and Calamuños all standing at the nurses' station talking. None of them were smiling. Matt decided not to interrupt them but to go on to Samuel's room and get a report from them after they talked. Maggie, Anna, and Ruth were sitting in their usual spots; and none of them were smiling either. Matt looked at Samuel, and he looked bad. He had an oxygen mask on, and his breathing was labored. Matt went over and spoke to him, but he could barely talk. Charlie was there watching the monitors. She did not look at Matt, probably to avoid any questions.

Matt looked in the direction of Anna and asked, "What's going on this morning?"

Anna said, "Samuel's breathing has been getting worse and worse. The doctors are talking about it now."

"What's causing it?"

"His heart and the plasma leaking from his vessels."

"When did it start getting this bad?"

"Early this morning."

Matt was getting upset and asked, "What's the plan?"

Anna kept her cool and said, "We are waiting to hear from the doctors. They were going to check on some tests."

Matt said, "Charlie, do you know what tests they ran this morning?"

"A lot of blood work, the usual chest x-ray, and they repeated his cardiac echo."

"Have you heard the results of any of those yet?"

"Not yet."

Matt tried to be calmer. "How's his blood pressure?"

"It is running low this morning."

Matt continued, "I can see that his heart rate is 140. That's definitely higher than it has been."

Charlie was uncomfortable with all the questions and said, "I'm sure the doctors will be in in a few minutes, and we'll see what they say."

Matt did not ask any more questions. He started pacing the floor.

Ruth sat with her head lowered and didn't say a word. No one had seen her that way before. She was having a hard time with it all since she viewed Samuel as one of her own. Her faith was strong, but she also had the view that death was the ultimate form of God healing us. She did not know how she could handle that.

Maggie was her usual strong self, but the wear and tear of the last several days showed in her features. She became bothered by

Matt's pacing. She said, "Matt, you're making me nervous with all that pacing back and forth."

"Sorry, I have a hard time sitting still as you know."

Matt leaned against the wall but still fidgeted. In a few minutes, all four doctors came in. Dr. Sanders stood beside Maggie and put his hand on her shoulder. Dr. Romero had that worried look that they had all come to know. Dr. Calamuños had his usual smile, but it didn't look natural this morning. Dr. Ortega had the stoic look he always has and he was the spokesman. Samuel was asleep so he spoke directly to the family, "I am sorry to have to report to you all this morning that the news is not good."

He paused as if he wanted that to sink in, and continued, "The echo is showing a marked weakening of the heart, so we are looking at significant pump failure. This is contributing to very low blood pressure and is basically now close to shock level. The matter is made worse by what appears to be early adult respiratory distress syndrome. This has a bad effect on the lungs and makes it even harder to keep his oxygen level up. I do not like to tell you that we are going to have to insert a breathing tube because of that."

Anna gasped audibly. Ruth had her head in her hands and looked at the floor. Maggie turned pale but said nothing. Dr. Sanders squeezed her shoulder. Matt stared straight ahead and shook his head.

Dr. Ortega continued, "Let me get Dr. Calamuños to go over a couple of more things."

"Thank you, Dr. Ortega. I wanted to report on his kidney function. It is down some, which is caused by the low blood pressure. It is not that much of a worry now but will have some effect on how we handle his fluids. I have started the dobutamine for his heart and hope to see his blood pressure come up some. We cannot give him large amounts of fluid since he has heart failure, but I am going to give him some plasma this morning."

Dr. Ortega said, "Dr. Romero, would you like to add anything?"

Maggie said, "Carlos, I would like to know what we can expect."

Dr. Romero had a hard time getting started but finally said, "I don't think I can add anything medically except to say that I am concerned that this developed so rapidly."

Matt asked, "What can you infer from that, doctor?"

"Nothing for sure. Usually, it's not a good sign."

Maggie said, "Sounds like you are preparing us for the worst."

"Don't know an easy way to do that. I don't want anybody to have false hope."

Nobody said anything for a few minutes, and Dr. Ortega broke the silence, "If there are no more questions, I'm going to ask everybody to wait in the cafeteria for a few minutes. We have to insert the breathing tube now."

Anna asked, "Is he going to feel that?"

"No, he will be sedated, and he'll remain sedated as long as it's there."

*****

Everybody filed out, each one going by and patting Samuel on the head. He did not respond.

They all sat around a table in the cafeteria, and there wasn't much talk. Ruth remembered Isabella and called to give her a report. Matt called Daniel. Dr. Sanders was the only doctor with the group, the other three tending to Samuel. He could not imagine how it felt to go through everything that this family had in the last few months. He was having a hard time digesting everything they were just told. He felt that he had to be strong for Maggie, Matt, and Anna; but he had his doubts as to whether or not he could.

After what seemed like a long time, Charlie came into the cafeteria and said, "It will be okay for you all to come back in now. I need to warn you that Samuel has a breathing tube now and is sedated. He won't be able to communicate at all."

Matt asked, "How is he?"

"I'd like to say that he was a lot better, but they are having trouble getting his pressure up." Her eyes were moist, and she tried to hide it.

Daniel and Michael came in, and Michael was shaken up by the latest developments. He asked if he could see Samuel for a few minutes. Everybody was nodding their heads yes.

Back in the room, Michael took Samuel's hand and voiced a prayer in Spanish. He turned and walked out of the room.

Dr. Calamuños came in and studied the monitors. He explained that the ventilator settings had to be high to oxygenate Samuel and that was having a negative effect on his heart. That was one reason that the BP was staying low. He was okay with the oxygen being slightly lower to keep the blood pressure higher.

Everyone was sitting or standing and saying nothing. All of a sudden, Ruth got up, walked over to her purse, and took out her hairbrush. She walked over to the bed, sat down, and started combing Samuel's hair. Tears were streaming down her cheeks, and she started talking, "I don't care how sick you are, you are not going to keep this mop looking like this. And don't act like you can't hear me, Samuel Jackson Martin. That won't do you a bit of good." She kept combing, oblivious to whether anybody else was in the room or not.

Matt could not be still and said to Daniel, "Let's take a walk down to the apartment and check on Isabella."

Daniel replied, "Sounds good."

The two men were walking the short distance to the apartment and Matt said, "Daniel, I never accepted that we might get to this point."

"Me either."

"I don't know what to do."

"Nothing you can do but pray."

"I guess I'm wishing about now that I was better at that than I am."

"No right way or wrong way."

They walked into the apartment and found Isabella finishing lunch. She was packing individual lunches into Ziploc bags.

She asked, "Any new report on Samuel?"

Matt said, "Not really, still having problems with his blood pressure."

She asked how everybody was doing, and Daniel said as well as could be expected.

She asked Matt, "How do you think Anna is handling all of this?"

"Better than me, I think."

Isabella then said, "I sure do worry too much about that one."

Daniel said, "Well, let's get back to the hospital, and you can check on her yourself."

*****

Back in the ICU, Drs. Romero, Ortega, Simmons, and Calamuños were standing at the nurses station and appeared to be having a serious conversation. Dr. Calamuños threw up his hands, and Matt thought the gesture may mean he was doing all he could and was frustrated. At least that was how Matt read it.

Everybody in the room greeted Isabella, and Anna acted especially glad to see her. She said, "Isabella, you ought to stay here and don't worry about the cooking. We can eat in the cafeteria."

"You are right, Anna. I think I'll plan to be here for a while."

Charlie made another adjustment to the IV, then looked at the monitors. The doctors were in and out about as much as Charlie was. The worry was the blood pressure that was running between seventy and eighty systolic. They couldn't get it to stabilize.

Matt was agitated and felt helpless. He thought of the small church and knew he had to go. He told everybody that he would be back and walked out of the room.

*****

The church was the same as before. Not a soul was there, and Matt sat down in the same spot as before. He looked at the cross on the stage and began to pray: "Father in heaven, I do not know what to say other than to ask for healing for my brother, Samuel. I do not understand things as I should because I am late getting to you. I don't want that fact to cause harm to Samuel. Help him and heal him, Lord. I do not think my mother and Anna can take another death, Father. I see no purpose to be served by that. Help us, Lord. Do not let anything happen to my brother."

Matt paused for a minute and looked around to make sure no one had come in. The more he thought about the situation, the more upset he became. He resumed his prayer with passion, "Father, I do not understand this. You brought us here and put us through a process of reconciliation, and for what? Why, God, would you take my brother from me after all of that? What have we as a family done to deserve such losses in a short time?"

Matt was now mad at God and shaking his fist at the ceiling, "I don't understand. I don't understand. Take all I have, but not this one. Don't let this happen, Father. Nothing good can come from this. You took my father. Don't take my brother. It is too much for us to bear. It is too much!"

Matt leaned over, put his head in his hands, and couldn't say anything else. He was having trouble focusing. Suddenly, he felt a hand on his shoulder, and it startled him. He looked up to see a man standing beside him that he had never seen before. The man was directly under one of the skylights, giving him a ghostly appearance and seemed to have appeared out of nowhere. Matt thought that maybe he was the pastor of the church. Matt did not get up, but just sat there. The man kept his hand on Matt's shoulder, raised his other hand, and began praying. He prayed in Spanish, very passionately as if he somehow sensed Matt's need. He continued for several minutes and abruptly stopped. He said nothing else, turned, and walked out of the church. Matt sat there for a few minutes trying to process what had happened.

*****

When Matt walked back into the ICU, there was a lot of frantic activity in and around Samuel's room. Dr. Ortega was ushering the family members out of the room and shouted, "We need the code team in here now!" Matt could see Dr. Romero doing chest compressions on Samuel through the glass door. Dr. Calalmunos stepped up and relieved him. There was continuous activity with people coming and going. Matt couldn't move. It did not seem real to him. He was close enough to hear what Dr. Ortega said next, "We've lost him!"

Dr. Romero and Dr. Calamuños were saying something, but Matt heard nothing past Dr. Ortega's last statement.

"Samuel gone. How could that be? Is this how my prayer is answered?" His thoughts were a blur. "Should go over and comfort Mom and Anna. Can't do it right now...can't get my breath...have to go outside."

*****

Matt stood in front of the hospital, dialing his wife on his phone. His hands were shaking.

"Matt, what's the news this afternoon?"

There was a long silence and Matt said, "I'll be coming home soon."

His wife could tell something was wrong and asked, "Samuel?"

Matt broke down and started sobbing, "He...he..."

"What are you trying to tell me, Matt? Is it bad?"

"I can't say it...He...didn't make it."

"I am so sorry, Matt. I don't know what to say."

Matt couldn't say anything else but did manage to say, "I'll call you back."

He hung up the phone, kneeled down, and wept. He didn't see Daniel running toward him.

Chapter 41

Conclusion

The plane touched down, and Matt was glad of that. As always, he didn't do well sitting still. He was once again thankful that the flight between Atlanta and Managua was only a little over three hours. He looked over his shoulder and could see his wife, Carol, and their two children in the seat behind him. He caught himself feeling like he was checking to make sure they were still there. He laughed to himself, "Where else could they be?"

As they were walking up the gangway from the plane to the main building, Matt's daughter, Stephanie, said, "It sure is hot here."

Matt replied, "I told you that it would be. The main airport building is air conditioned, but don't get used to it. Where we are staying is not."

Carol said, "I'm still not sure why we are having this here."

"That's all Samuel, and of course, his bride may have had a little to do with it too."

"I can't wait to meet her. She is a jewel according to you and your mom."

"Yeah, you'll like her."

"Any girl with a name like Charlie would have to be special."

"She does seem to fit her name."

As they neared the end of the ramp, Matt spotted Jose Ramirez, who smiled and extended his hand. "Good to see you, Matt. And this time, I got here on time."

Matt shook his hand and said, "Jose, meet my wife Carol and children, Stephanie and Joseph."

Jose's face lit up. "Another Joseph Martin! Does he know how big the shoes are that he will walk in someday?"

Matt laughed, "Not yet."

Jose got them through customs quickly, and when they walked through the double doors to the hallway leading out of the airport, they were met by Daniel, Sharon, and Michael. They exchanged hugs and introductions, and went out to get in the van. They said goodbye to Jose, and he said that he would see them at the wedding that was set for day after tomorrow.

Joseph sat up front with Michael and was able to converse some in Spanish since he took it in school. Michael had a good time with that and said that Joseph was cool like Samuel. Carol and Sharon hit it off immediately and enjoyed each other's company. Matt and Daniel sat in the seat behind the driver and were catching up on lost time.

Matt asked, "So you had a team last week?"

"Yes, it was a construction team. Coincidentally, they built a house close to the one y'all built."

"Don't remind me of that day."

Daniel laughed and said, "I look at that as the turning point. Got to look at the good side."

"I guess you're right, but, man, what a bad day at the time." Matt asked, "Is everybody back at the compound now?"

"They are. They moved out of the presidential accommodations when the team left the day before yesterday."

Matt shook his head and said, "I can't believe that the president let them stay that long."

Daniel said, "As I told you when I first met you, your dad carried a lot of weight with him."

Matt laughed and said, "Talking about coming full circle, that was the first conversation we ever had, when we were talking about the legendary status of my father. Man, there has been a little water under the bridge since then."

"I'll say."

"On another note, are Anna and Dr. Calamuños becoming an item?"

"Not sure, but I hear they have gone out a couple of times."

Matt said, "I can tell you this, if I'm ever bad sick, he's the one that's gonna take care of me. I still can't believe that miracle. Dr. Sanders said that for him to think of giving an IV blood thinner as a last resort bordered on genius."

"Yeah, for him to think that a blood clot to the lungs may have triggered the cardiac arrest was what saved Samuel. Everybody still talks about it being a miracle, even Dr. Calamuños."

"I guess this story supports perseverance if anything does. I sure did give up a little early."

"I can't fault you there, Matt, considering how many others did too."

"Maybe so, but next time, I'll wait for a little more official pronouncement before spreading the word."

Daniel laughed and then got a little serious and said, "Hey, tell me a little more about your prayer in that church. You mentioned it to me briefly before you flew home."

"It's not much more to it than I told you. I went in the church and prayed like I never have before, and it was only minutes before Samuel's cardiac arrest."

"But you said that someone else was there?"

"Yeah, a guy just came out of nowhere and prayed. I thought he must be the pastor of the church."

"That's strange, Matt, because I checked around with several of the pastors I know in Managua, and the ones that were familiar with the church said it hasn't been used in years."

"Funny you should say that because I kept thinking it was strange that nobody was ever there. And that didn't seem right because it was real clean and well kept." That made me think that people must show up sometime."

Daniel asked, "Are you sure that somebody came in when you were praying?"

"Yeah, I'm sure! He put his hand on my shoulder! I don't think he was a ghost."

"Maybe he was the Holy Ghost," Daniel laughed when he said it.

"Don't laugh. The way things turned out, I feel sure that he at least had the Holy Ghost with him."

"Guess I would have to agree with that."

*****

Sharon and Carol were getting acquainted, and Sharon said, "I have really come to love your in-laws. They've kind of filled some of the void I feel with my family being so far away."

"They are great people. I've always felt fortunate to have married into that family."

"And there never seems to be any shortage of activity and excitement."

"I agree with that. We are so blessed to still have Samuel, and what a great thing that he and Matt are now close."

Sharon said, "And if all of that wasn't enough, now a wedding!"

Carol laughed and said, "Yeah, Anna said that Charlie fell for Samuel early on, and his recovery in the hospital became a courtship of sorts for them."

"Yes, I heard that Samuel just casually asked her to marry him one morning when she started her shift. At least he had Anna go and get a ring."

"Well, Samuel has always done things a little different."

*****

When they got to the compound, everybody was glad to see them. Maggie, Anna, Samuel, and Ruth were there, as well as Isabella and Dr. Romero. Maggie made a big fuss over her grandchildren as expected. Isabella, Ruth, and Anna were in the kitchen in their usual positions. Anna ran out and hugged Matt, then welcomed the rest. Isabella came out, met Matt's wife and children, and had her usual enthusiasm going. She took Joseph in her arms and said, "Look at this one, a chip from the old stump."

Daniel said, "A chip off the old block!"

Isabella gave him "the look."

Dr. Romero shook Matt's hand and said he was glad that he was back. Ruth stuck her head out of the door and waved at the new arrivals, and went back to her work in the kitchen.

Samuel came out of the house, spoke to Carol and the kids, walked over to Matt, extended his hand, and said, "Nice to see you. I'm Samuel, and like another Samuel, 'rumors of my death have been greatly exaggerated.'"

Matt replied, "I guess I'm gonna hear about that one for a long time to come."

Samuel replied, "Depends on how long you live."

"You better be nice or I'll back out of being your best man."

Matt saw one more person coming out of the kitchen door and was shocked to see that it was his grandmother, Mrs. Barrett. She looked good, as usual. He ran over to help her down the steps and said, "Gran, nobody told me you were going to be here!"

"I wanted you to be surprised, and besides, it's a little dramatic this way. You know I have a flare for it, and before you comment, remember you inherited a little touch of that yourself."

Matt was carrying on and said, "I can't believe this. Your being here kinda completes the circle, so to speak."

"It does. I sure wish you grandfather could have made it, but there was no way."

"What made you decide to come?"

"Couldn't miss a family wedding especially since it's Samuel. I had about given up on that one ever settling down."

"Amen to that. I guess it took somebody like Charlie to take the wandering adventurer out of him."

Elizabeth said, "She is something else. If I had picked one out for him, I don't think I could have done better."

Matt asked, "How long have you been here?"

"Flew in a week ago."

"That long? What have you been doing?"

"We girls have been doing the 'shop till you drop' thing, and I have enjoyed some sightseeing."

"What all did you get to see?"

"I got to see some of the sights of Managua, including the hospital where Samuel was. We went to Matagalpa one day and that was fun, and oh, Daniel took me to meet a man named Hernando."

Matt exclaimed, "I can't believe you got to meet Hernando! Did he do your profile for you?"

"Did he ever, and he was really accurate."

"What jumped out at you the most that he told you?"

"Something that I already knew. That I had some catching up to do with my oldest daughter."

*****

After a while, all of the excitement created by the new arrivals died down, and Matt and Samuel found a quiet spot on the porch to talk.

Matt started, "Man, I can't tell you how good it is to see you."

"Yeah, Matt. It's good to be here, and I'm glad you're here"

"You feel like you're fully recovered?"

"For the most part. I have some weakness but not much."

"Headaches gone?"

"Thank God, yes. If I never have another one of those, I'll be happy."

"How do you think Anna is doing?"

"Really good. Seems like her old self again."

"She and Mom okay?"

"They are. I'm not sure that they're not closer than before."

"I am really glad to hear that. What about Dr. Calamuños? Anything between him and Anna?"

"Hard to tell. I think Anna is a little gun shy, but who knows?"

"What about you? Have you and Daniel talked much about your future here?"

"We have. I'll start off helping him with teams, and we'll see where it goes."

"I did want to tell you that my company is going to be one of your sponsors. My partner is real interested in the work here and says he's planning on coming down in the near future."

Samuel replied, "I thank you for that, and I'll look forward to meeting him."

The two men sat without saying anything for a few minutes, then Matt said, "You know, I have given all of this a lot of thought over the last few weeks."

"Matt the analyst."

"You can't tell me that you haven't wondered about all of the things that happened."

"You're right. I have."

Matt went on, "Remember the day we got here and that prophetess prayed for you?"

"Yeah, I couldn't forget that."

"Remember that she said that you wouldn't be leaving Nicaragua?"

"I do distinctly remember that statement. She said it so many times."

"Well, you didn't leave."

"I think I may be missing your point."

"That statement bothered me because I thought that she may have meant that something bad was going to happen to you, and that is why you wouldn't be leaving. That really bothered me when you were so sick."

"I guess what she said didn't affect me quite the same as it did you."

"Well, remember too, she also mentioned the word brother a lot and fever. Both of those words ended up having a great deal of significance."

"I can't argue with you there."

"I think her prayer had a lot to do with our reconciliation and your healing."

"I can tell you that I sure did have a spiritual feeling when she was praying for me. I'm not sure how else to describe it."

"That's what I'm talking about. What if your healing started before you ever got sick? What if she knew all along that you would get sick, and her prayer had a lot to do with you being healed?"

"I guess I haven't given it as much thought as you have, but I don't disagree."

"Well, all the doctors and everybody with any medical knowledge says that your making it through was a miracle."

"I agree with that one hundred percent."

"And another thing, what about the man that came into the church and prayed with me shortly before your death and subsequent resurrection—I mean, resuscitation? I can't see how that could be a coincidence."

"I don't think there is any such thing as coincidences."

"So you see what I'm talking about?"

"You are preaching to the choir, Matt."

"I was just wondering if I was the only one grasping the significance of all of that."

"As the one who died, I think I got most of it."

"I was just making sure."

They talked more about all that went on during Samuel's illness and how it had affected everyone. They talked about Dr. Sanders and how great a friend he was and his help to them, especially their mother. Both men spent some time talking about Maggie and how they had always appreciated her, but now that appreciation had reached a new level. The doctors that took care of Samuel were mentioned, and Matt was glad when he heard that they would be coming to the wedding. Matt also carried on about how everybody was thrilled to be adding Charlie to the family.

After a pause in the conversation, Matt said, "Another thing I think about and analyze, as you call it, is the whole trip itself."

"What do you mean by that?"

"I wonder if our father was a genius or did he just get lucky."

"I have thought about that some myself."

Matt said, "Just think of everything that was accomplished, and how it all worked out."

"Yeah, it was remarkable for sure."

Matt rubbed his chin and said, "But there is still one thing that I can't, for the life of me, figure out."

Samuel looked at Matt and asked, "What's that?"

"Why did he pick you to be the one to get the dengue fever?"

Samuel was shaking his head and replied, "I'm not believing you're asking that. The answer is so obvious."

Matt wasn't expecting that response and looked at Samuel with a curious look on his face. "What's so obvious?"

Samuel replied, "He knew you wouldn't have made it."

"Still the golden boy!" Matt said it as he punched Samuel on the shoulder.

"Be careful, you know I let you get away with that once."

"Yeah, you did, didn't you?"

*****

Ruth stuck her head out the door and yelled, "Samuel, you need to come in here. The hairdresser is here to trim that mop!"